THE RECKONING

THE
RECKONING

A Jess Williams Novel

Robert J. Thomas

Copyright © 2002 Robert J. Thomas
ISBN: 0966830415
ISBN 13: 9780966830415

Library of Congress Control Number: 2002095662
R & T Enterprise, Incorporated

Publication Date: October 2003 Published by R & T Enterprise, Inc.

Cover Illustration by Dave Hile, Hile Illustration
and Design LLC, Ann Arbor, Michigan

Publisher's Cataloging-in-Publication
(Provided by Quality Books, Inc.)
Thomas, Robert J., 1950-
The reckoning : the first in a series of Jess
Jess Williams novels / by Robert J. Thomas.—1st ed.
p. cm.—(Jess Williams novels; 1)
AMAZON AISN NUMBER / B005C5Z31Y
LCCN 2002095662
1. Revenge—Fiction. 2. Western stories.
I. Title.
PS3620.H637R43 2003 813'.6
QBI33-1498

The Reckoning
The first in a series of Jess Williams Westerns
By – Robert J. Thomas

This one is for Mom, Blanche T. Thomas,
Who we lost in October 2002.
She will be missed by many, but especially by her three sons
Anthony, Daniel and me.
We love you Mom!

PROLOGUE

Year 2002

"What's the number?" asked Dave.

"Forty-nine hundredths of a second!" Pat replied loudly since the two of them were wearing shooting earmuffs.

"Not bad, but still not good enough!" said Dave.

The two shots were so close together they sounded like one shot, but there were definitely two shots flying out of the barrel of Dave Walters's custom built competition pistol. Dave was pulling the first shot by thumbing the specially designed hammer back as he drew the pistol and the second shot was fanned by the middle finger of his left hand. The two balloon targets were about five feet apart and about fifteen feet away. He was using the customary wax bullets, which were used for competition fast draw. Dave holstered his pistol and drew and fired two more shots.

"How about that time?" Dave asked.

"Forty-seven hundredths of a second! He replied. It's getting hot out here! How much longer?"

"I'm finished!"

Dave Walters had been at it for two hours trying to get his fast draw down under the four tenth of a second mark. That's where he needed to be in order to seriously compete in the world championship title for fast draw. Dave had been competing in fast draw competitions for several years now and he had won some matches, but he was hell-bent on being the fast draw champion of the world. Pat Johnson was his good friend and also competed in fast draw competition. They had spent the last two hours at The Shooting Corral, which was a local gun range with a specialty. It had an area where competitors in fast draw and cowboy action shooting could ply their trade and practice.

"Hey, you did okay, said Pat as the two of them removed their ear muffs. "Maybe after you pick up that new pistol you ordered, you'll break the four tenths of a second mark."

"I sure hope so. My wife has been giving me a real ass-full about buying a new pistol. She wanted some new bedroom furniture and she's getting impatient."

"Tell her that when you become the new fast draw champion of the world, you'll be able to buy her a whole house full of furniture," boasted Pat.

"Sure I will. You sure know how to help a guy out," replied Dave.

"So, when are you getting it?" he asked.

"I called Bob Graham today and he said it's ready," he replied. Want to go with me?"

"You bet! I'd love to meet Graham. I hear he's one of the top custom gun builders in the country. Maybe I can get him to build me one."

"Okay," said Dave, as he threw his stuff into the trunk of his car and closed it. "I'll pick you up on Saturday."

"I'll be waiting and breakfast is on you this time," said Pat.

Dave picked Pat up on Saturday at seven in the morning. They stopped to have breakfast and then drove the hundred and fifty miles to Bob Graham's house. Bob Graham had been building custom built competition guns for years and he was a skilled craftsman. He could build anything you needed or wanted. He was an artist extraordinaire. He greeted them at the front door of his house with his usual wide grin.

"Morning fellows, how was your drive?" asked Graham.

"Just fine," replied Dave. "This is my good friend Pat Johnson and he's a shooter, too."

"Well, I've got the gun all set and ready for you to check out," exclaimed Graham.

"Great," replied Dave. "You did say this morning that you got the FD7 model holster from Mernickle Custom Holsters, right?"

"It just came in yesterday; it's in the box here," said Graham as he opened the box. "It fits the gun beautifully and I think you're going to like the way it handles. Bob Mernickle sure knows how to work leather into a functional yet beautiful piece of art."

Graham walked into another room and came back out with the newly custom built pistol in a plastic case. When Dave opened the case, his expression was one of a kid who had just gotten the gift he had always wanted for Christmas, but never got. The gun was beautiful. When Dave ordered the gun, he asked Graham, who is also an accomplished artist, to carve him a custom set of handgrips for the new gun. The handgrips were carved from the stag horns of the Sambar deer from India.

"You like those handgrips, Dave?" asked Graham.

"They're beautiful," he agreed. "And the way the grips flare out at the bottom just makes the gun feel so much more comfortable in my hand."

"They're not just pretty, they're functional," replied Graham. "You'll find that they help get the gun out of the holster much easier than the stock grips the gun originally came with."

Dave looked the gun over some more. It was perfectly balanced. Graham explained how he had lathed the barrel small enough to be able to fit an aluminum shroud over the steel barrel. That made the gun lighter, perfectly balanced, easier to draw and allowed for the gun to shoot live .45 caliber ammunition as well as wax bullets; which was something else Dave had expressly wanted.

Graham explained to Dave that he started with a Ruger Blackhawk .41 magnum caliber single-shot revolver and customized just about everything. There was not much original left of the gun. Besides changing out the barrel and making it a .45 caliber, he cut the trigger guard in half and changed the trigger to one that was about three times as wide as the original one. He installed a special fanning-type hammer that could also be thumb-cocked. The hammer rose straight up instead of curving back, which made it much easier to fan. Graham replaced many of the gun's original parts with aluminum to lighten it. Any part that was not changed to aluminum was nickel-plated. It truly was a work of art.

"Bob, I think he's going to drool all over that gun," Pat said jokingly. Bob Graham patted Dave on the shoulder.

"Go ahead and put the holster on and try it out," exclaimed Graham. "I think you'll like the way it just glides out of the holster."

Dave picked up the holster and looked it over. It, too, was a work of art. *Bob Mernickle was born to work magic on leather,* Dave thought to himself. He gently slipped the gun into the holster and it fit perfectly. Dave worked the action of the gun and it was smooth. He dry-fired the gun several times, both thumbing and fanning it. It worked better than he ever dreamed it might.

"I love it!" Dave exclaimed, as he placed his hand on Graham's shoulder. "With this gun and this holster, I know I can get a chance at the championship title now."

"Probably; as long as I'm not competing at the same time," said Graham playfully. They all laughed. The men and women who competed in fast draw were fierce competitors, but also a friendly bunch who believed in good sportsmanship. Dave thanked Graham again and packed up his new pistol and holster. Pat spoke with Graham for a few minutes about building a custom gun for him.

Dave and Pat drove back and Dave dropped Pat off in the late afternoon and headed home; his new pistol and holster in the trunk of the car. When Dave got home, he took the gun out of the case and looked it over once more. He read the serial number on the side of the gun: 40-01079. He looked the holster over once more and took note of the serial number stamped on the back of the holster: SN020679. The name 'BOB MERNICKLE CUSTOM HOLSTERS' was stamped on the back as well as the model number, FD7, and the words 'MADE IN CANADA'. He put the gun in the holster and hung it up in his stand-up gun locker and locked it.

He was watching television when his wife came in the door. He waited for her to say something first since he didn't know how mad she still was over the purchase of a new gun and holster instead of the new furniture she had been asking for. After she put her things away, she walked up behind Dave who was sitting in an old ragged recliner with several holes in the leather.

"Well," she said sarcastically, "you're going to show me anyway, so why don't you just do it now and get it over with."

Dave jumped up out of the recliner and headed for the gun locker with a boyish grin on his face. Before he got around the corner, he heard her shout—"And I *am* going to get that new furniture before you get any more guns or holsters, agreed?"

"Agreed!" Dave hollered from the bedroom. He spun the dial on the gun case and opened the door with his combination. He reached in to pick the holster off the hook and his hand reached for air as he let out a gasp of absolute horror and stepped back until he reached the foot of the bed. He let out a loud moan as he sat down on the edge of the bed. Horror washed over him as the realization of what he was experiencing right now finally took hold of him. The new gun and holster he placed in his gun locker not more than one hour ago, were gone!

Dave didn't sleep very well that night. He tossed and turned repeatedly and he had several nightmares throughout the night. He woke earlier than usual and he was sweating profusely. He got up and went into the bathroom to wash off his face with some cool water. As he did, he thought about the nightmares, and while most of them were somewhat vague in his mind now, there was one that he remembered very vividly. It was one of a little girl lying in a pile of hay—with a bullet hole in the middle of her forehead.

CHAPTER ONE

May 1876

Jess Williams wasn't unlike most young men growing up in Kansas in the late 1800's. He worked on the family farm and did odd jobs around town for extra money to help his family. He never had much time for play. He just turned fourteen a few months ago. He was a slender young man, standing five foot eight inches high.

His father, John, built their ranch from the ground up. He started with only eight head of cattle and his herd had now grown to over one hundred head. He had crops planted on about ten acres of fertile rich black soil. John hadn't always been a farmer and a rancher. He worked cattle drives when he was younger and he worked as a sheriff in a few small towns in Texas where he grew up. Not tough towns though. His duties mostly consisted of breaking up fights in saloons and locking up the drunks who couldn't let go of the bar without falling flat on their asses.

After his last job as sheriff in a little town in Texas called Sparta, he decided to pack up and just roam around until he found somewhere he could call home. After almost a year of wandering around, he found some land just five miles outside of a small town called Black Creek, in the state of Kansas. Good fertile land and the Black Creek ran right through the middle of the property. He spent some time in the small town. He rode around the area visiting some of the other ranchers and farmers. Everyone he talked to seemed downright friendly. He liked the area and he decided he was going to spend the rest of his life there. He was sure of it. He spent some nights camped out on the land that he planned to settle on. One night, just before dusk, when he was getting a campfire started to cook him some beans and salt pork, he actually picked out the site for the family cemetery. There was a giant oak tree about five hundred feet from where he decided he would build the house. The oak tree would provide some shade for the future gravesites. John was a planner in life for sure.

John first met Jess's mom, Becky, in town and he thought she was just the prettiest woman he had ever laid eyes on. He decided right then and there he was going to marry Becky. John was just that way. He decided quickly about what he wanted to do and then he would set out to do it. He still had some of the money he saved from his work as a sheriff, but it wasn't enough to build the house. He worked several odd jobs around town and for some of the surrounding ranches to earn enough money to buy the lumber and materials he needed to build the house. Of course, he preferred working in town since it gave him more opportunities to see Becky.

Becky was a seamstress and a darn good one. She had a little shop behind Smythe's general store where the townspeople could drop off their clothes for repair or to be fitted for new ones. Mr. Smythe didn't charge her any rent. Instead, he took a small cut of what money she made and, of course, he had all his clothes tailored for free. Becky first saw John when he came into the general store for supplies. She knew right off he was different from most men. She was interested, but certainly had no idea that he had already fallen deeply in love with her.

Jess's sister, Samantha, was seven and full of brimstone and hellfire. She was always getting into trouble and usually getting away with everything. Although she sometimes helped Jess with chores, she usually caused him more work and grief. Mostly, she would tag along with him and bug him until he just wanted to thump her on the back of her head. The only thing that stopped him from doing so was the knowledge that he would get a switch taken to his backside and that was something he worked real hard to steer clear of. It was close to noon on a typical day around the ranch and Becky was in the house making some lunch for Jess to take out to his pa. Jess had finished throwing some hay in the stables to feed the cattle and he was walking up to the house to see if his mom had the food ready when Samantha came out of the stables with her hands full of hay. She was jumping up and down, each time letting a little hay drop here and there. Jess knew she was just egging him on.

"One of these days I'm going to thump you good, Samantha," he warned her, giving her a look of dissatisfaction.

"I don't think so, 'cause you know pa will switch your behind real good," she replied giggling. Jess gave her the evil eye for a moment and turned around and headed for the house. Just as he walked in his mother was wrapping John's lunch in a cloth.

"I'll bet your pa is mighty hungry by now Jess," said Becky. "You get this out to him right away, you hear?"

"I'll get it straight out to him, I promise," he replied.

"Make sure you do."

"Can I ride the paint today?"

"Didn't your father already tell you that you could?"

"Yeah, but I was just checking."

"Then I'm sure it's okay," said Becky. Jess took the lunch from his ma and headed for the stables to saddle up the paint.

Jess had the paint saddled up and out of the stable in less than five minutes. Out of the six horses they owned, Jess had always liked the paint the best. He was a gentle horse and Jess gave him a few apples or carrots every day. Jess always loved riding out on the ranch. Sometimes he would imagine he was on his own and roaming around the country going from one town to another. He was always wondering about what he would do when he grew up. Would he stay and work the ranch or go off and do something different? Maybe he'd be a sheriff like his pa had been, or maybe he'd own his own business in town. Of course; like most young boys, Jess would imagine himself as a gunfighter; and of course, the *fastest* gunfighter alive. Whenever Jess got some free time from his chores, he would find himself down by the creek drawing his hand-carved wooden pistol that his pa made for him. He asked his pa a while back to teach him how to shoot a real pistol, but John said he was too young for that yet. It only took fifteen minutes before Jess found his pa. He was looking over a new calf that seemed to be lost and not doing very well.

"About time you got here Jess," said John. "My stomach's been growling like a bear that just came out from a long winter nap."

"Sorry pa," replied Jess nervously. "I got here as soon as I could…honest. I never stopped or anything, I rode straight out here. The biscuits ma made you are still warm and she put some honey in a jar to go with them." John looked at Jess and gave him a big smile.

"Don't get you're britches all up in a bunch," laughed John. "Get down off that horse and let's have a biscuit or two." Jess always liked it when his pa let him have lunch with him out on the range.

"Jess, don't forget to stack up some more hay in the barn and stable tonight before supper," said John, as he finished up with his lunch.

"Okay, pa. If I get done early enough, can I go down to the creek and mess around a bit?" asked Jess, a pleading look on his face. John knew exactly what that meant.

"I guess so. As long as you get all of your chores finished."

"Will you come down to the creek and help me practice a little?"

"Maybe after dinner," he offered. "We'll see what kind of mood your ma is in. She's still mad about me carving you that wooden pistol."

"How come she's so dead set against it?"

"Well, let's just say she has her reasons."

Jess got back to the ranch as quickly as he could so he could finish his chores and go down to the creek to practice with his wooden pistol. On the way back, he imagined himself a sheriff tracking down a bad guy who robbed a bank in some town. When he arrived back at the ranch, he brushed down the paint and put him in his stall. Then he finished the chores his pa had told him to do.

Jess went over to the stables and got out his homemade wooden pistol and holster. He made the holster himself out of some scrap leather his pa gave him. He fashioned the holster a little different from most holsters. He attached it to the belt at an angle so the barrel of the pistol pointed slightly forward. He fashioned the belt so the gun rode lower on the hip and he tied it down to his thigh with a strip of leather. He ran down to the creek and began to practice

This time he imagined he was a sheriff in a small town and he had been called out on the street by a gunslinger wanted by the law. Of course, he outdrew the gunslinger. He was there about a half-hour when he heard his ma call him to supper. As he walked up toward the stable to put his wooden pistol away, he wondered if his pa would come back down to the creek after supper so he could show him how good he was doing on his own.

Dinner consisted of beef stew and bread. Becky was a pretty good cook. For dessert, they had apple pie. Jess ate a good helping of stew and then a big slice of pie. John finished his pie, washing it down with another cup of hot coffee, and pushed himself away from the table.

"Damn fine meal, woman. I don't know anyone who can make apple pie quite like you," John said with a look of pride on his face.

Becky blushed a little. She was very modest. "You're quite the charmer, Mr. Williams," she replied. "Quite the charmer indeed." Jess looked at his pa.

"Pa, do you think you could go down to the creek with me for a little while?" Jess asked nervously. His ma gave him that look she always gave him when he mentioned going down by the creek. She knew what that meant and it wasn't fishing. Jess kept looking at his pa figuring if he looked at his ma it would just get her started.

"You know I really don't like you fooling around with that gun, Jess," said Becky. Jess kept looking at his pa, waiting for a sign.

"Sweetheart," John said, as he got up from the dinner table, "you are about the best cook around these here parts. I don't know anyone who can bake a pie like you can. Course, women are good at certain things and men are good at other things. Women have to be good cooks else they won't ever get a man. On the other hand, men who don't know how to shoot a gun may never live to get married to a wonderful woman like you in the first place. Matter of fact, if I'd never learned to shoot a pistol, I wouldn't be here today, and you know that to be a fact." As he finished his last word he had walked slowly around to Becky at the other end of the table and gave her a kiss on the cheek.

"Well, I still don't like it and you know it," she replied.

"He's going to learn anyway, submitted John. "So he might as well learn it right."

Jess was already up and out the door heading for the stable to get his wooden pistol. He was excited that his pa was finally going to show him how to handle a gun, even if it *was* only a wooden one. John stopped by Samantha's seat and gave her a kiss on top of her head; and just as he reached the door, and without looking back he said, "By the way, you ought not to be kicking your brother under the table like that at supper." It was Samantha's turn to blush now. She dropped her head a little and looked at her empty plate.

"Yes, pa," she replied sheepishly.

Just as John walked out the door he heard Becky quietly say, "Quite the charmer indeed, Mr. Williams...indeed." John met Jess between the house and the stable and they both headed down to the creek. The creek wasn't very big. It was only about six to ten feet across and very shallow except for a few deep pools here and there.

"Pa, when are you gonna let me shoot a real pistol?" he asked.

"When I think you're ready, Jess...and not one minute before," he replied firmly.

"But I've been practicing with this here wooden pistol for months now," he reasoned, a pleading look in his eyes.

"I know." replied John patiently. "But you have to understand, you just turned fourteen a few months back and I'm still your pa and I'll decide when you're ready, understand?"

"Yes sir...I understand," he agreed reluctantly, his eyes glancing down at the ground.

"Okay, now, let's see you draw a few times," said John.

Jess got himself ready. He made sure the holster was tight and in just the right place. He drew the wooden pistol several times and each time he re-holstered the gun as quickly as he drew it. The first time he drew, John was actually quite surprised with his hand speed, though he shouldn't have been.

"How am I doing, pa?" he asked.

"Not bad, son...not bad at all, but speed isn't the only important thing," submitted John.

"Well pa, if I was in a gunfight, I'd want to be faster than the other guy so I wouldn't get shot!" he contested keenly.

"Yeah, but if you were one half of a second faster than the other guy, and you missed with your first shot, who would be laying in the street, gut shot, and looking up at the sky wondering what the heck happened?" he countered with a look of experience on his face.

Jess thought about that for a moment and said, "I think I get what you mean, pa."

"Okay Jess, here is your first and most important lesson," he explained. "Drawing fast is important; there's no doubt about that. But shooting straight and true is just as important. I've seen my share of gunfights and you wouldn't want to know how many times the quicker man lay dead in the street. Sure, if you're *that* much faster than the guy you're facing, you might get off another shot before he pulls the trigger, but not many men are *that* fast. You have to make your first shot count every time, understand?"

"I think I do pa," he said practically.

"Also remember this," John continued, "most men don't have nerves of steel. They're afraid of dying even though most men will never admit it. When it comes down to the last second before the draw, most men will be sweating bullets or pissing themselves. A lot of times their first shot goes astray and the next thing that happens is they're lying dead in the street. You have to be cool and deliberate in a gunfight. You have to focus on your target and make sure the first shot counts or it just might be your last."

"How'd you get to know so much about gun fighting, pa?" he asked.

"Watching a lot of people who thought they were *real* fast get shot *real* dead," he answered matter-of-factly.

"I guess I'm lucky to have a good teacher like you pa."

"Just remember what I said about making that first shot count. I'm going to go up and have a cup of coffee and another slice of that apple pie with your mother. You can stay down here a few more minutes, but then you get back and hit the sack, okay? You have chores to do in the morning and I need to send you into town tomorrow for some supplies," he told him.

"Okay, thanks pa," he said excitedly.

John turned and started to head up to the house. He was still surprised about how fast Jess could draw the wooden pistol, but he admitted to himself silently that he shouldn't be. That kind of speed was born and bred into the boy, but Jess had no idea of the truth of the matter.

Jess thought a lot about what his pa had told him, especially about how some men were quicker on the draw, but still lost a gunfight by missing with their first shot. He practiced for another fifteen minutes and then headed for the stables to put his gun away and then he turned in for the night. As he slowly fell asleep, he imagined he was drawing his pistol slow and deliberate. He imagined he was a sheriff in a big town and he had to stop a gunfight and...

CHAPTER TWO

Jess woke at the first sign of daylight peeking into his window. He dressed and headed for the barn and stables to do his chores. He threw hay, did some milking and picked some fresh eggs for breakfast. John was in the stables messing around with the saddles and changing some worn out cinch straps. He planned to start plowing a few extra acres today. Becky was already cooking up a huge breakfast. Jess could smell the bacon all the way out in the barn and his stomach started growling. While he was picking eggs in the chicken coop, Samantha came in and started bothering the hens.

"Samantha, stop fooling around and make yourself useful for a change," Jess complained. "Here, take these eggs in to ma for breakfast."

Samantha stopped and looked at Jess as if she could burn a hole right through his head with her stare. Then, she smiled and politely said, "Okay."

Jess was a little startled by her reaction, but glad to see her finally willing to do something productive. Jess finished up in the coop, and then heard his ma call everyone for breakfast. Just as he stepped out of the coop, he heard a crunch under his boot. When he lifted his boot, he discovered a smashed egg. Samantha put it right in his path knowing he would either step on it or have to carry it in to the house. He shook his head.

When Jess got to the table, everyone else was already filling their plates. Becky cooked bacon, eggs, ham, biscuits and honey; and it all looked good. After finishing his plate and taking another swallow of his coffee, John looked up at Jess.

"Jess, don't forget you have to go into town today and pick up some supplies," he said. Your ma's got the list and make sure you stop in and see Sheriff Diggs to ask him if he needs any more steaks."

"Sure thing pa," he replied. "I'll make sure to stop and ask him." Jess went out and got the wagon hooked up to the paint and went in to get the list from his ma.

"Jess, I need those supplies back here in good time so I can get them all put away and have supper ready in time," exclaimed Becky. "You know how your pa can be if supper is late."

"I won't be late," he replied.

Jess climbed up into the wagon and slapped the reins on the rear of the paint and headed for town. It was about a five-mile ride into town and Jess enjoyed every mile of it. The road was a winding one and it followed Black Creek almost all the way. He was about two miles from town when he noticed a cloud of dust in the distance. Jess watched the cloud of dust getting closer and closer. The road was lined with just enough trees that he couldn't make out who or what was coming. Finally, between the trees, he spotted three riders. Several moments passed before he rounded the last curve in the road before meeting up with them.

He saw three men on horseback. He reigned in the paint and stopped the wagon. The three men rode right up to the front of the paint and stopped. They didn't say anything at first. They just looked Jess over and then looked at one another, slightly evil grins on their faces. Jess could tell right off he didn't like these men. The man in the middle was the youngest. He looked to be in his early twenties. He wore a set of six-guns that were strapped low and tied down tight. The man to Jess's left was older, probably in his thirties. He wore a single six-shooter in a left-handed holster. The man had a bushy beard.

The man to Jess's right was by far the oldest. He was probably in his late forties or early fifties. He was clean looking with a neatly trimmed mustache. He wore a yellow bandanna around his neck, and he had what looked like a new pair of boots on. He was wearing a six-shooter, but he noticed he also had a double-barreled shotgun lying across his lap. he wondered if he rode like that all the time or if he had taken it out only because he seen someone coming. The older man's grin had changed to somewhat of a smile, but Jess's first impression of him was the same as that of the other two men. He didn't like him.

The older man spoke first and asked, "where you going, boy?"

"Just going into town to get supplies," replied Jess.

"What kind of supplies, kid?" the youngest one asked.

"I got a list," he replied in a sharp tone.

"Kind of mouthy for a boy your age," said the grubby one with the bushy beard. The older man took over the conversation again.

"You from around here, boy?" asked the older man.

"Yeah," he replied.

"Where from?" asked the older man.

"Down the road, that way," said Jess, pointing backwards not taking his eyes off the three men.

"You got family, boy?" asked the older man.

"Yeah," he replied.

"They live down the road that way, too?" the older man asked, as he nodded in the direction Jess had pointed in.

"Yeah," he replied again.

"You're not very friendly, are you boy?" asked the older man.

"Not with strangers," he retorted.

"Hell, we ain't strangers, boy," the youngest one cut in. "We've been talking now for almost a whole minute! Hell that almost makes us friends!"

"We ain't friends," countered Jess.

"You sure ain't very neighborly, boy," exclaimed the older man. "We're just trying to be friendly and all."

"You don't seem very friendly to me," replied Jess. "Besides, I got to get to town, else I'll be late getting back and my pa will be sore at me."

"Maybe we'll stop and see your pa and tell him what bad manners you got, boy," the youngest one groused.

"My pa ain't got no time for strangers, he's too busy," he argued.

Jess slapped the reins on the paint and the paint responded by walking right through the three men who had been sitting in their saddles in a straight line across the road. The oldest man moved to the creek side and the other two moved over to the left just enough for him to get through. As he was passing the two men on his left, he glanced over in their direction. Not directly at them though, keeping his eyes low as if he was looking at the ground. He could see both of them clearly out of his side vision, especially the one that looked like a gunslinger. That's when Jess noticed something odd. The youngest man's left boot heel was missing. They were old boots, but Jess wondered why he hadn't gotten the boot fixed in town. After a minute or so, Jess looked back. The three men were still sitting in the road watching him and talking to one another. He made up his mind right then and there that he was going to tell Sheriff Diggs about these men when he got to town. When he looked back a second time, the three men had turned their horses around and continued down the road. *Good riddance,* he thought to himself.

As Jess rounded the last turn and headed down the main street of town, he finally relaxed. He was worried the three men might come after him. He headed straight for Smythe's general store and he tied the wagon up in back. He walked around to the front of the store and went in.

"Hey, Jess, how are you and the rest of the family?" asked Jim Smythe with a happy smile.

"They're just dandy, sir," he replied. "Pa sent me in to pick up some supplies. I got the list here." Jess handed the list to him and Jim went about picking the stuff out for Jess and stacking it in wooden boxes to carry out.

"Are you going to look over the candy counter today?" asked Jim, looking in the direction of the front counter where he displayed all the hard candy in nice clear jars.

"Yes, sir!" he replied eagerly. "I'll pick some out when I get back. Right now I have to go see Sheriff Diggs."

"He might be a little cranky just yet," said Jim. "He had to run three drifters out of town this morning. Also, that hotheaded Red Carter came into town last night and kept the saloon open all night. He got himself pretty drunk and started a fight in Andy's saloon with one of the hands from the Hansen ranch not more than a half-hour ago. He had to lock Red up. Red wasn't too happy about the sheriff cracking his skull with the butt of that shotgun the sheriff carries." Jess stopped and turned around before he got to the front door.

"I'll bet it was the same three men I met on the road earlier on the way into town," submitted Jess.

"Probably was, they rode out that way," he said.

"I was going to tell the sheriff about them anyway," he said keenly. "I didn't like them much."

"Not much to like," agreed Jim.

"Why did the sheriff run them out of town?"

"He figured them for trouble, just from the looks of them," he replied. "Sheriff Diggs never even let them get off their horses. He met them in the street with that shotgun of his and told them they weren't welcome to stop and to keep on riding. Besides, he knew that Red was sleeping it off in the jail and when he let him out, he knew that Red would end up right back at the saloon. If the three drifters went to the saloon, the sheriff knew he would be picking up some bodies. You know how Red is; thinks he's the fastest thing in these here parts."

"Yeah, and one day he'll get himself shot, that's for sure," claimed Jess.

Red Carter was the only son of one of the biggest ranches in the area, the Carter 'D', and Red *was* pretty fast with a pistol. He had gotten into a gunfight a few years ago against some drifter who challenged Red after Red won his money in a hot game of poker. Red planted a bullet in the drifter's chest before the man got off a shot. Then, last year the drifter's brother came to town to settle up the score and Red disposed of him even easier. That officially made Red a gunslinger. Most of the townsfolk were afraid of him and steered clear of him when he was in town.

Jess walked out the front door and headed for Sheriff Diggs's office. When he opened the door, the sheriff was filling out some papers. His double-barreled shotgun was lying across his desk, always within easy reach. Jess saw Red lying on the bunk in the cell, still sleeping it off.

"Howdy, Sheriff," he said as he entered the jail.

The sheriff looked up and smiled at Jess. He had always liked him. He had always liked his mom, too. Everyone in town knew not to mess with Becky or they would have to answer to the sheriff.

"Well, how's my favorite young fellow?" asked Sheriff Diggs.

"Just fine," he replied "I heard you were having a bad day."

"I was, until you came through that door."

"How's your pa, and how is my little Becky?"

"They're both just dandy, Sheriff."

"That's good to hear, Jess."

"Oh, I think I'm just gonna puke or something listening to you two carry on," Red Carter said, while propping himself up on the bunk in the jail cell. "My head hurts like hell, Sheriff."

"You're lucky I didn't take that empty head of yours clean off. I've about had it with you coming into town and always causing trouble," barked Diggs angrily.

"I'm warning you Sheriff, if you ever hit me with that shotgun again, I swear I'll kill you!" threatened Red.

"Shut your yap before it gets you into more trouble," warned the sheriff. "As a matter of fact, you can stay in there for another day now just for getting smart with me." Red grumbled something under his breath, but the sheriff wasn't listening to him. He turned his attention back to Jess.

"Is your pa cutting up some more steaks soon?" he asked.

"Yes sir; he told me to ask you if you wanted some more."

"Tell your pa to cut me up a few extra this time," smiled the sheriff.

"Yes, sir, I sure will," he agreed. "Sheriff, I ran into three men on the way into town this morning. I think they must have been the same men you chased out of town earlier."

"How'd you hear about them?"

"Jim Smythe over at the general store told me about it."

"Well, you stay away from them if you run into them again, they're nothing but trouble, I'm sure of that," claimed Diggs. "I've been looking through my wanted posters to see if I have anything on them."

"Last I seen of them, they were headed down the road toward my pa's ranch. I hope they don't cause my pa any trouble," he said with a worried look on his face.

"They'll probably just keep riding, heading for the next town," replied Diggs. "I'll tell you what though. After I finish up a few more things around here, I'll ride out to your pa's ranch and make sure that things are okay."

"Thanks Sheriff," he replied gratefully.

Jess felt a little better as he left the sheriff's office and walked back to the general store. Mr. Smythe had everything in one pile and Jess made quick work of loading up the wagon. He went back in to get the bill to take to his pa. Jim smiled at him and darted his eyes over to the candy counter as he handed Jess the bill.

"Well, are you going to pick out a few pieces of that candy?" asked Jim.

"Yes, sir," he said smiling, as he looked over the candy counter. Jess picked out three different flavors of sugar sticks. Two sticks for him and one for his sister. Jess climbed up in the wagon and headed back to the ranch, his thoughts on the three men he met on the trail. He had a bad feeling and he just couldn't shake it off.

CHAPTER THREE

J ess rode back to the ranch and turned left onto the path going up to the house. The house sat about fifteen hundred feet back off the main trail. As he was riding up the path to the house, he looked over to the right to see if his pa was still plowing. He spotted the horse and plow sitting still in the middle of the field, but not his pa. He pulled the wagon up to the front of the house so he could unload the supplies. It seemed unusually quite around the house. He was hungry so he tied the paint to the front porch railing and quickly headed up the steps.

He swung the screen door open and just as he was about to say how hungry he was, he was frozen in a complete state of horror. He stood there motionless, his eyes fixed to the grizzly scene before him. He couldn't speak even though his mouth was stuck open. Tears began to well up in his eyes. His knees almost buckled, but somehow he caught himself. His muscles began to tremble and shake. The carnage before him was almost unbearable to look at, but he couldn't turn his gaze away.

His mother's body was hanging in the doorway going to the sleeping quarters of the house. The ropes that were tied around her wrists were tied to nails at the top corners of the doorway. There was a huge pool of blood on the floor surrounding her feet. Within the pool of blood was her dress, which was torn and ripped. The dress was soaked in blood. Her body had been slashed and stabbed repeatedly, and her throat had been cut. Her face was black and blue and one eye was so full of blood you couldn't tell if the eye was still there. Jess' legs finally buckled and he dropped to his knees.

It took him several attempts, but he finally got the strength to slowly stand up; but his legs were still trembling and he almost fell to his knees again. He knew he had to tear his eyes away from the grizzly scene in doorway. He finally found the will to turn away and go back out the front door. He looked out to where his pa had been plowing. The horse and plow was still there, but he still couldn't see his pa anywhere. He started to walk in that direction. As he did, he saw something on the ground behind the plow.

As he reached the horse and plow, he saw his pa's body lying beside the plow. Jess knelt down next to his pa. John had been shot several times. One shot in the chest, one in the stomach and two in the head. After what seemed like an eternity, Jess gathered enough strength to stand back up. He stumbled backwards from his pa toward the house a few dozen steps and then he fell backward into the deep rich black soil. He looked up at the sky and the tears streamed down both sides of his head. He stayed that way for almost five minutes, wondering if there was anyone looking down on him right now. He finally got the strength to stand back up and he slowly turned around and walked toward the house. He stopped about two hundred feet from the house, not sure if he could summon the courage to go back in there. Then, all of a sudden, he realized that he had not found his sister Samantha yet.

Jess took a few steps toward the house and then stopped as if he had hit an invisible wall. He swallowed hard and wiped the tears from his eyes. He knew he had to look for Samantha and that meant he had to go back into the house, but he couldn't gather the courage to do it. He decided to go to the back of the house and look in the windows. He walked around to the back of the house and got within two feet of the first window. He leaned his back against the outside wall of the house and tried to gain the courage to look inside.

He slowly stepped up to the window of his pa's room and looked inside. There was no sign of Samantha. He made his way over to the other window and looked inside, but Samantha was not there. He turned toward the barn and stable and he walked over to the barn. The door was already open. He walked into the barn and called out his sister's name. He looked around and was getting ready to climb the ladder to the top floor when he saw her arm sticking out of a pile of hay. Tears of fear filled his eyes again as he walked toward her. He knelt down and began to clear the hay from Samantha's body. Her clothes were torn apart. Jess sobbed uncontrollably. She had been beaten to a pulp and shot; a single bullet hole in the middle of her forehead.

He picked her up and carried her body out of the barn. As he stepped outside, he stopped for a moment and looked out toward his pa's body. He went around to the front of the house and up the steps and laid his sister's body gently down on the porch. Then, he sat down on the steps of the porch, laid his face on his arms, and sobbed for what seemed like an eternity. He couldn't believe this was happening. He wondered if this was just a bad dream and he would wake up soon. *How could anyone do something like this? This just can't be happening,* he thought to himself.

He wasn't sure if he had fallen asleep or was simply still in a daze when he began to hear the beating of hooves on the ground. He lifted his head as Sheriff Diggs quickly reined up his horse in front of the house and dismounted. As soon as Sheriff Diggs hit the ground, he knew things were bad. He already saw Samantha's body lying motionless on the porch. He ran up the steps of the front porch to get to Samantha's body to see if there was any chance that she was alive. There wasn't.

"My God, Jess. What in the hell happened here?" asked Sheriff Diggs. Jess tried to mouth the words, but he couldn't speak. He just sobbed more loudly.

"Where is your father, Jess?" asked Sheriff Diggs.

Jess lifted his head, tears still streaming from his eyes. He slowly pointed toward the field where he found his pa's dead body earlier. The sheriff saw the horse with the plow just sitting still out in the middle of the field. He could just barely make out what looked like a body on the ground behind the horse and plow. He began to head down the steps to run out to check where Jess was pointing, but before he got to the bottom step, Jess grabbed the sheriff's arm and stopped him in his tracks. The sheriff knelt down and put his hand on Jess's shoulder.

"I've got to go out there, Jess," explained Diggs.

Jess looked at the sheriff and shook his head as if to say no. He tilted his head slightly back and to the right. "Inside," he sobbed, so low that the sheriff didn't catch what he had said for a second or two. "Ma," added Jess weakly.

The sheriff started back up the steps to look inside the house. As he opened the screen door, he gasped and froze. He stopped breathing for several seconds and then he slowly let the air out of his lungs. "Damn it," he whispered under his breath.

He glanced back out at Jess still sitting on the steps; his head back down on his arms that were crossed on his knees. The sheriff fought back tears that welled up in his eyes and his throat felt like he had tried to swallow an apple whole. Becky had been like a daughter to him. He walked toward her, but stopped abruptly. He noticed boot prints in the blood on the floor. There were four distinct sets of boot prints. Jess was one of the four sets of boot prints, but he noticed something odd about one of the other boot prints. Some of the prints were made from a boot with a missing heel; a left heel. He scanned the rest of the room and spotted the murder weapon. A large kitchen knife covered with blood lay on the floor of the kitchen area, about ten feet from the body. There were no boot prints in that area so the sheriff surmised that it had been thrown over there. He walked over to the body. Another wave of sadness along with sheer hatred for the people responsible for this pulsated through his body, stopping him in his tracks again. If he ever found them, he would just shoot them where they stood. No trial. Then he would drag their bodies out in the woods and let the buzzards and coyotes pick their bones clean. They deserved nothing less.

He walked closer to Becky and squeezed past her to get around to the back of her body. When he got behind the body, he looked up at the nails and rope that tied her to the doorway. He decided to cut the body down. He went inside Becky's sleeping room and got a large blanket. He wrapped it around the body as best he could and reached down and pulled out the knife he always kept in his right boot. He carefully cut down Becky's body and placed it on her bed. He grabbed another blanket and made sure that she was completely covered. He grabbed another blanket to cover Samantha's body outside.

He walked back outside and Jess was still sitting on the steps. He gently placed the blanket on Samantha. Jess had stopped crying and had lifted his head up, looking out across the ranch toward the main road. The sheriff touched Jess's shoulder as he went down the steps and headed out to the field where John's body was. As he got close to the body he noticed one set of boot prints going in both directions. They were made from the same boots with the missing left heel. He looked over the body and surmised that whoever had done this had shot John with a rifle from a distance and then walked up and finished him with a few shots from a pistol. John's body was behind the plow and there was no evidence that it had been dragged there. Surely if he had seen anyone coming up the ranch road he would have walked toward the house to see who it was. He probably never saw it coming. The sheriff walked back to front of the house and looked at the footprints. Near as he could tell, there had been three men. He found the prints from the boot with the missing heel again. He turned to walk over to the steps and when he looked up at Jess, he was startled by what he saw.

Jess stared straight ahead with a look that the sheriff had seen more than once in his lifetime and it was not a look that should be on any man's face, much less a boy's. He walked back up the steps and sat next to Jess again putting his arm around him. He knew there was nothing he could say or do to comfort Jess in this moment, so he just sat there with his arm around him for a while. While the sheriff sat there, he thought about what he had to do next. He wanted to hit the trail and look for these murderers, but he would have to go into town and get some help. The blood on the floor was mostly dry except for the thick puddle that was around Becky's feet, so they had a good head start. He decided he would load up the bodies in the wagon and take the bodies and Jess to town. He knew he had to break the blank stare that Jess still had on his face. The sheriff could only imagine what thoughts could be going through his head.

"Jess?" asked Sheriff Diggs. Jess said nothing.

"Jess?" asked Diggs, a little louder. Jess still didn't respond. "Jess, I have to take the bodies into town, and you have to go with me."

Jess slowly turned his head to look at the sheriff. His voice was broken and quivering badly as he spoke. "Why would anyone want to kill my ma and pa, and little Samantha? Why? What sort of people would do something like this?" The sheriff knew there was no logical explanation he could give a fourteen-year old boy that would make any sense, and yet, he had to tell him something.

"There are a lot of good men in this world, Jess," he explained thoughtfully. "Unfortunately, there are some really bad men, too. There are men who kill just for the sake of killing and the pure pleasure it gives their cold black hearts. It never makes any sense, no matter how old you get or how many times you see it." Jess looked away from the sheriff and looked straight out at nothing again.

"Jess, why don't you sit here while I go get the horse loose from the plow and stable him?" The sheriff suggested. Jess nodded affirmatively.

The sheriff walked out into the field and unhitched the horse. When he was finished, he met Jess back at the front porch and told him to put the horse in the barn and feed the stock. He figured that would give him enough time to load the bodies into the wagon without him being around. He quickly unloaded the supplies from the wagon and loaded up Becky and Samantha. Then he drove the wagon out to John's body. Jess was coming out from the stables when the sheriff got back to the front porch.

"Time to go, Jess," the sheriff said. He nodded as he looked in the back of wagon at the three bodies. He crawled up in the wagon and took his seat next to the sheriff. As he sat down, he looked at the boot prints in the soft dirt in front of the house. He noticed a left boot print; with a missing boot heel. He planted that picture deeply into his mind.

It was a long ride back to town. Jess never said a word. He kept going over and over in his mind what had happened. He thought about the boot print with the missing left heel. He pictured the three men again in his mind. He never wanted to forget what they looked like. He would burn their images into his brain and remember everything he could about them. It was getting close to dusk when they pulled into town. The sheriff stopped the wagon in front of the general store. Jim had come out on the porch to see what the sheriff was doing driving a wagon back to town with Jess next to him in the front street. The sheriff explained what happened and Jim fought back the tears.

"Jim," the sheriff asked, "can you take their bodies over to the undertaker? I need to get Jess here set up for the night. Then I need to round up some men for a posse to head out at first light and hunt down the bastards that did this."

"Of course, Sheriff," replied Jim, "whatever you need. Are you going to put him up at the hotel?"

"Yeah, just for a few days until I can sort all this out," he replied.

"Sheriff, I have a better idea," said Jim. "Why don't you take the bodies over to the undertaker and let Sara and me take care of Jess? We have an extra room upstairs. He shouldn't be alone at a time like this. We can keep a close eye on him that way."

"That sounds fine to me, Jim," replied Diggs. "I'm sure he would be better off here than at the hotel. You sure your wife won't mind?"

"Not to worry," replied Jim. "Becky was like a daughter to us and Jess is like family. We'd be more than happy to look after him," he replied firmly. Sheriff Diggs looked at Jess.

"Jess," asked the sheriff, "would you rather stay with Jim and Sara?"

Jess shook his head affirming that it was okay with him. He, too, had always considered Jim and Sara as family. He looked in the back of the wagon as he stepped down from it. There was no sobbing, but you could see tears coming from his eyes.

"I'm tired," said Jess, barely audible.

"You go on in and Sara will fix you some supper."

"I'm not hungry," he said flatly. "I just want to go to sleep."

"That's okay, Jess," agreed Jim. "Whatever you need."

"Sara!" Jim called out to his wife.

"I'm right here," Sara said softly, tears streaming from her eyes. "I've been standing here all this time. Jess, you come on in and I'll set up your bed right away, okay?"

Jess nodded and followed Sara up the stairs.

"You go ahead and get comfortable," said Sara. "I'll get you a glass of water just in case you get thirsty later."

"Thank you, ma'am," he said politely. He got undressed and got into bed. The sheets felt clean and cool to him and yet they did not comfort him in the least. Sara brought him a glass of water and sat it down on a little table next to the bed. She put her hand on his head just for a moment as if to let him know that she would be right there if he needed anything. Sara closed the door most of the way leaving it open just enough so she could hear him in the night. Jess lay there thinking about all that happened. He slowly started to doze off. Just before he fell asleep, he imagined he was hunting down the killers who had murdered his family and that he would kill every last one of them. And he would make them suffer...

CHAPTER FOUR

J ess tossed and turned that night. His mind
replayed the horrors over and over again. He
woke several times and each time he did, Sara was
right there to comfort him. He finally woke to the
smell of freshly brewed coffee and bacon. For a brief
moment, when he first opened his eyes, he hoped it
was all just a bad dream. Then he realized where he
was and it all came back to him again in a thunder-
ing rush. He just stared at the ceiling. He wasn't sure
how he could or even *if* he could deal with what had
happened. Then his thoughts turned to the men
responsible. He knew he had to see justice done. He
didn't quite know how yet. He only knew that he
had to make things right. There would be plenty of
time to figure it all out. For now, he had to survive.
He had to figure out what to do today, next week,
and next month. He was a planner in life, just like
his pa had been.

He got dressed and splashed his face with some
cool clean water Sara had left in a large bowl on the
table by his bed. It felt good on his face. As he lifted
his head up in the mirror and reached for a small

towel, he noticed something different about the way he looked. It was surely his reflection in the mirror, but it didn't quite look like him. He was different in some odd sort of way that he couldn't quite put his finger on. He headed down the stairs to the kitchen and Jim was sitting at the table sipping some hot coffee, an empty plate in front of him. Sara was standing over the hot stove and when she heard Jess come into the room she turned around to see him.

"How about some eggs and bacon, Jess?" asked Sara.

"I don't know," replied Jess. "I'm not sure I'm hungry yet."

"Jess, you haven't eaten since early yesterday," pleaded Jim. "You've got to be mighty hungry by now."

"Well, I guess so," he replied, talking so low you could hardly hear the words.

"Then let Sara fix you a plate of vittles," submitted Jim. "You've got to eat eventually." Sara put a plate of eggs, bacon and biscuits in front of Jess.

"Thanks, ma'am," he said.

"You're welcome, Jess. If you need anything else, you just say so." Jess picked up a biscuit and began to pull it apart. He put a small piece of it in his mouth and began chewing it, a strange blank stare in his eyes. Sara fixed herself a plate and sat down next to Jess hoping she could coax him into eating some more.

"It sure looks good," said Jess, "but I just can't seem to eat much. If you'll excuse me, I'd like to go out and sit on the back steps." Jess got up from the table and looked at his plate and then looked over at Sara.

"Sorry, ma'am," he said. Sara put her hand on his arm gently.

"It's okay Jess," replied Sara. "I understand. You can eat whenever you're ready."

"Thanks, he said, as he walked down the back hallway and out the back door and sat on the steps of the porch. The view behind the store was less than exceptional. There was junk cluttered all around. The view off in the distance was much more pleasing. He could see rolling hills, most of them covered with trees. As he viewed the scenery, he realized to himself that the men who had killed his family could be hiding in those hills right now. He didn't even realize it yet, but his subconscious was mapping out his destiny and his future. Sara slowly picked at her eggs while looking down the hallway watching Jess on the back porch. Jim and Sara had not been able to have their own children and Sara had always been partial to Jess and had always treated him like her own son.

"It's hard to even imagine what that boy is going through," said Sara, her head hanging down looking at her food, which she hadn't touched yet.

"I know," added Jim. "Sara, did you notice something different about him this morning? I mean; I know his family being murdered and all has him all tore up inside, but something else is different about him. I swear he even looks older to me this morning."

Sara hung her head and closed her eyes. You could see the tears welling up in her eyes as Sara looked up at Jim.

"Last night, we put a fourteen year old grieving boy to bed," she said sadly. "But this morning, there is a fourteen-year-old young man with hatred and raw vengeance in his heart sitting on our back steps. I'm afraid for him, Jim, deathly afraid."

"I felt it too, Sara. Something has changed him on the inside. We'll have to help him as much as we can. That's all we can do."

Sara was crying quietly. She could feel in her soul what was manifesting itself in this fourteen year old boy and she knew there was nothing that she or anyone else in this world could do to stop it. She mourned for him more than for his family who would all be buried in the ground today. His family lost their lives. Jess, however, lost his very heart and soul.

❧ ❦

The burial went as well as burials go. Jim gathered up a few of the townspeople and the preacher, and hauled the bodies of John, Becky and Samantha back out to the ranch to be buried in the little cemetery plot John had spotted that very first night he had stayed on his land. The graves were dug in silence and the bodies placed in their gravesites. The preacher said a prayer over each of them and some of the men from town shoveled dirt until the graves were filled. Someone fixed up three wooden crosses for the graves and Jim pounded them into the ground with a rock. Sara cried the whole time. Jess, however, watched all of this in a strange silence. He never spoke a word nor shed another tear. It was as if he already let them go and this was all just a formality; something that needed to be done. Jim came up beside him and put his hand on Jess's shoulder.

"We should be getting back to town," Jim told him softly. "There is no more we can do for them. The Lord will take care of their souls."

"I'm not going back, I'm staying right here," replied Jess firmly.

"Jess, you can't stay here and run this ranch all by yourself," submitted Jim. "There's too much to do for one man, much less a fourteen year old boy."

"I'm not a boy anymore, *they* took care of that," Jess replied, not really signifying who *they* were, but Jim and Sara both knew who he was referring to.

"I know, Jess," argued Jim, "but taking care of a ranch is an awful lot of responsibility to take on. Are you sure you're ready for all that?"

"I guess I'll have to be," he replied, a tone of finality to his voice. Jim shook his head in frustration.

"Okay," Jim said reluctantly. "But you promise me that if you have any trouble or need any help, you'll let us know, okay?"

"I will...I promise," he replied.

"The sheriff and his posse will be back in a day or so," Jim said. "We'll let him know that you're out here. Is there anything else we can do for you right now?"

"No; I just need some time to myself," he replied bluntly.

"Okay then. Just don't forget, if you need anything…" Jim started saying when Sara took Jim's arm and he knew that meant for him to shut up.

"Thanks for everything," said Jess. "I won't forget it. Pa always told me to repay kindness with the same."

"Your pa was a smart man, Jess, and a damn good one," said Jim. "We're all going to miss him and your ma, and Samantha, too. We won't forget them; ever."

"I won't forget either," Jess said as he turned his stare from the gravesites to the rolling hills out past the field that his pa was plowing when he was shot down in his tracks. "I won't *ever* forget," he said softly to himself.

"Well, we best be going, Jess," said Jim.

Jim and Sara got into the back of the preacher's wagon and the other few townspeople rode out with the Blacksmith back to town. Jess found himself all alone for the first time in his life. It was a strange feeling. He didn't like it, but he knew he had to get used to it. Jess sat down in front of the three fresh gravesites. He sat there for almost an hour. He kept thinking about how he and Samantha had always fought and how she used to aggravate him to no end. He wished she were here right now to do it again, but that wasn't going to happen, ever again.

He remembered his ma and how she was always there to help him with anything. His thoughts turned to his pa. How he had finally come down to the creek to teach him how to draw the wooden pistol he carved for him. He was just going to have to finish learning all by himself. But not with the wooden pistol his pa had carved. No, he would have to begin to practice with his pa's .45 that was in the box under his pa's bed. Before it was just a challenge to see how fast he could draw, now there was a *need*. He had to learn to be the best. Without really knowing or planning it, his mind was formulating a mission. He would hunt down the people who had so savagely murdered his entire family and kill them, one by one and there would be no mercy. He would kill them and in the most vicious way he could. They would suffer. His pa always told him there were some pretty bad people in the world, but he never realized just how bad. People that bad had no right to live as far as he was concerned.

Jess finally got up and said a little prayer over his family. After the prayer, he made his solemn promise to them. He made an oath that he would not rest until he tracked down and killed everyone responsible for their deaths. He walked back up to the house and went inside. Someone cleaned up the large pool of blood where his ma's body hung; only a dark stain remaining.

The smell of food surprised him. There was a fire in the stove and Jess found some fried chicken in a pot along with some biscuits. *Sara*. She was a good person and he was thankful to have her as a friend. He wouldn't go hungry tonight, but tomorrow he would have to fend for himself. He would have to do everything by himself now.

He felt the loneliness begin to set in as he sat at the table alone and ate. He decided he would go out and finish plowing the field his pa had started on first thing in the morning. He figured he would have to run the ranch for the next year or so. Then, he would ride out and carry out the deadly oath he made to his family. He would let the sheriff go after the men, but if he didn't catch them, he would go after them himself. If the sheriff caught them, they would hang, and he would watch. Regardless, they will be reckoned with. Deep within himself, he hoped for the latter.

He finished the meal and then noticed there was a pie sitting by the window. It was an apple pie. *Sara.* Jess decided to have some later. Right now, he figured he would go and check the stock and throw some extra hay and then go down to the creek and practice with his pa's pistol.

He headed out to the barn and threw some hay. He turned around to put the pitchfork back into the pile when he noticed a slight glimmer off to his right. The reflection was coming from the wall where his pa always hung his hat. What he saw hanging on the peg was the most spectacular and unusual looking pistol and holster he had ever seen. He walked over to it and picked it up off the peg. The holster was brown and had a finish to it he had never seen on any leather before. On the back of the holster was a name stamped into the leather.

BOB MERNICKLE CUSTOM HOLSTERS. He also saw the words MADE IN CANADA. Another unusual feature of the holster is that it had no place to hold bullets. The pistol had a polished finish on it that was as perfect as any he had ever seen.

Jess strapped the holster on and it fit perfectly, as if it had been made for him. The holster held the pistol a little more out from his leg than a regular holster. The gun rode on Jess's right leg perfectly. The holster didn't cover as much of the gun as most holsters did. There was a nice one-inch wide leg strap that fit Jess's leg perfectly. Jess unhooked the hammer strap and pulled the gun out. The first thing he noticed was how easy the gun seemed to glide out of the holster. It was as if the holster was greased, but it wasn't. He reached inside the holster and felt the inside and it had a real smooth feel to it and it was harder than normal, which allowed the gun to glide out of the holster easier. Then he noticed there was no front or rear sights on the gun.

He looked the gun over carefully and noticed some printing stamped on it. On one side by the trigger he read the words RUGER BLACKHAWK .41 MAGNUM CAL. On the other side of the gun was a number: 40-01079. The handgrips were made out of some type of material he had never seen before. It looked like some type of horn material and the grips flared out at the bottom so as to make the gun extremely easy to grip.

Jess decided to take the gun into the house to study it some more. When he got in the house, he placed the gun and holster on the kitchen table. He sat there for several minutes trying to take this all in and wondering where this unusual gun had come from. He picked it up again. The gun was extremely light compared to the few pistols he had ever been able to hold. His pa's gun was a Colt .45 Peacemaker and he figured it had to weigh twice as much as this gun. He didn't know much about pistols, but he knew after handling this one for a few minutes that it was like no other pistol he had ever seen. This was something unique and special. He knew he would have to keep this gun and holster hidden for now. He walked outside and quickly went back to the barn and climbed up the ladder to the top floor. There were some wooden boxes that his pa kept there and he gently placed the gun and holster into one of the boxes and placed some more boxes around it to hide it.

He went back to the house and decided to have some of the apple pie Sara had left him. Before he cut it, he decided to make himself some coffee to go with it. The coffee was strong, but good and the pie was even better. As he sat there, he thought some more about the pistol. It couldn't have been his pa's gun or it wouldn't have been hanging on a peg in the barn, it would have been in the box with his pa's other gun.

By now, the sun was getting low in the sky. Jess decided against practicing this late and decided to turn in early tonight. He had a field to plow come morning. He had some more coffee and then he went into his pa's room and got the shotgun from the corner and took it into his bedroom along with a few extra shells. If anyone tried to bother him tonight or the killers returned, he would be ready. He would never be surprised by anyone like his family had been. He promised himself that he would always have a gun by his side at all times and always be on the ready. As he fell off to sleep, he imagined he was tracking his family's killers across the country. And he saw the pistol he found in the barn strapped to his waist. It looked like it belonged there.

He dreamed that night, but not nightmares. He dreamed good dreams of his family. He woke often through the night as he would for the rest of his life. The slightest sound would awaken him. His senses seemed more aware without him really knowing it. He would always be ready...always.

CHAPTER FIVE

Jess woke before sunrise. Before he got out of the bed, he thought about the pistol in the barn. All the same thoughts about the pistol and holster ran through his head again. He got up and cooked himself some breakfast. While he ate, he thought of all the things he would have to do on his own. He continued to plan out what he would do. He would work the ranch for the next two years. He would be a little over sixteen and, by that time; he planned to be the quickest draw with a pistol anyone had ever seen. In the meantime, he would plant crops and sell them. He would sell off all the livestock and stash away all the money and use it to do what he needed to do; what he knew he had to do.

It was a hot dusty day and he never figured plowing a field would be such hard work. He earned a new respect for his pa. It was just after high noon and he decided to stop and eat. After eating a simple meal of ham and a piece of apple pie, he went back at it again. When he finished for the day, he walked back to the house after throwing some hay and looked at the blisters beginning to form on his hands. He figured that he better wear the leather gloves his pa had in the barn or else he wouldn't be able to practice drawing a pistol in the evening, and that was something that he promised himself he would do every night.

After dinner, he went into his pa's room and got the wooden box out from under the bed. He took it to the table and opened it up. Inside, he found his pa's Colt .45 Peacemaker and the holster to go with it. He also found four boxes of .45 slugs in the bottom of the box. He strapped the gun and holster on and went down to the creek. Even with the blisters, he practiced for two hours straight. The first hour and a half he drew and dry fired the gun. Then, he loaded the pistol and spent the last half-hour using live ammunition. His practice took on a new fervor. It was not just a game anymore. Now it was something he had to do to make sure that he survived. He decided that tomorrow he would start practicing with both his pa's pistol and the one he found in the barn.

When he finished practicing, he took his pa's gun and holster and put it back in the house. Then, he climbed up in the top of the barn and looked at the pistol and holster he found. He decided to take it into the house. He finally turned in and as he lay there that night, he figured he would practice with his pa's pistol for the first part of his practice every night and then switch to the new pistol for the rest of his practice.

The next day found him back out plowing the field. It was just before noon when he noticed a dust cloud out on the main road. He stopped and reached over to grab his pa's rifle out of the scabbard that he kept strapped to the plow horse. The Winchester 44-40 still looked like new. He also had his pa's double-barreled shotgun tied to the horse. He watched the group of riders turn down the ranch road. He counted four of them. He finally caught a glimpse of who was approaching. It was Sheriff Diggs with three other men. They rode right up to the plow rig and Jess walked around the rig after putting the shotgun down.

"Hi, Jess," said Sheriff Diggs. "I sure didn't expect to find you out here and especially never expected to see you working the field. Hell, I thought someone was trying to squat and I'd have to run him off. I figured you would still be at Jim and Sara's. You expecting trouble?" he asked, nodding at the rifle and shotgun leaning on the plow.

"I wasn't expecting any, but if there was, I'd be ready for it," he replied. "I decided to stay here and work the ranch. Got to be a man and do a man's work now, Sheriff. They didn't leave me much choice about that the way I figure." The sheriff knew who *they* were. "I reckon you didn't find them unless you had to kill them and bury their carcasses out on the trail."

"No such luck," replied Sheriff Diggs dejectedly. "I would have loved to bury the bastards if I found them. We did find out who they were with the help of some other unfortunate people they robbed not more than ten miles from here. I also got some news from the sheriff in a little town about twenty miles east of here. They stopped there for a drink and someone overheard them bragging about how they killed some people and raped some women. The sheriff didn't have any wanted posters on them, but he did get a look at them and he gave me a pretty good description. We had a local artist in town draw up some wanted posters and I showed them to the couple that was robbed and they were able to identify all three of them. I need you to look at them to see if they are the same three men you met on the road that day." Jess took the drawings from the sheriff and looked at them, the look on his face hardening as he did. It was the same three men.

"The youngest one," the sheriff continued as Jess looked over the drawings, "is Randy Hastings. He's the one with the missing boot heel. He carries two six-guns with pearl handles. The other one is Blake Taggert. He's the one with the bushy beard unless he's shaved it off by now, but I doubt it. He carries a left-handed six-shooter. The oldest one is Frank Beard. He always wears a yellow bandana. He carries a six-shooter, but his specialty is a double barreled shotgun. Hear tell, he's killed several men with it."

Jess looked up at the sheriff with a blank hard look. "These are the three men I met on the road, Sheriff. I'm sure of it. The drawings are a good likeness, that's for sure. Can I keep these?"

"Of course," replied Diggs. "Jess, is there anything else I can do for you right now? Can we help with some of the work here? Running a ranch is a lot of responsibility for a young man."

"Thanks, Sheriff," he replied flatly, "but I can take care of the ranch and myself just fine."

"All right, then. You take care, Jess," the sheriff said as he and his three deputies started to turn their horses around. Just then Jess stopped the sheriff and asked him the one question the sheriff hoped he would never ask, and yet somehow he knew that he would.

"Sheriff; you said they bragged about raping some women; meaning more than one. Does that mean they raped my little sister Samantha?" he asked solemnly.

Sheriff Diggs' eyes fell to the ground. He didn't want to answer the question, but there was no way he could avoid it. He knew that in his heart. Jess deserved to know the truth no matter how terrible. The sheriff was a man who always figured the truth was the best way out of a bad situation. His eyes slowly raised from the ground and he looked Jess straight in the eyes and told Jess the cold terrible truth.

"Yes. I had hoped not to have to tell you about it," he replied sympathetically. "But the truth is those bastards did rape Samantha. I'm sorry to have to tell you that."

Jess's eyes glazed over and darkness seemed to emanate from the back of them and the sheriff had seen the look that he had in his eyes all too often lately. He knew the look; rage, revenge, love, hate, all wrapped up in one look. He saw it in these eyes of a boy not yet fifteen. He knew what Jess had on his mind and he knew there was nothing that he or anyone else for that matter could do to change it. Jess never changed his look or never lost his lock on the sheriff's eyes.

"Thanks for your honesty, Sheriff," he replied sharply.

"You're welcome. I only wish I could have done more," replied the sheriff sadly.

"That's okay, you're a good man, Sheriff, and I figure I owe you one," he replied. "I know you've done your best. I'll take care of it from here." The sheriff didn't have to try to figure out what that meant.

Sheriff Diggs and his men turned their horses and headed back down the ranch road out to the main trail leading into Black Creek. As they did, the other three men with the sheriff tipped their hats at Jess as if to say they understood what he was going through. Jess simply nodded back. As the men rode away, one of them looked over at the sheriff with an apprehensive look on his face.

"Did you see what that boy had in his eyes?" the man asked. "I ain't ever seen that much rage and coldness in any man's eyes, much less a boy."

"I know," replied the sheriff, "but he ain't no boy anymore. Hell, it's only been a few days since I've seen him and I swear he looks five years older already. And by the look in his eyes, he'll damn well do it that's for sure. I've seen that look before and it ain't a good look. I wouldn't want to be any of those three bastards."

Jess watched the sheriff and his three deputy's ride off down the main road until they were out of sight. He went back to plowing the field as if nothing happened. He thought about his sister Samantha. He thought of the fear and helplessness she must have went through as she was being raped and murdered. He could hardly contain the rage within him; but he continued to plow, never stopping. The rage would fuel him. The rage would keep him going. The rage would always be his edge.

He finished plowing for the day. He walked back up to the house with the rifle in one hand and the shotgun in his other and when he got to the porch, he noticed a large box sitting on the porch. He looked inside. He found several loaves of bread, a dozen biscuits, an apple pie and a big pot of stew. *Sara*. He had been so busy he never seen her drop it off.

He finished supper and got his pa's gun and holster along with the new pistol and holster he found and went out to the creek for his nightly practice. He spent the next two hours practicing. First, he practiced with his pa's gun. He would draw the gun over and over again. Sometimes he thumbed the hammer and sometimes he fanned the hammer. His pa's gun was much heavier than the other gun and much harder to get out of the holster quickly. He noticed as soon as he strapped the new gun on, everything worked so much smoother and faster. The very design of the new gun and holster made it much easier to draw it quicker. Fanning the gun was easier, too with the tall hammer that stuck straight up. Jess looked at the pistol where it had .41 Caliber stamped on it.

He took six .45 caliber shells out of a box of ammo and put them into the pistol. They fit perfectly. He took them back out and even tried to put the lead end one of the bullets into the front of the barrel of the gun and it looked as if it was the correct caliber. Somehow, and he would never find out why, someone had the wrong caliber stamped on this pistol. He loaded the gun again and placed it back in the holster. He drew and fired at a tree across the creek. He was amazed at how much easier and quicker his draw was with this new pistol. He finished his practice with the new gun going through almost fifty rounds of ammo, and went back to the house. After making some coffee to go along with a nice piece of Sara's apple pie, he went to bed with his pa's .45 loaded next to him on the bed.

In the morning he decided to go into town for some supplies. He stopped at the general store and thanked Sara for the food and Jim for all his help. He ordered some supplies he thought he needed, and some .45 cartridges for his pa's gun.

"Why do you need bullets, Jess?" asked Jim.

"Just doing some target shooting down by the creek," replied Jess.

"You need a dozen boxes for target shooting?"

"You do if you plan on target shooting a lot," he replied bluntly. "I hope you'll allow me credit like my pa."

"Why of course, Jess," he replied. "By the way, did you know that your pa had some money in the bank? I'm not saying that so you will pay me in cash, I just thought you should know."

"No, I never knew my pa had any money saved," he replied.

"Well, you go see Mr. Jameson at the bank and I'm sure he will let you know all about it," said Jim.

"Thanks Mr. Smythe," he replied.

The bank was small and there were only three windows with one man working the only window that was open. Mr. Jameson was sitting behind a desk over to the left of the teller windows. As soon as he spotted Jess, he got up immediately.

"Good afternoon, Jess. I'm really sorry about what happened to your family," exclaimed Mr. Jameson. "What can I do to help you today?"

"Jim Smythe says my pa had money in your bank and that it probably belongs to me. Is that right?" he asked.

"That's right, Jess. Why don't we go look at the account and see how much is there. He was a good man, your pa," said Jameson kindly.

"That's nice of you to say, Mr. Jameson, sir," replied Jess. Jameson went behind his desk and picked out a ledger book from a shelf. He leafed through some pages and found what he was looking for.

"Oh…yes…hmm…here we go," Jameson said in his low banker's voice, "yes, he has…or I guess you have…two hundred, seventy-two dollars, and sixteen cents. Do you need some of the money right now?"

"Well, I don't rightly know just yet," he replied, as he thought about it for a moment. "How about if I take out twenty dollars for now? That way I can pay off my pa's bill and pay cash for my supplies. I guess I can use credit when I really have to. Better to pay my way if I can, don't you think?"

"Absolutely," replied Jameson. "Banks are for borrowing money when you don't have it and credit is for people who can't pay right away. The less you use of either is a good way for a man to live, Jess."

"I agree," he replied.

Mr. Jameson filled out a slip of paper for Jess. "Here, take this to the teller and he'll get you your money."

"Thanks, Mr. Jameson. You've been a real big help. This will be my bank from now on."

"Why thank you, Jess. That's a mighty nice thing to say," said Jameson.

Jess walked out of the bank and headed to the general store. He loaded up his supplies and paid in cash even over Jim's repeated objections. Jim was a little more than curious when Jess also asked for two dozen boxes of .45 caliber rounds instead of the original dozen he had asked for when he first came in. Jess figured as long as he had the money, he might as well get plenty. He knew he was going to use that much and more.

"Jess, what in the hell are you going to do with all these bullets?" asked Jim awkwardly.

"Like I said, just doing some target shooting down at the creek," he replied. "As a matter-of-fact, do you have some empty bottles I could have to use for targets?"

"Well…yes; you'll find all you want behind the store, but you be careful with your target shooting, you hear?" cautioned a worried Jim. "We don't want anything happening to you."

"Oh, I'll be careful; honest. My pa was starting to show me how to shoot just before…well, you know," he replied.

"I know, buy just be careful, okay. You promise me," Jim pleaded.

"I can promise you this; I plan on being real careful for the rest of my life," he replied emphatically, as he walked out and picked up a dozen or so of the bottles on the ground out back and headed back to the ranch.

Jess finished his work, had supper and went down to the creek with his pa's gun strapped on. He carried the new gun and holster over his left shoulder. He set up some bottles across the creek. Some he stood up on the ground and some were stuck upside down on branches waving in the slight breeze. He began the practice that would become a ritual for the next two years. He would draw the guns several times very slow, but very deliberately. That way he made sure he was doing everything just right. He would dry fire both guns; going through the entire motion perfectly. Cocking the pistol on the draw and then squeezing the trigger as he pointed the gun at the target. Then he would load the gun with .45 cartridges and go through the same motions again, firing live rounds. He would do it slowly at first and then finish with fast draws. He would repeat everything over and over again relentlessly. It didn't take long before he ran out of ammunition. He made another run into town to pick up a few supplies and another two dozen boxes of .45 cartridges. While he was at the general store, Sheriff Diggs walked in.

"How's my favorite young man, Jess?" Diggs said smiling.

"Hi, Sheriff; I'm just fine," he replied. Sheriff Diggs counted out the twenty-four boxes of .45 cartridges sitting on the counter and gave Jess a curious look.

"Twenty-four boxes of cartridges? Jess, what the hell are you doing with all this ammunition? I heard you're buying poor Jim clean out," the sheriff asked curiously.

"I'm just doing some target practice," he replied evasively. "A man has to know how to use a gun these days."

"How's it going so far?" asked Sheriff Diggs.

"Pretty good so far," he said bluntly.

"Well, you be careful with guns, Jess," replied Diggs. "They ain't toys you know."

"I know, Sheriff, I'll be careful," he said.

"Especially with that shotgun there," said Sheriff Diggs, as he nodded to the back of the wagon where Jess had put his pa's .44-.40 rifle and double barreled shotgun.

Jess picked up his supplies and the boxes of cartridges and loaded them in the wagon. He climbed up in the seat and slapped the reins on the paint's rear and headed out of town and back to the ranch. Jim looked at Sheriff Diggs.

"You need anything, Sheriff?" asked Jim.

"Not really; I was just checking on Jess," said Sheriff Diggs. "He makes me nervous messing with his pa's guns. I don't like him getting that close to a pistol at his age, especially with what's happened and all. There's something going on in that boy's head and I don't think it's anything good either."

"Hell Sheriff, his whole family was murdered in cold blood and he saw it with his own eyes," expressed Jim. "That would put a change in anyone's life including you, the hard-case that you are." The sheriff laughed at that and agreed.

"Well, let me know what he buys from you in the way of ammunition, okay?" asked Diggs. "I want to keep an eye on him. He's really starting to worry me."

"Sure thing, Sheriff," replied Jim. "Sara and I only want the best for him too, but he is a man now and he's going to have to find his own way."

"I know. I just don't want it to be the wrong way," cautioned Sheriff Diggs.

The sheriff walked out and looked down the main street and he could see Jess turning the corner out of town. There was a real bad feeling growing in the back of his head about him. Yet, somehow he knew there was nothing he could do about it.

He knew the boy was holding in a real rage about what had happened to his family and he understood that. He just wondered how all that rage would find its way out of the young man. Then he slowly hung his head and shuddered inside as he came to the realization that he already knew the answer to that question.

CHAPTER SIX

For the next two years, Jess pretty much followed the same routine every day. He worked the ranch, taking care of the stock and working the fields. He sold off small groups of cattle here and there and put the money in the bank. He made many trips to town for supplies and ammunition. Every evening, he went down to the creek and practiced with his pa's .45 and the new pistol. He was getting pretty fast with his pa's gun, but he was like greased lightning when he drew his new gun. His accuracy was getting much better, too. He rarely missed a bottle whether it was standing still or even waving in the breeze hanging on a branch. He had even taken to throwing bottles up in the air and hitting them on the way down. He made it more difficult by wearing a hat while looking straight ahead and not up and then only drawing the gun when the bottle came into his field of view. This only gave him a fraction of a second to hit the target. At first, he missed most of the bottles. Later on, he rarely missed one.

He learned to point and shoot accurately. He learned to rapid fire and to fan the trigger, especially the second shot; which would become his trademark shot. He would cock the hammer back as he pulled the pistol out for the first shot and then use the middle finger of his left hand to fan the second shot a split second later. Before he drew, his right hand was down by the butt of his pistol and his left hand was just above his right hand, ready to fan the second shot. He would even go upstream and throw several bottles in the creek and run back and wait for them to come into his side vision. When they did, he drew and blasted them out of the water, one by one.

The new gun seemed to jump out of the holster with the least of effort. He was well on his way to being the fastest man to draw and shoot a pistol because he had an advantage that no other man had; the gun. Without it, he could learn to draw as fast as any of the best. But with it, he would become unbeatable.

Not only did he practice with pistols; he practiced with the rifle and the shotgun. With the shotgun, he made a special holster that was strapped to his back so that the handle of the shotgun stuck up just over his right shoulder. He practiced loading both shells into the shotgun in one fluid motion. He sewed some pockets onto his shirt that held two shotgun shells together so that he could grab and reload the shotgun quickly. He had to carry his pistol cartridges in his front pants pockets since the holster had no holders for bullets. He didn't understand why, but it didn't matter to him. He learned to throw a knife. He made a scabbard for the knife and tucked it behind him under the holster and tied it in place with a small leather thong.

During all this time, the sheriff was out to talk to Jess several times. He knew what Jess was planning and he knew it from the start. About a week before Jess was ready to head out for the trail, he decided to pay a visit to Sheriff Diggs and see if there was any news about the three men who had murdered his family. As he walked into the sheriff's office, the sheriff was checking out the lock on one of his three jail cells.

"Need help with that, Sheriff?" asked Jess. The sheriff turned around.

"Well it's about time you came to visit me," exclaimed Diggs. "Naw, I'll get the blacksmith down here to fix it. Damn thing won't stay locked and I sure can't have that. What can I do for you?"

"I'm just checking one last time to see if you've heard anything new about the three men who killed my family," replied Jess.

"Actually, you're in luck," exclaimed Sheriff Diggs. "I just got some information on one of them. Remember the one with the missing boot heel?"

"I remember every one of them, Sheriff," he replied candidly.

"Well, Sheriff Manley, up in Tarkenton, about two hundred miles northwest of here, says some-one fitting his description got into a shootout with the local hothead there and got himself wounded," exclaimed Sheriff Diggs. "He killed the other man, but needed surgery to remove a bullet from his left thigh so he's been recuperating in the town's local cathouse for the last couple of weeks. I've got no information on the other two, but at least it's a start."

"Why doesn't the sheriff arrest him and lock him up?"

Sheriff Diggs let out a sigh as he sat down behind his desk. "Jess, you need to understand that most lawmen are not tough men," he explained. "Some of them can't even handle a gun and quite frankly, most of the lawmen in small towns just do it for the money so they don't starve. They can't handle or won't handle most hardened criminals."

"Then they need to get new lawmen," he countered.

"No one else will take the jobs in those small towns," said Diggs shaking his head. "I ain't saying it's right, I'm only telling you how it really is, okay?" Jess just shook his head, not wanting to understand how things really were.

"Anyway," the sheriff continued, "he's the one called Randy Hastings. The only murder he's known to have committed is your family, although I have to believe he's guilty of more. The wanted poster says there's a five hundred dollar bounty on his head, dead or alive. I thought about heading up there and seeing if I can bring him in."

"No, don't bother, Sheriff," he replied sharply. "Leave him to me."

Sheriff Diggs had a look of frustration on his face as he took on a fatherly tone. "Jess, don't talk that way," he said. "Hell, Jess, I know what you've been planning since that day I met you at your house when you were plowing the fields. I've watched you come into town and buy every round of ammunition Jim Smythe has ordered over the last two years. I know about your practice with your pa's gun and I know what's in that skull of yours. But it just ain't a good idea to go off and hunt men down and kill 'em. It'll change your life forever. It'll turn you into a cold-blooded killer and you'll never be able to come back from that. Once you start, you can't stop and then you'll end up dead before it's over. Trust me, I've seen it over and over again and I don't want to see it happen to you."

"Sheriff, I understand what you're trying to do, and I appreciate it, I really do," he said thoughtfully. "But you have to understand something. I died inside that day I sat on the porch of my pa's house after finding my entire family murdered. That's the day I changed, not today. I have only one mission left in life and it's to hunt those bastards down and make them pay. I'll kill every one of them along with anyone else who gets in my way. Look in these eyes, Sheriff. What do you see?" He walked closer to the sheriff. The sheriff looked into Jess's eyes, which were black and cold, devoid of anything but death and vengeance. Diggs lowered his eyes to the paperwork on his desk, a sad look on his face, even though he understood.

"Okay, here is everything I have on Randy Hastings," exclaimed Sheriff Diggs. "As soon as I get anything on the other two, I will get it to you. You just promise me you're going to be careful. These men are cold and callous killers Jess," replied the sheriff.

"Thanks, Sheriff," he said, as he took the copy of the wanted poster of Randy Hastings. "You can be sure of one thing. Their killing days are coming to an end." Jess said it with such a meaning in his voice that the sheriff truly believed it.

Jess headed over to the bank to see Mr. Jameson. He wanted to go over the account before he left town. He had sold everything that he figured he wouldn't need and now had over nine hundred dollars in the bank. As always, Mr. Jameson was working at his desk. He was always glad to see Jess because he was usually bringing money to deposit.

"Howdy, Jess. Making a deposit again?" asked Mr. Jameson.

"Not today. Actually, I need to take some money out," he replied.

"Well, how much do you need, Jess?"

"I'd like two hundred dollars."

"Alright," said Jameson, as he filled out a slip for him to take to the teller. Jess remained seated. "Anything else I can do for you today, Jess?"

"I was wondering how I can get money when I'm on the trail?" he asked.

Jameson explained about how he could wire for money if he needed any while away from town. Then Jess went to the general store and visited with Jim and Sara. He explained that he would be leaving town and he paid up his bill and purchased all the boxes of .45 cartridges Jim had in stock, as well as rounds for the rifle and more shotgun shells. He told Jim and Sara that he would stop by next week and see them one more time before he left and then he headed out of town and back to the ranch. Jim and Sara were standing on the front porch of the store watching Jess ride out. Sara looked up at Jim with tears in her eyes.

"Do you think we should tell him?" asked Sara.

"I don't know, Sara. I've got to think about it. We can decide before he leaves town next week."

"He deserves to know, Jim," she pleaded. "We should tell him before he finds out for himself."

"We'll see, Sara, we'll see," he replied.

Jess went back to the ranch and spent his last week there. That last week at the ranch was a week full of memories. He spent a lot of time sitting at the gravesites remembering all the good times. Jess knew that someday he would come back, but not for a while. He knew he was in for a long and hard journey. On the last day, he made his last breakfast in the cabin, saddled up and headed for town to say his last goodbyes. Before he climbed in the saddle he strapped his new gun on, put his pa's rifle in the scabbard and put the shotgun into the special back holster he had made from his pa's scraps of leather. He stuck his pa's Colt .45 Peacemaker in the front of his holster belt. He checked his knife and it was sharp and in its place strapped to the back of his gun belt. He was ready. He was ready for anything or anybody. Yet, he had something more. Something most men didn't have. He had rage—and he had reason. Jess looked over the ranch once more before he started down the ranch road toward the main road leading into Black Creek.

Something happened to him when he rode down the ranch road. Something he couldn't quite put a finger on. His life instantly changed forever at that moment. He felt like he had crossed an imaginary line of some sort. There was no feeling inside him one way or another. There was nothing he was afraid of and nothing that could stand in his way. God help the men he hunted or anyone who got in his way. They were destined for death, and he was destined to do the killing. It felt right.

CHAPTER SEVEN

On his way into Black Creek, Jess stopped along the way at his old favorite stop by the big boulder at the bend in the creek. Not for himself though, just for his horse to drink. While Gray drank, Jess remembered the confrontation with the three men on that fateful day. He could picture the three men as if they were right there in front of him right now. Gray finished drinking and Jess continued toward town. As soon as he rode around the last bend toward the main street of town, he noticed the town was busier than usual. There were people gathering together and talking to one another. He noticed one man who ran across the street to the saloon. He put himself on high alert. He pulled up in the front of Jim and Sara's general store. He dismounted and was tying up Gray when Jim walked out of the store.

"Jess, I have some bad news for you…" he stopped in mid-sentence…"What the hell…?" he said, surprised to see Jess with a gun and holster strapped to his waist, another pistol tucked in the front of the holster, and a shotgun handle sticking up behind his back. Jim stared at him for a few seconds before he spoke again.

"Jess; are you okay?" he asked in a concerned tone.

"Yes sir; I'm just fine."

Jim was looking Jess over and he finally got a good look at the gun strapped around Jess's waist. It was like no other pistol and holster he'd ever seen before. "Jess, where the hell did you get that holster? And what kind of gun is that?" asked Jim.

"I found it in the bottom of my pa's lock box," he replied, not wanting to explain how he had really found the gun.

"That doesn't look like any pistol I've ever seen before, and I've never seen a holster quite like that either," submitted Jim, still looking at the pistol and holster Jess was wearing.

"Jim, you said you had some bad news? What news?" he asked, trying to get Jim to tell him what was going on. Jim hesitated, still not sure what to make of Jess.

"Oh, I'm sorry to have to tell you this, but the sheriff was shot dead not more than a half-hour ago," replied Jim, still staring at the pistol and holster Jess was wearing. If Jess was surprised, he didn't show it, but Jim could see a coldness washing across Jess's face and a darkness looming in the back of his eyes.

"Who did it?" he demanded in a harsh tone.

"That no good son-of-a-bitch Red Carter. He came into town and got drunk again at Andy's Saloon and he was trying to pick a fight with some drifter. The sheriff went into the saloon and warned Red he was going to put him in jail again. Red told the sheriff he wasn't going to let him crack him on the head again with that shotgun. The sheriff gave him his last warning and Red just skinned leather and shot him. Then he went back to drinking at the bar again like nothing happened. That cold-blooded bastard is still over there drinking."

"And the drifter?"

"Folks say he high tailed it out of there before the shootout. Sara went over to Doc Johnson's place to see if she could help, but the sheriff was dead before they got him there. Shot right through the heart. I swear it seems like it's always the good ones who go down." Jim replied sadly.

"Not today," said Jess coldly as he turned around and headed for the Doctor's office to see for himself. As he walked away, and without looking back at Jim he said, "Jim, let me know if Red tries to leave town while I go over to the Doc's."

"Well, okay. I guess so," replied Jim, a little worried about the different way Jess was acting.

Jess walked down to the Doctor's office. Doc Johnson was a fair doctor, but not a great one. When Jess walked in, he saw the sheriff lying still on the table. There was blood all over him and his shirt was torn open. The Doc was standing over him with a grim look on his face and Sara was sitting in a chair in the corner of the small room with her head in her hands sobbing. Doc Johnson looked up at Jess.

"He never had a chance," he said gravely.

Jess nodded at the Doc, but said nothing. The Doc pulled a sheet up over the sheriff. Sara had slowed with her sobbing only because she noticed that Jess had come in. She looked up at Jess with tears streaming from her red eyes, but before she could say anything she noticed what Jess was wearing. She was speechless for a moment and she just kept looking back and forth between him and the gun strapped around his waist.

"Jess, what...why are you wearing that?" she said as she nodded to the gun, "and where did you get such a thing?"

"That's not important," replied Jess. "Are you okay?"

"Yes, I'm not hurt, if that's what you mean."

"Alright then, you stay in here with the Doc, okay?"

"Okay; but why?" she asked. "The Doctor doesn't need my help now."

"Just do as I say please." he insisted. She nodded and started sobbing again. Doc Johnson said nothing else. He kept staring at Jess, startled at the change in the young man that, up until now, he had always thought of as a young kid.

Jess walked out and headed across the street straight for Andy's Saloon. He wasn't really thinking about what he was going to do. He just knew he had to deal with Red Carter. This town had been good to him and his family. They were there when he needed them and they were terrified of Red Carter. They would be even more terrified now, since there was no law in town and no one was going to step up to replace the sheriff now after what Red had done. He stopped in the middle of the street. He looked up and down the main road. He glanced over to the general store and saw Jim standing just outside the door, watching. He glanced over his shoulder and saw Sara looking out of the Doc's office window. He looked down to the sheriff's office and then looked back to the saloon. He realized once he walked in there, his life would take another turn and there was no coming back from it. He was ready.

He walked through the swinging doors of the saloon. As soon as he stepped inside the saloon, he stopped to look around. There were four men at a poker table, but they weren't really playing cards anymore. They were just going through the motions, terrified that Red Carter would start in on them next. The barkeep was standing behind the bar cleaning up just so he'd have something to do. Red Carter was standing at the bar with a bottle of whiskey and a shot glass. He looked up at Jess.

"Why, little Jess Williams," Red said sarcastically, "What the hell are you doing in a saloon? And what the hell is all that you've got on you? Are you wearing a six-shooter now?" Jess didn't reply, he simply glared at Red.

"What the hell you got behind you," continued Red. "Is that a shotgun? Are you going rabbit hunting or something? Speak up, boy, I'm talking to you!"

Jess looked him straight in the eyes with no discernable emotion. "You shouldn't have killed the sheriff, Red. He was my friend and a good man. He didn't deserve to be shot down like that."

"The hell he didn't," he retorted. "He was gonna crack me on the head with that damn shotgun again."

"You still shouldn't have killed him."

"What the hell is it to you, boy?" he asked sarcastically. "You gonna do something about it? Oh, you ain't really going rabbit hunting are you? You mean to tell me that you came in here to square off with me for killing a two-bit sheriff? You gotta be kidding me, boy. You ain't got the gonads to face me or any other man for that matter."

The barkeep, William, who hadn't said anything up to now, finally got up enough courage to speak. "Jess, do us all a favor and go on home," implored William. "We've had enough killing here today. Red, you leave the boy alone."

"You shut the hell up, barkeep, or there'll be some more killing real soon, starting with you!" hollered Red. The barkeep quickly went back to minding his business.

Jess moved over to the left of the saloon. He knew that Sara was still looking out of the window across the street, and he didn't want to chance a stray bullet hitting her. He moved toward a corner where no one could get behind him. He never took his eyes off Red. Red finally realized Jess was serious. Red moved himself away from the bar a little and straightened up his stance and dropped his hand a little closer to the butt of his pistol.

"Boy, why don't you go home now before you get hurt," warned Red. "I ain't ever shot a boy, but if you plan on pulling for that gun you've got, I'll kill you for sure. Don't you ever doubt it, not even for one second."

"You're killing days are over," replied Jess with a coldness in his voice. The cheeks on Red's face quivered. His ears turned a cherry red and he was about all out of what little patience he had.

"Why you cocky little bastard!" hollered Red. "You think you can come in here and threaten me? I ain't scared of no man, much less a wet behind the ears little shit head punk like you. You've got about five seconds to clear out of here before you catch a case of lead poisoning from this lead pusher on got on my right hip!"

"Then I guess you've got about five seconds to live; so I gotta ask, what're you planning on doing with the time you have left?" he asked, his eyes locking firmly on Red's.

"I guess I'm gonna kill me a punk ass kid," he retorted angrily.

Red moved his hand a little closer to the butt of his pistol. Jess had already placed his hands into position without Red even knowing it. Jess could see in Red's eyes that he was going to draw. Jess never moved. He waited until Red went for his pistol and Jess still never moved. Red finally got his hand on the butt of his pistol and pulled. Red's gun barrel just cleared the top of his holster and then the gun fell backward and Red's hand was no longer holding it. Instead, his hand was clutching his chest where the bullet from Jess's pistol had burned through his heart exploding it instantly. Red slumped to his knees. He looked at Jess with a look of utter surprise. An instant later, he was lying face down in a pool of blood not more than ten feet from the drying pool of blood that had been left from Sheriff Diggs's body. Jess watched Red's death with no emotion. After Red fell to the floor, Jess put his gun back in his holster in one quick smooth movement.

"Jesus Christ!" exclaimed the barkeep. "I ain't ever seen anyone draw like that before. If I hadn't seen if for myself, I would have thought you drew on him before he had a chance. Jess, you're lucky you got a witness or else they'd say it wasn't a fair fight."

Jess said nothing. He just looked at Red Carter's dead body lying face down on the floor. Jess walked over to Red's body and using his left boot, he rolled him over. He unbelted his holster and reached down and picked up Red's gun and stuck it back in the holster. He checked Red's pockets and found about fifty dollars and he placed ten dollars of it on the bar.

"This should help pay for any damages," exclaimed Jess.

"I don't know if you should be taking his stuff, Jess. It doesn't seem right," alleged the barkeep.

"He won't need it anymore," he replied briskly. "Besides, as far as I see it, I've earned it. Is that his horse out there?" The barkeep nodded affirmatively.

"I'll be taking that, too then."

"Don't matter to me. I mind my own business, Jess," the barkeep said timidly.

"I'll be selling the horse and saddle. If you need any more money to clean up or fix any damages, you see Mr. Jameson at the bank and he'll give you the money, okay?" Jess stated.

"Sure thing, but this is more than enough," he countered. Jess walked out of the saloon and Sara was standing in the middle of the street with her hands over her mouth.

"Oh my Lord, Jess, what have you done?" asked Sara.

"I did what was needed, Sara," he answered briskly. "I've got some business to take care of. When I'm done, I'll stop by and see you and Jim before I leave, okay?"

Sara nodded and headed down the street toward the general store. Jess walked the horse over to the stables and sold the horse and the saddle. He sold the rifle he found on Red's horse to the gunsmith and he took the money to Jameson and deposited it. He kept Red's .45. He figured it was always good to have extra weapons handy. Then he walked over to Jim and Sara's store. He found Jim behind the counter and Sara sitting in a chair at the end of the counter by the small wood stove that Jim used to heat up the front of the store. They both looked up at Jess when he walked in as if they didn't even know him anymore.

"Jess," said Jim, "I know what you're planning to do and it's no life for a young man. Is there any way we can talk you out of this?" Jess looked Jim straight in the eyes and gave a simple one word answer.

"No," he stated firmly.

Sara wiped more tears from her eyes and said, "Jess, you just killed a man over at the saloon and you don't seem the slightest bit bothered by it. I swear you are not the same boy."

"I'm not a boy anymore and I'm surely not the same person you knew before," he replied softly. "Red Carter needed to be killed and I won't apologize for it to anyone. I only hope that you won't hate me for it."

"We could never hate you, Jess," said Sara. "We will always consider you family. We just don't want to see you turn to this way of life. Using a gun is not a good way to live. It's a good way to die."

"I don't plan on dying, but I'm not afraid of it either," he said with meaning.

"Jess, where in the hell did you get that gun?" asked Jim.

Jess let his palm touch the butt of the pistol. "Let's just say it came to me."

"Was it your pa's?" pressed Jim.

"I'm not rightly sure, but it's my gun now," he replied. "Anyway, I have to leave now. The sheriff told me last week that he had a lead on one of the men who killed my family. He said that he was involved in a shooting up in Tarkenton about two hundred miles northwest of here. I intend to hunt the bastard down and kill him."

"Like Red Carter?" asked Sara, still wiping tears from her eyes.

"Yes, only worse," he replied ominously. "I plan on letting that son-of-a-bitch die a little bit slower."

"Oh Jess," Sara said in almost a whisper. Jim looked at Sara and he knew what she was thinking. She figured it was time to tell Jess something she would never reveal if his family was still alive, but there was no reason to hold back the truth any longer.

"Jess, there is something that we need to tell you," said Sara, still trying to compose herself. "Your parents swore us to never tell you about this, but now they're gone and we think you should know."

"Know what?" he asked.

"Jess, you have other family," interjected Jim. Jess turned to look at Jim with a look of disbelief.

"What the hell are you talking about?" he asked intensely, a bewildered look on his face. "I don't have any other family. My family was murdered." Jim hung his head and began to speak in a quiet, deliberate tone.

"Jess, John Williams was a good man and a better friend; but he wasn't your real pa..."

"That's not true!" retorted Jess, cutting Jim off in midsentence. Jim cleared his throat and gathered his emotions so he could continue.

"Jess, your real father was a man by the name of Ed Sloan. He's a gunslinger and a gambler who was taken with your ma the minute he saw her. I tried to tell her he was no good for her, but she wouldn't listen. Don't blame your ma, Jess. She was young and he was as slick as they come. She spent some time with him and she ended up pregnant with you...and your brother, Tim." Jess sat down in the other chair in the front of the store stunned by this revelation about another part of his family he had never known about. Jim cleared his throat and continued.

"After your ma had the two of you, your real father took off with your twin brother and a gal from Dixie's he'd gotten close to while your ma was with child. Her name was Sally. He was a no good son-of-a-bitch and he hurt your ma. Last we heard about your brother Tim, he'd taken up the gun and hear tell he's mighty fast with one. Your father, Ed, is even faster. The two of them are no good and you should think twice before you have anything to do with them if you have any sense, Jess. Anyway, we figured you had a right to know," explained Jim.

Jess couldn't believe what he was hearing. The thought of all this just balled his nerves up in a knot that found its way to his throat. Then, he made a decision right then and there. He couldn't let all this distract him now. He would have to deal with it later.

He stood up and looked at Jim and Sara. "Do you know where they are now?"

"Last we heard they were both in Wichita," replied Jim. "That was quite a while ago though. They could be almost anywhere by now."

"Thanks for telling me," replied Jess. "But, I still have to go."

"No you don't," cried Sara, almost desperately, "you can stay here with us."

Jess thought for a moment, but he knew in his mind there was no turning back now. His mind was made up. Sara and Jim saw the look in his eyes and they both realized it too. They both knew he was going to live or die by the gun. Sara stood up and walked to Jess and gave him a long hug. Jess turned to Jim and extended his hand. Jim shook Jess's hand, hoping it wouldn't be the last time he did so.

"I'm going to miss the both of you," said Jess. "I'll keep in touch and if you need anything, tell Jameson over at the bank. He'll know where I am most of the time."

Jess hung his head for a moment and without another word he walked down the steps and to his horse, climbed up in the saddle and headed out of Black Creek. He never looked back. Jim and Sara were both standing on the front porch of the store watching him ride away. They were holding hands and exchanging glances. Sara looked at Jim as Jess finally turned the corner.

"Do you think we'll ever see him again?" she asked.

"I hope so, Sara, I surely hope so."

"Me too," she said, starting to cry again.

As Jess turned the corner at the end of the street, his thoughts turned to what Jim and Sara just told him about his brother and father. He knew he would eventually track them down, but not until he finished his business at hand. He made up his mind right then and there that he would always consider John as his real pa no matter what else was true.

His thoughts turned to Randy Hastings. There was one thing he was sure of. He knew that Randy Hastings was one of the three men who murdered his family. He also knew he was going to find him, confront him and then kill him. Of that, he was certain. His journey had begun. It would not be over until all three of the men who murdered his family were in their graves. Only then would justice be served. He rode out of Black Creek and headed for Tarkenton. Destiny would meet him there…at least part of it.

CHAPTER EIGHT

Jess rode all day watching the landscape change as he went along. He had never been anywhere away from his home and was seeing everything for the first time. He stopped along a creek for some lunch that consisted of jerky and biscuits Sara had given him. He continued along until he found a nice place to bed down for the night. He picked a site several hundred feet off the trail in a clump of trees and bushes to give him plenty of cover. He leaned his saddle against the largest of the trees to give his back some cover while he slept. He started a very small fire and warmed up some beans. He had another biscuit with the beans and then he made some coffee. Just after dark, he leaned back against the saddle to sleep. He covered himself with a light blanket. Not because he was cold, but mostly to cover his weapon in case someone came in the night. He laid the shotgun across his lap and he slept with his gun strapped on. He did not sleep well that night.

He rose at dawn and made some coffee, salt pork and pan bread. Then he took some time to practice with his pistol, which was something he would do every day. He broke camp and saddled up and headed back on the trail. Gray was a sturdy horse and Jess pushed him hard. It took Jess six days to reach the outskirts of Tarkenton, where he camped about two miles outside of town. After breaking camp in the morning, he rode up to the end of the main street of Tarkenton. He stopped for a few minutes to look the town over. It was a small town with only about fifteen buildings. There were several people along the street and a couple of people standing together in front of one of the buildings. He dismounted and walked his horse into town. One of the first buildings in town he came to was the livery. He walked Gray over to it and a young boy came out and greeted him.

"Howdy, mister," he said, "do you need me to take care of your horse?"

"What's your name, son?" he asked.

"Billy; and yours?" he asked.

"It's nice to meet you, Billy. My name is Jess and I'd like you to take care of my horse Gray here. He's had a long, hard ride and he needs a good brushing and some of your best feed. If you promise to take extra care of him, there's a dollar a day in it for you."

"Golly, a whole dollar each day?" exclaimed Billy. "That's more than I make in any day, mister. You got yourself a deal, only don't say anything to the owner. He's a mean old cuss. And don't tell him about the good feed or he'll want to charge you extra for it."

"You've got a deal, son," replied Jess. "Where does a man get a good room and a good meal around here?"

"You can get both at the same place," he replied keenly. "The town hotel has rooms and they serve some pretty good food. It's right across from the saloon. Right over there," he said, pointing over to the hotel.

"Thanks Billy. Is Sheriff Manley around?"

"Yeah, he's probably over at the saloon. He ain't much of a sheriff though. Scared of his own shadow."

Jess remembered the little speech that Sheriff Diggs gave him about some of the small-town lawmen not really willing and able to do their jobs. Jess tossed Billy a silver dollar and he caught it and quickly dropped it into his front pocket. He smiled and took Gray into the livery.

Jess looked down the street and spotted the saloon. He felt his stomach growl and decided to go to the hotel and get a hot bath and some grub before he spoke to the sheriff. He walked into the hotel and up to the counter. The desk clerk smiled nervously.

"Need a room?" asked the clerk.

"Yeah, and if you throw in a hot bath and a good meal, I'll consider you a friend," replied Jess.

"Well, we can take care of all that right here," he offered. "Dining room is right in the back and I'll give you room twelve upstairs with a view of the street. I'll take your stuff up to your room if you want," said the clerk. Jess signed the register and paid the clerk for one day, not knowing how long he would be in town.

"I'll take my stuff up myself and I don't want any visitors. I also don't want anyone in my room, not even to clean the linens, understand?" he asked firmly. The clerk looked at him kind of funny and smiled.

"No problem, it's your room as long as you're paying for it. I'll have someone prepare you a nice hot bath."

"Thanks," he replied. I'll be down in a few minutes after I get settled in my room. Make the water extra hot."

"Hot and clean and an extra towel to boot," exclaimed the clerk. "You look like you've been on the trail for a while."

"Long enough," said Jess, as he took the key and went upstairs. He looked out the window to see what view he had and to see if anyone could come in the window easily.

He never realized just how good a hot bath could feel, especially when you haven't had the chance to get one for some time. He soaked in the bath until the water started to cool. He kept his gun within easy reach by pulling a table up to the bath. He got dressed and headed to the dining room. The dining room was small and there were only a few people inside eating. There was a barkeep standing behind the bar and he looked up at Jess as he entered the dining area.

"You hungry?" asked the barkeep.

"As a bear," replied Jess, rubbing his stomach. "What have you got on the menu today?"

"We only have one special a day," said the barkeep. "Today is ham and potatoes and it's really good."

"Then I guess I'm eating ham and potatoes."

"Martha will be out in a minute to get your order," said the barkeep.

Jess sat down at a table in the corner, away from the door and the few people who were in the dining room. The barkeep kept looking Jess over, paying close attention to the shotgun Jess had strapped to his back. The barkeep came over to Jess' table with a pot of coffee and poured Jess a cup of it.

"You expecting trouble, son?" the barkeep asked.

"Why do you ask?"

"You sure got enough hardware hanging on you," he replied. "Are you one of those bounty hunters?"

"I could be," replied Jess. "Is there someone in town that has a bounty on his head?"

The barkeep smiled. "Hell, there's always someone in this town that needs hunting. If you're looking for trouble, you'll sure find plenty of it here."

"I ain't exactly looking for trouble, but I ain't shying from any either."

"Well, enjoy your lunch," said the barkeep. "Martha will be out soon."

Less than a minute later, a young girl with dark red hair came out of the kitchen and stopped at a table and dropped off two plates of food. As she did, she noticed Jess sitting at the table in the corner. She headed for Jess's table and smiled as she walked toward him. The smile turned to a look of concern when she spotted the butt of the shotgun sticking up over his right shoulder. She almost paused, but continued.

"What can I get for you today?" asked Martha.

"I've given it a lot of thought and decided to take the special," he said smiling.

Martha smiled again. "So, Sam told you about the special already, did he?"

"Yes. I'm afraid he beat you to it," he said. "You wouldn't happen to have any apple pie today, would you?"

"You're in luck," she said. Fresh baked this morning. You'll like it. It's the best apple pie anywhere around here."

"You make it?"

"Of course; don't I look like a woman who can make great apple pie?" she asked smartly, her hands on her hips now.

"As a matter-of-fact, you look just like a woman who can make great apple pie."

Martha turned and walked back into the kitchen. Jess tried the coffee. It was just how he liked it, hot and strong. Jess turned his glance toward the door as he saw a man enter the doorway. The man acted like he wasn't sure if he was going to come in or not. The man carried a single six-shooter slung extra low, but not tied down. Jess sized him up and figured him for a local troublemaker and one who was not as fast with a gun as he thought he was.

The man was Scott Vogan, a local ranch hand who worked for a ranch called the Last "C" and he came into town a few times a week to get serviced at the local cathouse, as well as get drunk and raise a little hell. Scott had a slight crush on the waitress

Martha, which is what kept him coming back to the hotel. The barkeep, Sam, noticed Vogan standing in the doorway.

"Scott," Sam said with a stern voice, "I thought I told you not to come back in here today."

"Yeah, well you ain't the owner here and what you say don't mean shit," argued Vogan, as he walked over to the bar and leaned on it. "Now give me a shot of that good stuff you keep under the bar."

"Alright," protested Sam, "but this is the last one today and I mean it. You want anymore and you'll have to see the boss. I don't care how tough you *think* you are."

"Well, that's a start, barkeep," Vogan said with an ugly sneer.

Martha came out carrying Jess's plate of food and as she walked toward his table, she noticed Vogan. She ignored his stare and took Jess his plate of food.

"It sure looks and smells good," Jess said.

"You'll like it," she replied. "You want some more coffee?"

"Yes and keep it coming."

"Hey, Martha," Scott hollered across the room, "how about you take the rest of the afternoon off and spend some time with me? I'll make it well worth your while." Martha shot Vogan a glaring look.

"I've got work to do, Scott," she said tensely. "And even if I didn't, I wouldn't spend any of my time with the likes of you. I thought I'd made that quite clear to you on more than one occasion. I'm not one of them whores down at Julie's place that you can buy for a few silver dollars. Now leave me alone, you hear?"

Jess took another sip of coffee and looked up at Martha.

"Problem?" asked Jess.

"Nothing I can't handle," she replied. What's your name? I haven't seen you around here before."

"I'm not from around here. My name is Jess; Jess Williams."

"Well, it's nice to meet you Jess Williams and welcome to Tarkenton," said Martha smiling.

"Thanks, but I don't plan on staying around too long. I'm looking for someone, a man by the name of Randy Hastings. Heard of him?"

"Who hasn't?" she said plainly. "Just about everyone around here knows Randy. He's a pain in the ass and a cold-blooded killer. He came to town a few weeks ago with two other men. He killed one of the local toughs and then decided to stick around and make the rest of us miserable. He's not someone you want to mess with. He'd just as soon kill you as look at you. What's your business with him?"

"Personal," he replied bluntly.

"Well, you watch yourself around him," she warned as she walked back into the kitchen.

Jess nodded and took a bite of the ham. It was so tender you could cut it with a fork. During the conversation with Martha, Scott was leaning sideways on the bar listening to them. He was jealous and it showed by the scrunched up scowl on his face. As soon as Martha walked away from Jess, Vogan picked up his drink and started to walk over to Jess's table. Jess was listening to his footsteps and paying attention to everything in the room. He was listening for any sound of a gun being slid out of a holster or a hammer being eared back. He heard neither.

"What's your name, son?" asked Scott in a snide tone. Scott slowly walked around the table to face Jess. Jess put his fork down and looked up at Scott with a cold stare that seemed to make the man take a step back.

"I'm not your son and my name ain't any of your business," replied Jess, in a harsh voice and a cold look on his face. "Anything else you want to ask that you've got no business asking about in the first place?"

"You're a cocky little son-of-a-bitch, ain't ya?" asked Vogan.

"Mister, let me make this real easy for you to understand," he said sharply. "My business ain't your business. I just had me a nice hot bath and now I'm trying to enjoy a good hot meal, which is something I haven't had in a week. Now, I plan to eat this meal before it gets cold; so if you're looking for trouble let's get it over with right quick. If not, haul your ass back over to the bar and don't make me tell you twice, because if I have to, I'm grabbing some iron and I'd suggest you do the same." Jess said all of this so matter-of-factly that it took Vogan totally by surprise, and he knew when to fold up and move on and this was surely one of those times.

"Didn't mean to rile you up, mister," he said as he headed back to the bar and leaned on it looking at the empty glass. The barkeep had a smirk on his face. He had enjoyed watching Vogan get his ass ripped.

"Would you like another shot, Scott?" Sam asked sarcastically knowing that his nerves may need a little settling after all.

"Hell yeah, might as well," retorted Vogan. "And wipe that damn smirk off your face."

Jess finished his meal and Martha brought him a nice slab of apple pie. She had watched the confrontation between Jess and Scott from the doorway and she had a smile on her face when she glanced over at Vogan.

Vogan was leaning on the bar just looking down at the shot glass. Jess savored the pie and another hot cup of coffee, paid his bill and headed down the street to the saloon to find Sheriff Manley. After Jess left, Martha came back out from the kitchen. Scott was still nursing his wounded pride along with his whiskey. She walked up behind the bar and started to help Sam wash a few glasses. Scott watched her and wondered what she thought of him after getting told off by a young kid who barely looked like he'd reached manhood yet.

"He didn't look all that tough," said Vogan. Martha eyed him quizzically.

"Then why'd you back down?" asked Martha. "You're always looking for trouble. You had it right in the palm of your hand." Scott let his gaze fall back to his drink.

"Yeah," added Sam, "for a man always looking to give someone a hard time, you sure got a case of the frights."

"Nobody asked you for your opinion," muttered Vogan. "I just didn't think it right to shoot a kid. Hell, he can't be more than sixteen or so."

"He may be young, but he ain't no kid," replied Sam with a knowing look.

"Hell yes he is," chided Vogan. "You saw him. He's still wet behind the ears for Christ's sake."

"Sam's right," interjected Martha. "He might be a little wet behind the ears, but there's something different about that young man. You can see it in his eyes and tell by his demeanor."

"Hell, that punk didn't scare me," rebuked Vogan. "I've taken on tougher men than him and I'm still standing."

"You tell yourself whatever you want," she said as she walked back to the kitchen.

Jess walked into the saloon and quickly looked around. The place was dirty and reeked of cheap whiskey and cigar smoke. The barkeep gave Jess a look and then glanced over at the men playing cards. One of the men looked to be in his fifties and had a tin star on his shirt. He nodded at the barkeep as if to say that he noticed Jess, and then went back to playing his hand.

The barkeep looked back to Jess and asked, "Can I help you, mister?"

"I'm looking for Sheriff Manley." Jess looked over to the man with the badge. "I assume that would be you?"

"You assumed right, son. Now you just wait until I finish this hand. I've been losing at this game all day and I think this hand will make me whole," bragged Manley as he finished his hand and lost.

"Damn it!" carped Manley, throwing his cards on the table. "How can I be such a lousy player?"

"Maybe you ain't such a lousy player," said one of the other men at the table. "Maybe it's just that we're better at the game than you, Sheriff."

"Kiss my ass," groused Manley. "I'll get my money back tonight from you cheatin' bastards."

"Aw, come on now, Sheriff," claimed one of the other men in the game. "We've been playing fair. You've just been playing lousy like always."

"Well, you can still kiss my ass," the sheriff countered as he pushed back his chair from the table and looked up at Jess.

"What can I do for you stranger?" the sheriff asked.

"I'm looking for a man who goes by the name of Randy Hastings. What can you tell me about him?"

"That you shouldn't be looking for him," replied Manley directly. "He ain't nothin' but trouble. He's wanted by the law and has a bounty on his head. What's your business with him?"

"If he's who I think he is, he's one of three men who murdered my family."

Sheriff Manley put his head down for a moment and let out a long sigh then said, "He was heard bragging one night over at the saloon after having a few too many that he had raped and killed some women some years back. No one knew if he was just braggin' or tellin' the truth. He killed one of the local boys here in the saloon recently. Wish he would just take off and leave this place for good."

"Do you know where he is now?"

"Left town a few days ago, but he told a few people that he'd be back. You're kinda young for a bounty hunter, ain't ya?" asked the sheriff.

"I never said I was."

"Sure do look like one," he said. "Why the shotgun? And where did you get a pistol and holster like that?"

"I came here to ask the questions, not answer them," he replied crossly. "What is the bounty on Hastings?"

"Kind of a smart-ass for such a young one," observed Manley.

"Maybe; now what about the bounty?"

"Five hundred dollars the last time I checked."

"I'll be collecting it when he comes back to town."

"I thought you said you weren't a bounty hunter."

"I never said I wasn't."

"There's that smart-ass thing again."

"Don't push me on it, Sheriff," Jess warned.

"I'm the one wearing the star," countered Manley.

"Yeah, and you had a murderer in your town and didn't do a damn thing to arrest him," complained Jess angrily.

"Don't tell me how to do my job," Manley snapped back.

"Then don't make me do yours." argued Jess.

"You gonna go at Hastings?" asked Sheriff Manley.

"I thought I made that pretty clear."

"You seem kinda sure about how things are gonna turn out. Hastings ain't gonna surrender that easy, especially to a young one like you," said the sheriff.

"Who said I was going to ask him to surrender?" replied Jess. "I'm staying over at the hotel. I expect you'll let me know when he comes back to town."

"And just why in the hell should I do that?" demanded Manley, getting agitated at Jess's harsh demeanor.

"Well Sheriff, if you won't do your job, at least be man enough to let someone else do it for you," he barked. "Now I expect you to let me know when he comes to town. If not, you'll answer to me."

"Who the hell do you think you are talking to me like that!" cried out Manley in an embarrassed tone.

Jess took another step toward Manley and spoke calmly and directly. "I'm the man who plans on killing at least *one* man before I leave your town," he warned him. "It's up to you whether or not it's more than one. Enjoy the rest of your game, Sheriff."

Jess turned and walked out of the saloon, ignoring the curse words coming from the sheriff's mouth. He had already figured that Sheriff Manley was nothing more than a coward and he wasn't going to waste any time on him. He had also noticed that Scott Vogan had sauntered into the bar during his discussion with Manley. Vogan had leaned on the bar saying nothing and listening closely. Jess knew that he would probably have to deal with Vogan before he left town, but that would be Vogan's choice. Manley had watched Jess walk out of the saloon and then slowly slid his chair back up to the card table. The other three men at the table were getting ready to start on Manley about the kid telling him off.

"Don't even start on me," advised Manley.

"Start what?" one of the men said, acting as if he didn't know what the sheriff meant.

"You know damn well what I mean!" argued Manley. "Damn young kid thinks he can come in here and tell me what to do."

"I think that's exactly what he did, Sheriff," one of the men said and all three of them starting to chuckle.

"Kiss my ass, the bunch of you," muttered Manley.

They started up the game again and one of the men got a serious tone in his voice. "You know, Sheriff, I saw something in that young man. I don't think I'd cross him if I were you."

"What the hell are you talking about?" asked Manley.

"I don't know," replied the man. "It's just a feeling. The way he carries himself and that gun he's wearing. Did you ever see anything like that before?"

"I heard of some gunslingers making up their own holsters, but I never seen one like that," one of the other men said.

"Well, I ain't messing with that kid anyway," interjected Sheriff Manley. "This damn job don't pay enough. I just run in the drunks and sweep out the jail. If the town wants more than that, they can hire themselves another sheriff."

Jess took a stroll around town and checked out the buildings and back entrances to them. He wanted to know more about his surroundings before Hastings came back to town. He stopped at the livery to check on Gray.

"How's he doing?" Jess asked Billy. The stable boy had been brushing Gray down when Jess walked up.

"He's doing just fine, mister," he replied. "He sure likes apples. I hope it's okay that I gave him a few earlier."

"He loves apples," he said. "Just don't give him too many, he's quite the hog. I'll be staying in town a few days over at the hotel. How would you like to make ten dollars?"

"Golly, ten dollars! That's a lot of money. What do I have to do for it?" he asked excitedly.

"All you have to do is let me know when Hastings gets back to town."

"What if he finds out I told you?" he asked, a worried look on his face. "He'll beat me for sure and I'll lose my job and I need this job mister. I have to help my ma. She's got a bum leg and can't do much work. Besides, how am I supposed to let you know without getting caught?"

"I'll tell you how, Billy," he replied. "I'm staying at the hotel in room twelve. If it's late at night, just knock on my door three times, wait a few seconds, and knock twice more. If it's during the day, just find me and look me in the eyes from a distance. I'll know what it means. And I'll make it twenty dollars instead, how's that?"

"Well, my ma can sure use twenty dollars."

"Thanks, Billy, I owe you," he said as he turned to walk out. Before he got to the front door, he turned and said, "Hey, Billy?"

"Yeah?"

"I never saw a dead man give anyone a beating," he said with a knowing look.

Jess went back to the hotel and picked up his clean set of clothes. He went to his room and packed his clothes in his bag. He always had to be ready to move at an instant. After that, he went back down to the dining room of the hotel and had supper. He turned in early and arranged his room very carefully. He put the chair in front of the door and put his pistol on the table next to his bed. The bed was comfortable, much more so than the cold hard ground he had been sleeping on the last several days. He drifted off to sleep wondering how he would kill Randy Hastings. He wanted to make him suffer as much as possible. He imagined putting the last bullet between his eyes.

CHAPTER NINE

Jess rose before dawn, dressed and went down to the dining room. There were a few people already eating. He sat down in the corner again. Before long, Martha came out of the kitchen and took a few orders and then she noticed him. She brought him a cup and poured him some coffee.

"Are you hungry this morning?" asked Martha.

"How about some scrambled eggs and a pile of bacon?"

"Be right out with it," she said smiling.

"Still got any of that apple pie left for dessert?" he asked before she walked away.

"I saved a piece just for you."

"And maybe you could throw in some flapjacks, too?"

"My, my; aren't we hungry this morning?" she asked playfully.

"I'm still a growing boy," he replied, shrugging his shoulders. Martha laughed as she headed for the kitchen.

Jess finished breakfast and washed it down with several cups of hot coffee. He noticed Sheriff Manley eating at another table. Jess left Martha a nice tip and once again she smiled. It was the best tip she'd ever got waiting tables. She walked over and began cleaning off Sheriff Manley's table. He had been joined by one of his poker pals, a man by the name of Ron Butler.

"Well, Martha," the sheriff asked, "what do you think about our young new guest we have in town."

"I don't rightly know yet, Sheriff, but he seems like a mighty interesting young man. I think he acts a lot older than he really is."

"What do you mean by that?"

"Sheriff, he may be all of sixteen or seventeen, but he acts more like a man of twenty. He backed down Scott Vogan yesterday and the look in his eyes when he was doing it…well…it scared Vogan, and quite frankly, it scared me a little, too."

"Really; what kind of look?" asked the sheriff.

"The kind of look that could burn a hole straight through you," she replied frankly. "A look of torment and hatred all rolled up into one. If that look didn't kill you, I'm sure he would in a heartbeat. Yet, he seems like such a nice young man. It's a little strange; like he's two people all wrapped up as one."

"Well, you don't have to worry about him much longer," said the sheriff. "He's looking for Randy Hastings."

"He told me that yesterday," she said fatefully. "I sure wouldn't want to be him."

"You mean our young guest over there?"

"No, I'm saying I wouldn't want to be Randy Hastings," replied Martha with caution.

Ron Butler finally chimed in. "Hastings is pretty damn fast with those twin six-shooters," said Butler. "I watched him draw in that gunfight over at the saloon and he was pretty quick. Hastings won't be a pushover when it comes to a gunfight."

"Call it a hunch, but I think Hastings may have met his match," she said as she walked back to the kitchen.

"What do you think, Sheriff?" asked Butler.

"I don't know, but I'll put ten bucks on Hastings if you'll take the bet," said the sheriff. Butler thought about what Martha had said about the young man called Jess Williams and took the bet.

Jess went out on the porch of the hotel and sat in one of the chairs. He watched the town wake up and watched the local townspeople going about their daily business. Sheriff Manley left the hotel and headed for the saloon. Jess took another stroll around town and stopped in to see Billy at the livery. The old man who owned the livery was there and he was yelling at Billy for taking too much time caring for Jess's horse. Jess showed up just as the old man slapped Billy on the back of the head.

"Damn it boy, quit fussing over that damn horse and clean up this shit here!" hollered the old man. "I ain't telling you again, you hear?"

"Yes, sir," replied Billy. "I'll get to it right now."

"Well, see to it that you do," grumbled the old man.

ROBERT J. THOMAS

Billy grabbed a shovel and started to scoop up the horse droppings. Jess walked into the livery. The old man noticed him when Jess said good morning to Billy. Billy just nodded at Jess and kept working for fear he'd get another slap on the head.

"What can I do for you?" the old man asked in a grumpy voice.

"Well, first off, you can stop slapping the boy around," replied Jess. "That horse he's fussing over is mine. I expect him to be taken care of properly, and I made him promise me to do so." Jess didn't mention the extra money he was paying Billy to take care of Gray, remembering what Billy said about the old man taking the money if he found out.

"Hell, that boy ain't got a lick of sense that ain't been beat into him. Besides, what's it to you anyway?" barked the old man. Jess looked at Billy and smiled.

"Well, let's just say that I've taken a liking to the boy and don't want to see him mistreated. You got a problem with that?" he asked, turning to glare at the old man.

The old man looked at Jess and didn't say anything for a moment or two, studying him.

"Sure, if that's what makes you happy," replied the old man in a softer tone of voice.

"I'm glad we have an understanding," he implied. "And billy, don't forget a few apples for Gray today."

"No problem," said Billy with a big smile on his face.

"So what're you in town for anyway?" asked the old man, spitting out some tobacco juice on the ground.

"I'm looking for a man by the name of Randy Hastings. You know him?"

"Hell yes, I know him," said the old man. "I take care of his horse. He should be back tomorrow. What's your business with him?"

"Personal."

The old man laughed, "Hope it's not too personal."

"Why do you say that?"

"You'll find out when he gets back in town," replied the old man with a strange smile on his face.

"I suppose I will," he replied, glaring at the old man again, quickly wiping the strange smile off his face.

⌐ ¬

Scott Vogan and Saul Littman had been bellied up to the bar in Spurs Saloon for at least two hours now. They shared a bottle of whiskey and neither of the two was feeling much pain. Ray, the barkeep, didn't like Vogan; but he didn't say anything to him because he knew that Littman was a hired gun with a nasty disposition and pretty good with a pistol.

"So who was this punk who gave you a hatful of shit today?" Saul asked Vogan.

"I never saw him around before. I think I overheard the sheriff say his name was Jess Williams or something like that."

"Why didn't you just pull leather on him and smack a bullet into his smart mouth?"

"I don't rightly know. I guess it was that look in his eyes. It was unnatural like. I thought maybe he was just plumb loco."

"Hells-fire!" bellowed Littman. "A look ain't ever killed anyone as far as I know."

"I suppose so, but you had to be there," explained Vogan in a defensive tone. I'm telling you, it wasn't normal. I think the kid's got the devil inside him or something."

Saul laughed at that notion. "You leave the little shit head to me. I'll straighten him out right quick." Saul looked up just in time to see Ray with a funny look on his face.

"What the hell you smirking about?" asked Saul.

"Nothing," replied Ray, sheepishly.

"Don't give me that shit," refuted Saul. "I saw that little smirk on your face. You best tell me what you think is so funny else I'll wipe that smirk off your face with the butt of my pistol."

Ray was a barkeep, not a fighter, so he answered timidly. "I was just remembering how Sam over at the hotel bar was telling me about how that William's kid backed Scott down yesterday. According to Sam, he's got the look of death in his eyes. I saw it yesterday with my own eyes when he was talkin' to the sheriff."

"Hell, ain't no kid that young gonna be that fast with a pistol and looks don't kill," argued Saul. "He comes in here, I'll show you how to handle a punk ass kid. Now get us another bottle of that whiskey and make sure it's a full one this time."

Jess left the livery and walked back to the hotel and paid for another night. Then he headed for the saloon. He walked in and noticed the sheriff playing a poker game at the same table as before. Jess noticed Scott Vogan at the bar along with several other men. There was one at the far end of the bar next to Scott that Jess picked up on right away. He looked like trouble. He was a tall slender man, wearing a hat that looked too big on him and two pistols worn low and tied down. Jess kept an eye on him along with Vogan as he walked to the bar and ordered a beer. Ray brought Jess a cold beer. Jess took a long drink and noticed an empty table over in the corner. He walked over to it and sat down, deftly removing his hammer strap as he did.

Scott and the man with the oversized hat turned around at the bar facing Jess's table. Vogan, feeling braver after several shots of whiskey and having Littman with him, decided to pay Jess back for humiliating him earlier in the hotel bar.

"So, what are you really in town for, mister?" asked Vogan sharply looking directly at Jess.

"I'm looking for someone."

"Anyone I know?"

"Could be."

"Could be?"

"That's what I said," he replied harshly.

"So, who you looking for?"

"His name is Randy Hastings; you know him?"

"Maybe."

"Maybe?"

"That's what I said," Vogan replied sarcastically.

"Hey, you're the one who asked, and frankly, I don't really care."

"You don't care about what?"

"Neither."

"What do you mean, neither?"

"I don't care if you know him and I don't care if you tell me," countered Jess. The smirk that was on Vogan's face suddenly disappeared and he got a more serious tone in his voice.

"Yeah, I heard of him," admitted Vogan. "He's out of town right now, but he'll be back any day now." Jess simply nodded and didn't respond. Vogan pushed some more.

"So why are you looking for him?" he asked.

"It's personal."

"You and him friends then?"

"Not exactly."

"Well, Hastings ain't someone to mess with."

"Is that right?"

"Yeah, and he don't take kindly to strangers either."

"We ain't exactly strangers."

"So he knows you then?"

"No, we've only met once before and I don't think he'd remember me," replied Jess cagily.

Saul Littman had been listening to all of this, letting Vogan have him fun. Saul put his drink down and took his hat off and sat it on the bar. He reached into his front pocket and took out a half-smoked cigar and lit it. He took a long drag and blew the smoke slowly up toward the ceiling. He took another sip of his whiskey, all the while, studying Jess. He looked at the shotgun handle sticking up over Jess's right shoulder and he took some time to look over the gun strapped to his waist. Jess ignored his stare, but he was well aware of it.

Saul, without taking his stare off Jess, hollered to the barkeep, "Ray, pour me another."

Ray filled the shot glass and Saul reached back and picked it up and tipped his head back and downed the whiskey. He sat the glass down on the bar with a hard thump. He hollered at the barkeep again. "Ray, one more time." Ray filled the glass again as Saul stared straight at Jess.

"So tell me, what do you use that shotgun for?" asked Saul.

Jess still didn't look directly at Saul. He took one quick glance around the saloon and took another sip of his beer and put the glass down gently. Then, he slowly lifted his eyes up and locked them onto Saul's. He figured Vogan was going to be involved in this, but he already decided that this man was the one to worry about first.

"And you are?" asked Jess calmly.

"Who wants to know?" he replied nastily.

"Well, when a man asks me a question, I figure I deserve to know his name before I feel a need to answer him," he stated firmly.

Saul's cocky smile turned to a nasty scowl. "You're quite an arrogant little bastard, ain't you?"

"Yeah, I've heard that," he replied, smiling at Saul now, which only got deeper under his skin.

"What if I don't feel like telling you my name?"

"Well, then I guess I don't feel like answering your question." Saul smiled a cynical smile. He looked over at Vogan who was watching as if he was enjoying the banter.

"Well, if you must know, my name is Saul Littman," he replied as if the name was important to everyone listening. "What's yours?"

"Jess Williams."

"Never heard of you before."

"And that matters?"

"So, now that we know each other, what's the shotgun for?"

"Shootin' rabbits; and sometimes people."

"So, how many people have you killed so far?" asked Saul.

"One."

"Only one?" he asked sarcastically.

"So far."

Saul laughed and so did Vogan.

"And did you kill him with that shotgun or with that fancy looking lead pusher you got there?" asked Saul.

"Does it really matter?"

"Guess not. You pretty good with that pistol?"

"Good enough."

"You sure?"

"Pretty sure."

"And how good is that?"

"How good do I need to be?"

"I don't know," sneered Saul. "Maybe good enough to take me."

Jess noticed an immediate change in Saul and knew that things were coming to a head fast.

"Ray," Saul hollered back at the barkeep, "you forgot to wipe up that dirty table he's sitting at. I can see spilt beer on the table. Is that any way to run a place?"

Ray, who had been watching and listening to the banter between Jess and the two at the bar, was caught completely off guard by the question. "Huh...oh yeah...I'll get it." Ray said as he started to walk over to where he had left a towel to wipe the tables down.

"Don't bother," said Saul, as he reached for the towel that was lying only a foot away from him, "I'm sure he wouldn't mind cleaning up his own table." Saul picked up the towel and threw it at Jess.

What happened in the next few seconds was something that no man in the bar would ever forget. The towel was in the air heading for Jess as Jess reached back with his right hand and found the handle of his bowie knife and he brought the knife out of its sheath and up, going straight for the towel. In one quick fluid motion, Jess caught the towel on the point of the knife and slammed the knife down into the table, and as he did he stood up facing both men. Saul had begun to move his hand toward his right pistol and Vogan's hand was moving for his gun at the same time. Jess drew his pistol, thumbing the first shot, which hit Saul square in the chest. Before the hammer hit the firing pin, Jess's left hand began its movement toward the gun with the middle finger hanging down. Jess fanned the second shot and the bullet slammed into Vogan's chest just above his heart.

Both shots were kill shots, and yet, they were only a fraction of a second apart. Before the two men hit the floor dead, Jess stepped to his right and placed his back against the wall and took a quick glance around to see if anyone else was going to be involved. He quickly glanced over at the sheriff who had a stunned look on his face.

Ray, the barkeep, was the first to speak. "Damn, I can't believe what I just saw. I saw it, but I still don't believe it."

Jess replaced the two spent cartridges and holstered his pistol. He sat back down at his table, able to see the entire place including the door and took another sip of his beer. Sheriff Manley slowly rose from his chair and walked over to the two dead men lying on the floor. Vogan had fallen face forward while Saul had slunk down, banging the back of his head on the bar before hitting the floor. Manley looked up at Jess and just stared at him for what seemed to be forever. The sheriff took in a deep breath and let it out slowly. Then he spoke. "So, you say you're looking for Randy Hastings, hey?"

"I thought I already made myself clear on that matter, Sheriff."

"Well, you'll surely find him now."

"Why's that?"

"Because Hastings only has a few friends around these parts, and you just killed two of them," replied Manley. "I imagine he'll be looking for you once he gets back in town. Sure as hell hope I don't miss that fight. You gonna pay to bury these men?"

"Is there any bounty on either of them?"

"Don't believe so."

"Well then, I'll be taking their horses, saddles, guns and any cash they have on them," he replied plainly. "You can tell the caretaker to bury them and I'll pay for it out of what I get from the sale of their belongings. Tell him nothing fancy, only what's necessary."

"Why the hell should I?"

"Because if you're not going to enforce the law, then at least you can clean up the mess after someone else takes care of it for you," he said bluntly.

Jess stood up and walked over to the two dead men and stripped them of their valuables. He walked the two men's horses over to the stables and tied them up and left a note for Billy. Sheriff Manley walked back to his table. Ron had a funny grin on his face.

"What's that big grin for?" asked Manley.

"Just wondering if you want to cancel your bet?"

"I ain't canceling anything," he muttered. "That kid got lucky is all."

"What I just saw wasn't luck, Sheriff," submitted Butler. "That boy is faster than a whore running out of a church on a Sunday morning."

"Kiss my ass and deal me a winning hand for a change," groused Manley, as he sat back down. He sure hoped he got a good hand because he had a feeling that he was going to lose some money to Ron Butler soon.

Jess headed back to his room and went straight up and turned in for the night. When he woke, he splashed some water on his face and headed down for breakfast. Martha took his order and the place was eerily quiet. Sheriff Manley was sipping coffee with one of the men Jess had noticed at the poker table last night. They both glanced at him repeatedly.

"Well, I heard you had quite a night last night," said Martha as she sat Jess's breakfast on the table.

"It would seem so," he replied.

"Everyone in town is talking about it," she said. "They said you were fast; really fast."

"Is that what they're saying?"

"Yes," she replied cautiously. "Why don't you leave town while you're ahead? You seem like a fairly nice young man, except for the fact that you just killed two men last night."

"Why thank you, Martha. I think you're a fairly nice woman too. But I can't leave town until Randy Hastings is dead. I'm not looking for a fight with anyone else. I didn't ask for one last night. It wasn't my choice."

"There are two men dead, just the same."

"They made an error in judgment."

"And you won't?"

"No."

"How can you be so sure?"

"A good man knows his abilities."

"Oh, and they didn't?"

"That's kind of obvious now, isn't it."

"And you do?"

"Yes."

"It must be nice to be so sure of yourself."

"It does help," he replied flatly.

Martha turned and walked back into the kitchen. Jess finished his breakfast and headed out to the porch to sit. He wasn't there more than five minutes when Billy walked across the street and up to him.

"I got your note about the horses. What should I tell the old man?" Billy asked, referring to the owner of the livery.

"Tell him to sell the one horse and saddle or to buy it himself," he replied. "And tell him to take ten percent and not to even think about cheating me."

"Okay," Billy said as he turned away. He stopped suddenly and turned back to Jess. "What about the other horse?"

"Oh, that one's yours to keep, Billy," he replied. "You pick out which one you want. Every young man needs a horse and now you've got one."

"Thanks Mr. Williams!" exclaimed a very excited Billy. "I never had me a horse. I don't know how to thank you. Can I pay you something for him? I don't have much money, but what I got, you can have."

"Tell you what, Billy," he replied. "You can pay me one silver dollar when I leave town. How's that?"

"That's just fine," he replied keenly. "Wait till my ma finds out I got me a horse. She won't believe it. Thanks again Mr. Williams."

"Just don't forget about our little secret," he reminded Billy.

"I won't. You can be sure of that," he replied.

Billy headed back to the livery and Jess sat on the porch outside the hotel for a while. Then he went up to his room and took a little nap. As he lay there, he thought about Randy Hastings and what he and the other two men had done to his family. Whenever he had any doubts about what he was doing, he thought of his little sister Samantha lying with a bullet hole in her head and pictured his ma hanging in the doorway in a pool of drying blood. Whenever he thought of those things, he knew what he was doing was not only right, it was justified.

CHAPTER TEN

Jess woke before daylight and headed down to the café in the hotel. Jess sat down just as Sheriff Manley walked in. He noticed Jess and sat at a table on the other side of the room. Martha finally came out of the kitchen and stopped by the sheriff's table and took his order. Another man came in and sat next to Manley. Jess recognized the man as one of the men who played poker with Manley at the saloon. Martha walked up to Jess's table and the normal smile was replaced with a frown.

"I guess you didn't take my advice about leaving town while you're still alive," she said dryly.

"Guess not. I just couldn't pass up another helping of those biscuits."

"Biscuits ain't worth dying for, no matter how good they are."

"Some men have died for less."

"You're probably right," she said. "None of it makes any sense to me no matter how much I try to understand it. I suppose it must be something that men just think they have to do."

"Maybe so," he said.

"You want the same as yesterday?"

"You bet. And don't hold back on those biscuits. I could eat a dozen of them," he answered as Martha headed back into the kitchen. Jess thought for a minute and then got up and walked over to Sheriff Manley's table.

"Sheriff, I'd like to come over and talk to you at your office later today," said Jess. The sheriff waited a minute to look up at Jess. When he did, he had an odd look of both fear and anger on his face.

"Well, I suppose that would be okay," replied Manley. "Say about noon?"

"Noon it is," he agreed.

"Can I ask what this is about?"

"I'll let you know when I see you there."

Jess went back to his table to eat his breakfast. After that, he took a stroll around town again, stopping in to visit Billy and check on Gray. Then he went to his room to take a short nap. His eyes opened before the first knock. He had unconsciously heard the noise of footsteps while he was dozing. He had the double barreled shotgun up and ready before the knock on his door was finished.

"Who is it?" he asked.

"It's Billy," said a quiet voice. "Please open the door before anyone sees me." Jess got up and slowly opened the door to let Billy in.

"Hastings came back," said Billy nervously.

"When?"

"About ten minutes ago, but he left already."

"He left?" asked Jess. "Why and where?"

"Well, he saw the horse you gave me," he explained. He noticed it right away and asked about it. The old man told him what had happened and he got really mad when he found out you had killed his two friends. He took off for the Last "C" ranch. He told me to tell the sheriff that he'll be coming back to town later today and if you're still here, he was going to shoot you down like a dog. I'm really scared."

"Don't be," he replied calmly. "I plan on seeing the sheriff today at noon. You go find the sheriff and tell him everything you just told me and then go back to work like nothing else happened. As far as anyone else is concerned, we never talked, okay?"

"Okay. But I'm still scared," he said. "Are you sure you can take him? He's pretty fast."

"There's not much I'm certain about in life Billy, but there is one thing I am sure of and that is before this day is over, Randy Hasting will be dead." Billy nodded and headed out to find the sheriff like he was told.

Jess spent a few minutes getting his gear ready knowing he would probably leave town today after he killed Hastings. He walked down to the general store and picked up some supplies and packed his saddlebags. He noticed the townspeople staring at him and he knew it was because they knew what was about to happen. He headed over to the sheriff's office to talk to Manley about the other two men he was hunting. Manley was sitting on the front porch in a chair when Jess arrived.

"Sheriff, do you have any information about Randy Hastings's other two partners that he came to town with originally?" asked Jess.

"Not really," replied Manley. "They didn't stay long after they hit town. I heard Hastings say something about meeting them down in Red Rock, Texas, later."

"You got any wanted posters on those two?" asked Jess.

"Don't think so," replied the sheriff.

"When is the last time you looked at any wanted posters?"

"Hell, I don't know," he answered agitatedly. It's not like I keep a schedule to look at them," retorted Sheriff Manley.

"Maybe you should."

"Well maybe you outta…" the sheriff never finished what he was about to say after he saw the look in Jess's eyes quickly change, a dark look coming forth.

"Here are some sketches of them I got from Sheriff Diggs over in Black Creek," said Jess, as he reached into his front pocket and pulled out the two drawings. "Why don't you take a look at any posters you have and see if any match up?"

"Ain't you got something bigger to worry about?" the sheriff asked sarcastically.

"Like what?"

"Like getting shot dead this afternoon," replied Manley. "You know, Hastings is just plain mean and he don't fight fair. He'll probably have some help with him. He didn't ride out to the Last "C" ranch just to visit 'cause he was lonely. He'll most likely bring back a couple of toughs with him."

"That'll be his choice," barked Jess. "They might even get me, but not before I get Hastings; you can bet on that." The sheriff's expression changed to more of a look of respect for Jess. It had been a long time since the sheriff had seen such confidence and tenacity; especially in someone so young.

"You sure got the gonads of a grown man, I'll give you that," admitted Manley. "You'd better hope that those gonads don't get you killed."

"You let me worry about that Sheriff."

"Well, I'll check my posters for you," he replied. "You be on the lookout for trouble though, 'cause it's coming at you for sure."

"I suppose so, but I'm ready," he replied.

"I'll just bet you are," the sheriff replied, nodding his head.

Jess walked away and headed for the saloon. He figured that's probably where Hastings would look for him when he returned to town. He took a seat at the table in the corner. He had a good view of the batwing doors and the street so he could see trouble coming early. Ray brought Jess a beer and sat it down on the table. Jess thanked him and took a long slow drink as Ray wiped up the table.

"What are you going to do when Hastings gets back in town later?" asked Ray.

"Kill him," he replied candidly.

"I guess that's one way of handling it."

"I reckon it is."

"He'll probably have help with him."

"I already figured as much. It'll be their choice to throw in with him, not mine. Whoever does is going to die with him."

"Well, good luck, Jess. I hope you get to ride out of here."

"Me too, since I have two more men to hunt down after Hastings," he said looking up at Ray with a determined look.

There were at least a dozen people in the bar. That was more than usual this early in the afternoon, but they knew that the show would soon begin. They heard about the gunfight between Jess and the other two men the other day and knew Jess was good enough to give Hastings a challenge. Jess had been sitting there for about two hours when all of a sudden a few more men rushed into the saloon. When they did, Jess could tell that trouble wasn't far behind. He could tell by the way the men were looking at him. He stood up and walked over to the end of the bar by the wall so no one could get behind him. All of a sudden it got real quiet in the saloon. Jess removed his hammer strap from his pistol. He had a clear view of the swinging doors as well as the door at the other end of the bar going to the back of the saloon. He knew he would have to keep an eye on both doors.

Jess heard spurs jingling and footsteps coming up the stairs. A man wearing a six-shooter tied down low walked in and made his way to the opposite end of the bar. Jess noticed that the man had already removed his hammer strap. He was slightly heavy-set and acted like he'd been drinking. He ordered a whiskey from the barkeep while keeping a close eye on Jess. Then, the moment Jess was waiting for finally happened. He heard footsteps this time, but no spurs. Jess stared at the man as he came through the door. He wanted to make sure who it was and he wanted it to be Randy Hastings. He wasn't disappointed. He remembered the two pearl handled Colts that Hastings had been wearing on that fateful day he met him out on the road going into Black Creek, Kansas. He was still wearing the Colts, tied down tight and low on both legs. A flood of emotions hit Jess. He felt excitement, hatred, revenge and satisfaction all rolled up as one.

Hastings glanced over at his friend at the bar and his friend looked over at Jess, letting Hastings know which one of the men in the saloon had been looking for him. Hastings would have been able to easily pick him out anyway. The strange looking pistol and holster and the shotgun handle sticking up behind Jess's back were dead giveaways, but that's not how he would have known; the look on Jess's face was enough. It was a look that would make most men shudder with fear, but Hastings wasn't like most men; he was a cold-blooded killer.

Hastings took a moment to look Jess over. Jess glared back at him. Hastings had a cocky smirk on his face. It was eerily quiet in the saloon as Jess and Hastings just continued to stare at one another for what seemed an eternity. Jess was savoring the moment of finally catching up with one of the men who murdered his family. Hastings was curiously wondering why this young man was hunting him. No one said a word until Hastings decided to break the silence.

"I hear you've been looking for me?"

"You heard right."

"I also heard you killed two of my friends."

"That almost makes us even."

"Do I know you?" Hastings asked inquisitively. "What's your name, boy?"

"You don't remember me, do you?" asked Jess.

"Now why would I remember you?"

"We met once before."

"Really, where was that?"

"Black Creek, Kansas."

"Okay; Black Creek, Kansas. Now who in the hell *are* you?"

"My name is Jess Williams."

"Well, Jess Williams, what's your beef with me?"

"Almost two years ago, three men murdered my family," replied Jess. "They shot my pa down like a bunch of cowards. Then they raped and murdered my ma, but that wasn't enough; they also raped and murdered my little seven-year-old sister. *You* were one of those three men. I remember you from the road that day. I was riding in the wagon. Does that help your memory? Do you remember me now? Do you remember murdering my family?"

Hastings never flinched. He just stood there, with that same smirk still on his face. The truth was; he did remember that day. He just wasn't about to admit it.

"Mind if I have a drink first?" asked Hastings.

"Go ahead," replied Jess. Jess watched Hastings slowly walk to the bar and order a whiskey. Jess noticed that Hastings had gotten his left boot heel fixed.

"I see you got your left boot fixed," observed Jess.

"How'd you know that?" asked Hastings cagily.

"I saw it that day on the trail into town," he replied bluntly.

"Really?"

"I saw your tracks in the dirt in front of my pa's house, too."

"You don't say."

"I saw your tracks in the blood on the floor where you killed my ma too."

"Maybe I ain't the only one who's ever lost a boot heel," retorted Hastings.

"Maybe not; but probably not someone who wears two pearl handle Colts," replied Jess firmly. Hastings downed his whiskey and glared at Jess.

"You know, you've made some serious accusations," he said in a sinister way. "You got any proof?"

"Don't need any."

"Really?"

"Really."

"Why not?" asked Hastings.

"You're wanted by the law, dead or alive," he replied smartly.

"Well, if I was one of those three men, and I'm not saying I was, what the hell you plan on doing about it anyway?" replied Hastings, showing no remorse at all.

"I plan to do what I promised my family I'd do," replied Jess. "I plan to shoot you down like the dog you are, and I plan to make you suffer like my family did."

Hastings was getting a little agitated now. Jess could see Hastings ears actually starting to turn red.

"Better men than you have tried and died," retorted Hastings. "You sure you still want to do this? I believe you're outgunned and outclassed." Jess looked around the bar and looked back at Hastings.

"Are all these men in the saloon throwing in with you or just the chubby one down at the end of the bar?" Hastings' friend straightened up at the insult.

"Just me and my friend over there," replied Hastings. "The rest of these men are only here to watch you die."

"Well then, I'm neither outgunned or out-classed," replied Jess defiantly. "The only one who is going to die here today is you and your friend if he reaches for his pistol. Now, I don't know about you, but I'm done talking unless you want to confess before I kill you. Not that it will matter much. I don't plan on taking you in alive. Just killing you and col-lecting the five hundred dollar bounty on your sorry ass."

Hastings put his right hand down by the butt of his gun. "You know what punk?" said Hastings. "I'm the one that put that bullet in your sister's head. What do you think about that?"

"I think your day of reckoning has finally arrived," retorted Jess.

Everything happened at lightning speed. Hastings and his friend both went for their guns at the same time. Jess drew and shot the man at the end of bar first, the bullet ripping through his chest. He didn't turn his body, he just snapped off the shot from the hip keeping the gun close to his side. The man had just barely got his hand on the butt of his pistol. As Jess brought the pistol back toward Hastings, he fanned the next shot with his left hand and the slug hit Hastings in the left arm, but that was no mistake. Hastings hadn't quite got his gun out of the holster when Jess's first shot hit him. Hastings dropped his gun and grabbed his left arm where he had been hit. Jess slowly walked forward and shot Hastings in his right arm. Hastings let out another scream.

"You bastard!" wailed Hastings.

Jess said nothing as he slowly moved toward Hastings, who continued to back up. Jess fired another shot that hit Hastings in the gut. Hastings fell back against the wall and slid down to the floor. He was screaming in pain trying vainly to cover his stomach wound. Jess smiled at Hastings as he shot him in his left kneecap, shattering it into little pieces. His sixth shot took out the right kneecap, bits of blood and bone splattering Hastings in the face. Jess walked up to him and looked at him for a moment, worming around on the floor holding his gut with both hands, which wasn't easy since both his arms had been shot. There was blood all over. The only noise in the bar was coming from Hastings who was moaning and cursing. Everyone else in the bar was silent watching the event unfold.

Jess reloaded quickly and watched the room carefully. If anyone tried anything, he still had his pa's Peacemaker tucked in his front belt. Then, Jess brought the pistol in line with Hastings' forehead and pulled the hammer back slowly allowing Hastings to hear all four clicks of the hammer separately.

"What do you think my sister felt when you put that bullet in her head? Ever wonder? Will you actually hear the gunshot? What do think it will feel like? Well, you're about to find out because that's exactly what's going to happen next," Jess said with deadly intent.

The bullet sprayed Hastings's brains all over the wall and floor. It was an ugly sight, but not one that hadn't been seen before by most of the men in the bar. Jess replaced the spent cartridge, holstered his gun and walked back to the bar taking another long drink from his beer. No one said a word. He looked over at the barkeep and Ray brought him another beer.

Sheriff Manley walked into the saloon. He was surprised by what he saw, but he sure wouldn't miss

Hastings. He'd been nothing but trouble since he arrived in town. Manley walked over to the bar and Ray brought him a shot of whiskey. Manley slugged it down and turned around to survey the scene. The man at the end of the bar was lying face up on the floor in a pool of blood, shot in the middle of the chest. Hastings' head was still leaning up against the wall and there were pieces of his brain matter all over the wall and floor. Manley turned back around to the bar and ordered another whiskey.

"Well, I guess you did what you came here to do," said Manley.

"I suppose I did," replied Jess.

"Don't suppose you feel bad about it neither, do you?" Manley asked, already knowing the answer.

"Not even a little," Jess responded.

"Well, you earned six hundred dollars in the process," offered Manley. "I'll make arrangements to have the money transferred to that Jameson fellow at your bank in Black Creek."

"I thought the bounty was five hundred?" inquired Jess.

"Well, I looked through those wanted posters like you asked me. I found another poster on Hastings and wouldn't you know, they raised it," exclaimed Sheriff Manley. "I also found a wanted poster on one of the other two men you're looking for. The man's name is Hank Beard. He's wanted for murder and two bank robberies. The last bank robbery was in a town called Halstad, down in Texas. There's a three hundred dollar bounty on his head. I also found an old telegraph notice from the sheriff in Halstad. The notice said that Beard had been spotted around a small town called Timber, about one hundred miles southeast of Halstad. I got nothin' on the other guy you showed me. I'm sure he'll surface sooner or later though. Those types usually do. Hell, he may even be with Beard. Suppose you're leaving town and heading down that way?"

"Matter of fact, I've decided to stay in town tonight and leave tomorrow. I have one more thing to do," said Jess curiously.

"Can you do me a favor?" asked Manley.

"What?"

"Try not shootin' anyone else before you go?"

"I'll sure try, Sheriff."

Jess finished his beer and headed to his room to turn in for the night. He felt good about killing Hastings. He had no business living after what he had done to other people. He hadn't wanted to kill the other man, but that was his choice. As he dozed off, he kept thinking about Texas and a little town called Timber, and what he would find there. Hopefully, he would find the next part of his destiny.

⌘

Back in Black Creek, Kansas, the funeral for Red Carter was a quiet and solemn one. No one from town came to the funeral. No one really liked Red except for his father Dick Carter. Carter owned the largest ranch in the area, the Carter "D." He was a hard man who had no problem with stepping on anybody who tried to get in his way. He bought out some of the smaller ranches around his, and the ones he couldn't buy, he simply forced them out. Carter didn't have much use for Red either, but Red was his only son and he loved him despite all the problems Red had caused him.

Dick Carter had mixed emotions about Jess Williams. Jess had worked for him on the ranch doing odd jobs and he had always liked Jess, but that was before. He felt bad for what happened to Jess and his family; and he was sorry about Red killing the sheriff, but that was still no excuse to kill his only son; at least in his mind it wasn't. Dick needed something and he needed it real bad. That something was revenge and that's why he hired the two best gun handlers he could find. Their job was to kill Jess, and it didn't matter to Dick Carter how they did it. They could kill him when they found him or they could drag his ass back to Carter so he could personally hang Jess himself. The two men were Frank Reedy and Todd Spicer and Dick was meeting with them this afternoon.

They were both hard men and fast with a pistol. Each had killed their share of men in their line of work. Frank Reedy was a former lawman who had turned to bounty hunting because it was more profitable, at least most of the time. He wasn't really a bad man, just one who had lost his way in a land where you lived and died by the gun. Todd Spicer was different. He was just plain mean and he had no conscience about anything. He killed for money and he could change sides depending on who paid the most. They had worked as a team for the last three years and they split all their earnings right down the middle. They both knew that Carter was one of the largest ranch owners in the area and could pay big money, which is why they dropped what they were doing and high-tailed it to Carter's ranch.

They arrived at Carter's ranch after two days of hard riding. They were met by one of Carter's foremen who took care of their horses and arranged for them to have a nice hot bath and good meal before meeting with Carter. That was just fine with them.

"Must be pretty important for Carter to give us the royal treatment like this," Spicer said, as he soaked in the tub next to Reedy. A young cowboy was bringing in more buckets of hot water and adding them to their tubs. The foreman had also put a good bottle of whiskey and two glasses on a table between the two tubs.

"Yeah, this ain't bad at all, partner," said Reedy. "You know, I've been sitting here thinking and I have a hunch I know what he wants."

"Really, how the hell you know that?" he asked. "You got a crystal ball in that tub of yours?"

"I don't need no crystal ball, you idiot," replied Reedy. "Don't you ever read the papers or listen to what's going on?"

"I only read the numbers on the money we get paid and I only listen to what I want to hear," he said as he shook some water from his head.

"You're one hell of a partner, Spicer," retorted Reedy. "I don't quite know what I'd do without you."

"Probably starve and have to beg for food."

"Then you don't know that Dick Carter's only boy Red bit the dust recently?" asked Reedy.

"Hell, I didn't even know Carter had a son."

"I'm sure glad I'm the brains of this outfit," said Reedy, as he lay back in the tub after scrubbing his feet with a brush. "Anyway, I guess some young kid put a slug into Carter's boy, Red."

"Why the hell did he do that?"

"I guess it had something to do with the fact that Red killed old Sheriff Diggs, who was the sheriff here in Black Creek. For some reason, that riled the boy and he came to town and braced Red and killed him for it."

"Did he back shoot him?"

"The way I heard it, he faced him fair and square," replied Reedy. "I heard he was damn fast, too."

"So you figure old man Carter wants to hire us to go after the kid who killed Red?"

"You catch on real quick sometimes," said Reedy sarcastically.

"Don't make me pay that young cowpoke to throw a bucket of hot water on your sorry ass," retorted Spicer.

"Too bad about Sheriff Diggs though. I worked with him a few times and he was a pretty good law dog. Tough but fair."

"Don't get all mushy on me," said Spicer. "Pour me another shot of that good stuff and let's get on to our little parley with Carter. Maybe we can separate him from some of his money."

They both finished their baths and got dressed. Carter's foreman led them up to the main house. It was a grand looking place with huge rooms and high ceilings. The foreman led them to a room that had a nice spread of food laid out and told them to make themselves comfortable and that Carter would be in to see them in a little while. They both dug in and filled up. The food was as good as the whiskey. They were sitting down, sipping on some more good whiskey when the door opened and a large man with graying hair entered. Dick Carter wasn't what you would call fat or heavy. He was big boned and made of muscle. He was over six feet tall and weighed almost three hundred pounds and not one pound of it was fat. He tried to force a smile, but you could see the look of torment on his face.

"Welcome, boys. I hope my foreman treated you well so far?" he asked.

"Hell, we ain't been treated this good in a long time," said Reedy. "A nice hot bath, the best whiskey I can remember and all this good grub. What else could a man ask for?"

"How about three thousand dollars?" Carter said, almost nonchalantly. Spicer, who had been gnawing on a chicken leg, almost choked.

"Excuse me?" said Spicer with a mouth full of chicken. "Did I hear you right? Did you just say three thousand dollars?"

"That's exactly what I said, three thousand dollars," he replied bluntly. "You would each get paid a five hundred dollar advance and then one thousand dollars each when you finish the job." Carter poured himself a glass of whiskey. Spicer glanced quickly at Reedy and swallowed the mouthful of chicken.

"And all we have to do for it is hunt down the kid who killed your son, Red?" asked Reedy.

Carter looked surprised. "So you know about what happened?"

"I can read and I hear things," added Reedy.

"Well, do you boys want the job?"

"Hell yes!" replied Spicer, who had put the chicken leg down and was already figuring what he could do with his half of three thousand dollars.

"Hold on there, partner," debated Reedy. "I'd like to at least find out who it is he wants us to hunt down. Who is this kid who shot your boy?"

"His name is Jess Williams," replied Carter. "His family owns a small ranch the other side of town. He's the one who shot my boy and now he's got to pay."

"Don't you mean *used* to own a small ranch on the other side of town?" asked Reedy.

Both Carter and Spicer looked up at Reedy with a surprised look on their faces.

"So you heard about what happened to his family," Carter said, not really asking since he sensed that Reedy knew all about it already.

"Like I said," observed Reedy. "I read and I hear things."

"Well, that doesn't matter none to me," countered Carter. "My boy didn't have anything to do with his family being murdered. I even hired Jess to do odd jobs around here to help him out 'cause I felt sorry for him. He had no right to kill my boy and he damn well is going to pay for it." Spicer just sat there listening to the conversation between Reedy and Carter.

"Well, do you want the job or not?" asked Carter plainly, leaning forward in his chair.

"Three thousand dollars is a whole lot of money," submitted Reedy. "You want him dead or alive?"

"I don't really give a shit," replied Carter. "You can kill him, hang him or bring him back to me and I'll hang him myself. It doesn't really matter to me. Just as long as he ends up dead just like my son. I won't rest until that happens."

"I don't know about my partner, but I'll take the job for that kind of money," said Spicer.

"I'd really like the both of you to take the job," said Carter. "I hear you work pretty well as a team and you don't fail to bring back your man, which is why I sent for you. I'll hire just one of you if I have to, but I'd much rather have you both on the job."

Reedy knew that his partner would take the job alone anyway and as long as it was going to happen, he might as well cut himself in for a part of the action. He felt odd though. Something about this job just stuck in his craw like when a piece of meat that gets stuck between your teeth and you just can't get it out, no matter how hard you work at it. But three thousand dollars was a lot of money, especially for just one man; or boy. That kind of money was hard to turn down under any circumstances.

"Okay, we're in. Do you have any idea where he is?" asked Reedy.

"I hear he headed out to Tarkenton to look for one of the men who killed his family," replied Carter.

"At least that's a start," said Reedy. "Can you give us a description of the boy?"

"You can't miss him," replied Carter. "He's wearing a pistol and holster that sticks out like a sore thumb. I didn't see it, but those that did said it was like no other pistol and holster they'd ever seen before. Other than that, he's about sixteen, dark hair, slender, and wears a sawed-off shotgun strapped to his back so that the butt sticks up over his shoulder."

"That should separate him from the crowd," implied Reedy. "We'll head out first thing in the morning. Mind if we bunk down here tonight?"

"I've got a nice room for you boys," said Carter, smiling for the first time in a while. "And I'll make sure you're provisioned up real good when you leave tomorrow. Anything you need to get the job done, you just ask for it."

"I wouldn't mind a few bottles of this fine whiskey to take along with us. A man gets mighty thirsty on the trail," Spicer said with a grin.

"I'll have a case of it on the pack horse along with food, ammunition and water. I'll give you the cash in the morning before you leave," offered Dick responded.

They shook hands with Carter to seal the deal and Carter left them in the room. They ate and drank some more and then turned in for the night. In the morning, Carter paid them five hundred dollars each in cash and supplied them with a packhorse loaded with everything they could possibly need. They left Carter's ranch and headed in the direction of Tarkenton, but both men had enough experience at chasing men down to know that anything could have made Jess detour. Once they reached the outskirts of town, they found a campsite where they decided to stay overnight. They would go into Tarkenton in the morning. Their hope was that Jess would still be in town when they arrived. They could make their kill; collect their money and move on to the next job.

Both men settled in just before dark and Reedy was pouring them both another cup of hot coffee and Reedy gave his partner a concerned look. "You know what partner; I'm still not sure about this job. It just doesn't set well with me," he said as he put the pot back on the fire. He had become increasingly uncomfortable about the job.

"A job is a job, Frank," he argued. "Hell, I told you if you want to back out, I'll do the job myself. Just give me the five hundred dollars Carter already paid you and head out tomorrow. Then, after I kill that kid, I'll collect the other two thousand dollars. Hell, that's more money than I made all of last year."

"It's just that the kid doesn't seem all that bad," debated Reedy. "They said it was a fair fight and that Red drew on the kid first."

"Now who the hell told you that?" he asked skeptically.

"I talked to the owner of the general store back in Black Creek when I went there to get us some more supplies before we met with Carter," replied Reedy. "He's known the kid since he was a baby. He told me the whole story about his family and all."

"Well, he ain't no baby now," retorted Spicer. "He's a man-killer, and we've been hired to take him down."

"Let's not forget about Red killing the sheriff either," added Reedy. "You know I don't stand for killing a lawman."

"Frank, you gonna shine up that old badge of yours and pin it back on?" he asked sarcastically.

"I ain't saying that," he argued. "I'm just saying there are a lot of things I don't like about this job. It doesn't feel right. Hell, if my family was murdered like that, I'd track down the men who did it and shoot 'em down like dogs, too."

"Hell, so would I, but that's got nothing to do with the job we've been hired for," countered Spicer. "The kid killed Red Carter and red didn't have anything to do with the kid's family being murdered. And now Red's dad wants him dead and he's willing to pay three thousand dollars to get the job done whether we do it or someone else does. It seems pretty plain and simple to me. What part of that don't you understand?"

"I'll tell you what, Todd," decided Reedy. "I'll go into Tarkenton with you, but I want to talk with the kid before we finish the job. I'm not going in there and put him down without hearing his side of all of this. Good enough?"

"Suit yourself, Frank. Just remember, once you're done talking, if you ain't in, turn around and leave your share of the money," he replied. "I'll finish the job myself."

"Can't ask for more than that, I guess." replied Reedy as he put a few more pieces of wood on the fire and both men turned in.

CHAPTER ELEVEN

In the morning, Jess woke and gathered up his things and headed to the dining room. He had breakfast and thanked Martha for her hospitality. He asked Martha about Billy's ma and how she got the bad leg. Jess had spotted her a few times down at the stables talking to Billy. She told him the story of how Billy was playing in the street when a bunch of hooligans raced their horses through town and Billy's ma had to grab him and pull him out of the way of the horses. Unfortunately, not before she had her leg broken by one of the horses. They had no money for a doctor and she had to set the bone herself. It never healed right and she's limped since. Jess walked over to the stables and found Billy, who was brushing down a horse.

"Hey, Billy, got my horse ready?" he asked.

"Morning Mister Williams," he said excitedly. "I can have him ready to go in just a few minutes." Billy went about getting Gray ready.

"Billy, how's your ma doing lately? I noticed her visiting you a few times. Does she work?"

"Well, she cleans houses, but has a hard time getting much work," he replied sadly. "That bum leg sure slows her down a lot. She can't get around very well, but we do the best we can. That's why I work here so much. The twenty dollars you said you were going to pay me will sure help a lot. We still have a deal, don't we?"

"Yes we do, but I figure I need to change the deal a little," he said.

A worried look came over Billy's face, as if he was about to be let down.

"Actually, I figure with all the risks you took, I should pay you say...how about one hundred dollars?" Jess asked him.

Billy's mouth opened, but nothing came out right away. Finally, he responded, "Why would you give me that much money?"

"I figure maybe your ma could go and see a good doctor and set that leg right," he replied.

"Mister Williams, you've got a friend for life for sure," exclaimed Billy.

"Well, Billy, I need all the friends I can get. Listen, if you need more money for your ma's leg, you just get hold of a man named Jameson at the bank in Black Creek, Kansas," said Jess. "He'll know how to reach me and I'll do what I can to help. Killing bad men seems to pay off right nicely."

"As long as you don't get shot doing it," he agreed with a grin.

"Can't argue with you on that point, Billy," he said. "Listen, you take care of yourself and your ma, okay?"

"Sure thing," replied Billy. "Where are you headed?"

"Heading for Texas," replied Jess. "Seems one of the other men I'm looking for has been seen down there in a little town called Timber."

"Boy, I sure wouldn't want to be him, that's for sure," said Billy.

"No, you surely wouldn't," replied Jess. He took the reins from Billy and walked his horse down to the sheriff's office. As Billy watched Jess, he thought to himself that he wanted to grow up to be just like him. A bounty hunter who was fast with a gun and yet could still be a nice fellow.

Sheriff Manley was sitting out in front. He looked sober and he seemed to be in a surprisingly good mood.

"Good morning to you, Mr. Williams. "I suppose your heading for Timber?"

"Yeah, got a date with a dead man there, hopefully," he replied.

"Well, I want to thank you for cleaning up the town here a little," offered Manley. "I know I ain't the best sheriff in these parts, but what you did will make my job a lot easier for sure."

"I guess there's a silver lining in every cloud. Sheriff, will you do me one more favor?"

"Sure, you name it," he replied.

"Take five hundred dollars of my bounty money and wire it to my bank in Black Creek, Kansas," he said, handing Manley a piece of paper. "Take the other hundred and give it to the boy at the stables."

"Billy?" asked Manley, a look of puzzlement slowly forming on his face.

"Yeah, he and his ma need the help, especially with her bad leg and all, and he did take good care of my horse." The sheriff grinned. He had gained a lot of respect for this young man, Jess Williams. Truth be known, Manley always had a soft spot in his heart for Billy and his ma. If he had been doing his job right, maybe that accident with the horses would've never happened. Manley had always felt a little guilty about it.

"That's a mighty nice thing for you to do Mr. Williams, mighty nice," exclaimed Sheriff Manley. "If you ever come back to my little town, look me up; I'd like to buy you a drink."

"Thanks, Sheriff. You take care."

"I will and you do the same," he replied.

Jess climbed up in the saddle and headed slowly down the main street. Martha was standing in the doorway and she waved goodbye. Jess smiled and tipped his hat at her. As he rode out of town, he thought that maybe he would come back again and take Manley up on his drink offer. That way he would get another chance to see Martha, but not yet; not until he finished his task and killed the other two men he was hunting.

Hank Beard and Blake Taggert had left Tarkenton about two weeks after they had arrived there. They headed for Red Rock first. Blake still had some family there. The plan was for all three of them to meet up at the Taggert house in Red Rock after a while. Hank was in Red Rock for less than a week when he heard from his old pal Ben Grady, who was in a small town in Texas called Timber. Grady had wired a message to Taggert's family for Hank figuring they would get it to him sooner or later. Hank wired him back and they continued to send some messages back and forth. Ben Grady had a plan to rob the man he worked for in Timber and wanted Hank in on the deal. Hank thought it was a good way to make some quick money so he agreed to meet Grady.

"So, are you heading for Timber?" Taggert asked Beard.

"I guess so," he replied. "We're running low on funds. Hell, we haven't robbed anyone or anything in a while. We'll have to do something soon or we'll all have to get a real job."

"No chance of that happening," replied Taggert plainly. "I ain't working for money as long as I can take someone else's."

"Hey, barkeep, how about two more whiskeys?" asked Beard, waving at the barkeep. Beard and Taggert had been bellied up to the bar in one of the saloons in Red Rock for over two hours and both of them had had their share of whiskey.

"Well, one of us has got to do something," added Beard. "That dog Randy hasn't done a thing but chase skirts back in Tarkenton. I ain't seen any money from him or you."

"Simmer down," replied Taggert. "I told you I had a plan to rob that family out the other side of town. I hear they keep their money hidden in the house 'cause they're afraid of putting the money in the bank."

"Yeah, well planning is one thing and doing is another," retorted Beard. "You best get to it and real soon."

"You can count on it," he replied deviously. "You know what else they got there?"

"What?"

"A nice young pretty daughter," he replied with an evil smile on his face. "She looks to be about fourteen and pretty as a cactus flower."

"You just can't pass up a pretty face, can you?" asked Beard. "Why can't you pick on some older women instead of the young ones? I didn't like what you did to that little one back in Black Creek."

"Hastings in the one who shot her after I was finished with her," he argued, as if that made what he did okay. "Anyway, I hear this family has several hundred dollars stashed."

"We can sure use it," said Beard. "I'm going to head for Timber in the next few days and if that works out as planned, we'll have enough money to take care of all three of us for quite some time." They finished their whiskeys and ordered two more.

☙ ❧

Jess headed southwest and made camp at dusk. He woke at dawn and rode for about two weeks without seeing a soul. That kind of solitude bothered some men, but Jess rather enjoyed it. It gave him a lot of time to think and to practice with his pistol. One morning, he had ridden only about two hours before he finally crested the top of a hill and looked down on a lovely sight. There was a large meadow with a river running through it. The river meandered through the meadow and just before it headed back into a wooded area; it took a ninety-degree turn.

Right at the point of the turn, Jess spotted a tent with a smokestack poking through the top of it. There was a horse grazing the meadow untied and a rocking chair outside the tent. It was about noon and Jess figured he had to be close to the town of Timber. He figured that whoever was living in that tent might know something about the man he was hunting. Jess made his way down to the tent. When he was about one hundred yards from the tent, he heard a low raspy voice holler out. "That's close enough, mister!"

Jess reined Gray up and stopped. He could see a man peeking out of the front of the tent holding a long rifle that looked like an old beat up buffalo gun. Jess got down from his horse.

"I mean no harm," he explained. "Just need a cup of coffee and maybe some talk, that's all. I'm not looking for any trouble."

"Well, come on then and let me get a good look at ya," said the raspy voice.

Jess slowly walked up to the front of the tent. A rough looking man with a bushy beard came out and looked him over real good. Jess stood very still not wanting to set the man off, especially while he had that rifle pointed at him.

"You one of them bounty hunters?" asked the man.

"I don't really think of myself as a bounty hunter."

"Sure do look like one."

"I've been told that before."

"Who you looking for?"

"I'm looking for a man by the name of Hank Beard; you know him?"

"Name don't ring a bell, but I'm not good with names anyway," he said. He put the rifle down as if he was no longer worried about Jess's intentions.

"Speaking of names, I'm called River Bend Bill. What's yours?" he asked.

"Jess Williams."

"Nice to meet ya, Jess Williams."

"How long have you been living out here?" he asked, looking at the raggedy old tent.

"Oh, 'bout five years or so," he replied. "I can't recall for sure. How 'bout that coffee? I got the pot, if you got the coffee." Jess tied Gray off and got some coffee out. After Jess poured them both a cup, he showed him the drawing of Hank Beard, but Bill didn't recognize him.

"So, how'd you get the name of River Bend Bill?" asked Jess.

"Well, I suppose it's 'cause of where I live. Right here, by this bend in the river," he replied. "Can't live in town, they'd just throw me out."

"Why?"

"Well, it's a long story you see," he explained. "There's a woman by the name of Patti Nate in town. I guess I kinda like her, but so does the sheriff, Mark Steele. Every time I go into town and try to talk with her, he gets all riled up and runs my ass out. I keep going back and he just keeps running me out. I think she's sweet on him, but she was with me first, so I figure I'll keep trying as long as she ain't hitched to him yet."

"Sounds like you got a fight on your hands," implied Jess. "I wish you luck."

"Yeah, thanks," he replied. "I'd a wupped his ass already, exceptin' he wears that badge and that gives him a lot of leeway, you know. Plus, I think she's impressed with that badge, course I guess most women are, don't ya think?"

"I reckon you're right about that, Bill. Besides your problem with the sheriff, is he a good lawman?"

"It pains me to say it, but yeah. He keeps the peace and takes no shit. Maybe he'll have some information on your fellow," added Bill.

"What's it like in town?"

"It's usually a pretty quiet town, but right now a few of the ranches are feuding over water rights. Been a few gunfights between the ranch hands so if you go to town, you best be careful. Them boys don't care who they pick a fight with after they've been drinking. Town's about two miles straight that-a-way, through the woods. When you see Sheriff Steele, tell him River Bend Bill says hi. That'll get his dander up," Bill said with a smirk.

"I'll be sure to," replied Jess. "Thanks for the company and good luck with Patti Nate."

"Hey, you stop in the saloon and have a drink on me and say hi to Patti. She works there. Tell her River Bend Bill still loves her and will be in to see her soon!" he said.

"I'll be sure to tell her."

Jess left the bag of coffee there and rode through the woods until he came to a clearing by a road. He could see the town about a half mile away. He walked his horse into town. It did seem like a quiet town, not much going on; but then again, the town wasn't much. There were only about a dozen buildings. He stopped at the only saloon and tied Gray up and walked inside after looking down both sides of the main street. Jess walked in and up to the bar and ordered a drink. He had noticed that there were men sitting at several tables in the saloon and four men standing at the bar. Jess could feel tension in the room. He had taken his usual spot, always at the end of the bar and always in the corner with a wall to his backside. They had all eyed him as he walked in, but they were paying more attention to each other at the moment.

Another man walked in the bar and Jess felt the tension in the room tighten up even more. He could smell trouble. The man walked to the bar and joined the other four who had been standing there. He ordered a drink and turned around to face one of the tables where three men had been sharing a bottle of whiskey.

"Since when did you let girls drink in this saloon, Jed?" the new man asked the barkeep. The other four men had turned around. The barkeep was nervous and heading slowly toward the end of the bar where Jess had spotted a short double-barreled shotgun.

"I don't want no trouble in here, Johnson. You heard the sheriff the last time you started a fight in here," the barkeep said as he reached for the butt of the shotgun.

"Well, you wouldn't have any trouble if you didn't let girls drink in here, ain't that right boys?" asked Johnson sarcastically. All four of the other men nodded affirmatively. The three men quietly sitting at the table didn't say a word. They worked for the Triple Bar ranch, which owned most of the land that the river flowed through. They just finished up their drinks and left some money on the table and stood up slowly and started to leave.

"Where you girls goin' now? Down to the store to get some lace for them britches?" asked Johnson, still trying to goad them. One of three men stopped and turned slowly. He didn't say anything for a moment as if he was contemplating what his next move would be. The other two men stopped and turned. You could have cut the heavy air with a knife.

"Johnson," the man said, "you know we can't have any trouble or we'll lose our jobs and we all got families to feed. Why don't you give it up and leave it alone."

"Because I don't give a shit about your families or your jobs," retorted Johnson. "If your damn boss wasn't such a hard-ass, maybe we wouldn't have a problem."

"We can't control that and you know full well that it's his water, even Judge Hawkins said so. Why don't you just let it drop?" replied the man.

"I don't know. Maybe I'm just a hard-ass, like your boss," sniggered Johnson.

Just when Jess figured things were about to blow, a tall lanky man walked into the saloon. He wore a badge on the front of his shirt. It was Sheriff Mark Steele. When he walked into the room, you could sense that he was immediately in control of the situation.

"What's going on, boys?" the sheriff asked, in a very quiet, yet deliberate tone.

"Johnson's been trying to pick a fight again and those boys were just trying to leave, Sheriff," Jed offered quickly, before anyone else could speak.

"That right, Johnson?" asked Sheriff Steele.

"This is unfinished business and you know it, Sheriff," retorted Johnson. Johnson was getting mad and nervous at the same time. He was obviously afraid of Sheriff Steele, as were the other four men that were with him and Jess could see that.

"When I ask you a question, I expect an answer, not an explanation to a question I didn't ask. So, what's the answer?" The sheriff's voice was as firm as a steel blade.

"I…I guess that's right, Sheriff…but…" Johnson began to say when the sheriff cut him off mid-sentence.

"Okay, now I want you boys to unbuckle those gun belts so that Jed here can deliver them to me at the jail, which is where you boys are going for the rest of the day," ordered the sheriff.

"But Sheriff…that ain't right!" retorted Johnson angrily.

"I ain't going to ask you again boys and you know I mean it," the sheriff answered, his hand going to the butt of his pistol and the look on Sheriff Steele's face said he would use it if he had to.

"Damn it!" hollered Johnson, as he unbuckled his gun belt and let it fall to the floor. The other four quickly followed suit.

"Thanks, Sheriff. We didn't want any more trouble. We'll be going now," offered the man from the other group.

"Good day, gentlemen," said Sheriff Steele. "And thanks for not acting like these fools, and tell your boss I appreciate it." Sheriff Steele was leading the five men out of the saloon when Jess spoke up.

"Sheriff, could I get a word with you later?" asked Jess.

"Sure thing, stranger," replied Steele. "I was wondering who you were anyway. Give me about an hour to lock these hooligans up and stop in at the jail."

"Thanks, Sheriff," he replied.

Jess drank his beer and ordered another one. He asked Jed where he could find a room for the night. Jess thanked him and headed down to see the sheriff. Sheriff Steele was sitting at his desk writing when Jess knocked on the half-opened door.

"Come on in," he said.

"Hi, Sheriff," said Jess, as he stuck his hand out and shook hands with him. "My name is Jess Williams. I'm looking for a man by the name of Hank Beard." Jess pulled the sketch of Beard from his front pocket and showed it to Steele. "He's one of three men who murdered my family and raped my ma and little sister. He's got a bounty on his head and I heard he was last seen in this area. Do you have any information on him?"

"Raped your little sister?" Steele asked with a disgusted look. "How old was she?"

"Seven," he said as his gut knotted up.

"Damn. A man who would do something like that should be shot on sight. No judge, no jury, and no trial; just shot," said Steele.

"He will be, Sheriff. As soon as I find him."

"You a bounty hunter?"

"No, not really."

"Could've fooled me," he said plainly. "You sure look like one although you seem awfully young to be in the bounty hunting business. Well, this picture doesn't ring any bells, but let me look through some posters and ask around. How about I meet you at the saloon about suppertime and let you know what

I find out. They have good food there. I know the cook real well. Can you leave the sketch?"

"Sure, but I need it back," he replied. "I'll see you later, Sheriff." Jess started to walk out and stopped and turned around. "Oh, I almost forgot. A friend of yours said to say hello to you."

"A friend? Who might that be?" he asked.

"River Bend Bill," replied Jess, smiling. The sheriff shook his head in disgust.

"That old codger can kiss my ass," he said sharply. "You tell him exactly that when you see him again and tell him not to show up in town or I'll lock his ass up and throw away the key!"

"If I get the chance to see him again, I will."

Jess left the sheriff's office and headed for the only hotel in town. He stopped at the livery, but there was no one there so he brushed Gray down and stabled him. He got a room and took a nice hot bath. He decided he would try the food at the saloon since the sheriff had recommended it. He headed down to the saloon to wait for the sheriff. There were a dozen or so men in the saloon. Jess picked the table in the corner at the end of the bar and sat down to have a cold beer before eating. There was one man who was standing at the bar and the man was paying a little more attention to Jess than normal and Jess knew it. The man was short, but lean and tough looking. He wore a single six-shooter. Jess counted four notches on the man's gun handle and if they were honest notches, that made him a very dangerous man. It wasn't long before the man put his drink down and turned to face his table.

"So, which ranch you working for, son," asked the man.

Jess looked up to face the man. He figured him for a gunslinger or a hired gun. His demeanor and the way he acted told Jess all he needed to know about the man. He knew he had to be careful with him. It was just something that one could see in a man's eyes.

"I'm not working for any ranch," replied Jess. "I'm here looking for someone." The man kept looking at Jess, studying him. He was intrigued by the pistol and holster Jess wore.

"You a bounty hunter?"

"Maybe; what's it to you if I am?"

"That depends on whether or not you're hunting any of my friends," replied the man.

"I'm looking for a man by the name of Hank Beard. Is he one of your friends?" Jess asked. The man stiffened a little and Jess immediately picked up on it.

"As a matter of fact, I do know Hank. We've worked together a few times," replied the man.

Jess figured that any man who could be friends with a cold-blooded killer like Hank Beard had to be just as bad as Beard. Jess deftly removed his hammer strap and slowly stood up from his table, keeping a careful watch on the man's gun hand. Some of the men left the bar slowly and the rest moved around a little and watched, sensing that a gunfight was about to happen. Jess watched the room out of the corner of his eyes, but never took his eyes off the man.

"You didn't work with him on any jobs in the town of Black Creek, Kansas, did you?" asked Jess, a hint of anger in his voice.

"Depends what the job was."

"Murdering my pa and raping and killing my ma and my little sister," clarified Jess crossly. The man seemed to think a moment about what he had told him.

"He never mentioned any of that to me, so it ain't any of my business," replied the man. "I don't cotton to raping women myself, but I don't judge other men."

"The way I see it, any man who would have anything to do with a man like Hank Beard ain't much better than Beard," he barked.

"Hey, you kiss my ass, kid," he retorted. "If you've got a lick of sense, you'll get the hell out of town and forget about hunting Beard. He ain't worth dying for."

"I'm not the one who's going to die."

"You sure about that?"

"I believe that's what I said," snapped Jess. The man took a step away from the bar and removed his hammer strap and when he noticed that Jess's hammer strap was already removed, the man smiled.

"Pretty fancy pistol and holster you got there," observed the man.

"Guess so," he replied.

"You better know how to use it."

"I do."

"How old are you?"

"What does that matter?"

"Well, you look awful young to be wearing all those guns you have," he said.

"I need every one of them," replied Jess. The man looked at Jess's pistol again.

"Where did you buy a pistol like that?"

"I didn't."

"Didn't what?"

"I didn't buy it."

"Then where did you get it?"

"I found it."

"Where?"

"You sure ask a lot of questions."

"Just asking."

"You should be asking yourself one question."

"Yeah, what should I be asking myself?"

"Am I ready to die today?"

"Are you?"

Jess took two steps closer to the man and stared deep into the man's eyes. "I'm always ready to die," he warned with an ominous look. "And I'm willing to take you with me."

"You talk mighty tough for a kid," stated the man.

"I ain't a kid anymore," he said plainly. A few more of the men in the bar began to move out of the way, sensing that lead would soon be flying.

The man began to slowly move his hand down closer to the butt of his pistol, all the while staring into Jess's eyes trying to get a read on him. He couldn't see anything but a darkness that seemed to slowly edge forward. Jess did the same and he saw it in the man's eyes just before the man went for his pistol.

The man was fast, but a fraction of a second later, the man was dead. Jess's shot was right on target, dead center in the middle of the man's chest. The man had barely cleared leather. He fell back onto a table, bounced off it and landed face down, dead.

Jess holstered his gun after checking the room and replacing the spent cartridge. The saloon had gone silent for a whole minute. The men in the saloon just stared at Jess as if they couldn't believe what they had just seen. Most of them had seen their share of gunfights and some of the gunslingers they saw were pretty fast. They had seen men shoot off their toes and empty their guns without hitting the man in front of them. Most men just weren't cool-headed and fearless. But this young man was not only cool-headed and fearless; he was faster than anyone they had ever seen before. Most of the men swore they couldn't even see Jess draw his pistol. One moment, his gun was in the holster, and then, before they realized anything had happened, it was pointed at the other man with smoke still coming from the barrel. Jess sat down at his table again. It wasn't long before Sheriff Steele came into the saloon. He walked up to the body lying on the floor and then looked over at Jess.

"This your work, son?" he asked.

"I'm afraid so, Sheriff."

"Boy, you don't waste any time. You've been in town less than two hours and I already have one man to bury. How long you plan on staying?" he asked.

"No longer than I have to, Sheriff."

"That's good, because you just killed Ben Grady," replied Sheriff Steele. "He was a hired gun working for the Mason ranch. Paul Mason was paying Ben here good money for his skills with a pistol. You must be damn good with that gun of yours because Ben here was one of the best. I was avoiding going up against him as long as I could."

"He's damn good," said the barkeep, who was still staring at Jess, having a hard time believing what he had just seen. "Grady never even had a chance."

Just then, Jess noticed a woman standing in the doorway going back behind the bar to the kitchen area. She was middle-aged, but quite attractive. She was slender and had beautiful blond hair that hung down to her shoulders. She was wiping her hands with a towel and she acted as if this wasn't the first dead man she had seen, which was true.

"Well, Sheriff, seems like you got more paperwork to do," she said.

"Guess so, Patti. And you know how I hate paperwork," he replied.

"Well, it wasn't his fault," she said nodding in Jess's direction. "Ben drew first and this young man finished it. I watched it from behind the doorway. I have to say, it was something to see for sure."

"Why thank you, ma'am," Jess said politely.

"Well, at least someone around here has manners," she said. "What's your name, young man?"

"Jess Williams, ma'am," he replied. "Sorry for the trouble."

"I've seen trouble before and I plan on seeing it again, Jess. My name is Patti. Can I get you some dinner?" she offered.

"If you wouldn't mind," I'd love some grub," he replied. "Sheriff here says you're a great cook."

"Well, he's right," boasted Patti proudly. "I'll bring you something right out. Meat and potatoes man, am I right?"

"Yes, ma'am," he replied. "And some hot biscuits if you got some."

Patti went back into the kitchen to fix Jess a plate of food while the sheriff and Jed carried Ben Grady's dead body out of the saloon. Jed had the floor cleaned up before Patti brought out the food. Sheriff Steele sat down with Jess and ordered a beer. Patti brought out two big plates of food and plenty of hot biscuits.

"I figured both of you were hungry," she said as she put the plates on the table.

"Thank you," said Jess. "By the way, would your last name be Nate?"

"Why, yes it is. How did you know that?"

"An old friend of yours said to say hi to you if I had a chance to meet you," he said. Sheriff Steele looked up at Jess with a glaring look in his eyes, but Jess was ignoring him.

"Really, and who might that be?" asked Patti, wondering who Jess might know that was a friend of hers.

"River Bend Bill," he replied, now turning to see the look on Steele's face. Jess could see the sheriff was less than happy. Patti's surprised look went from Jess to the sheriff and all she could say as she turned and started back toward the kitchen was; "Oh no, not this again!"

CHAPTER TWELVE

Sheriff Mark Steele was definitely a hard case. One who didn't fool around with anyone causing him trouble or breaking the law. He'd rather lock them up as talk to them. If they resisted, he'd just as soon shoot them. He had lived in Timber for ten years now. He had moved to Timber from another small town in Texas where his father had been a lawman. His father had always carried a shotgun along with a forty-five. Steele didn't carry a shotgun much, only when he was facing a crowd. He'd only had to do that twice so far. Once when he had a cowhand in jail who had raped one of the young girls in town while in a drunken stupor, and another time when he was trying to break up a fight between the ranch hands of two competing landowners. They were always fighting over the water rights concerning the only river that flowed year round through Timber and the surrounding area. He was good enough with his pistol skills to handle most situations. It was his attitude, however, that always carried him through trouble.

He had a confident air about him that most men could sense right off. He showed no fear in a gunfight even though, as most men did, he surely feared getting shot. Even when he took a bullet in the left shoulder five years back when he tried to get a hotheaded gunslinger to give up his gun and go to jail willingly. He simply stuffed a bar towel in his shirt, told a few men in the saloon to carry the body over to the undertaker's office, and then walked over to the doc's office. After the doc fixed him up, he went right back to work doing his final check for the night around town. He hurt like hell, but he would never show it. He figured that's what the townspeople expected out of a sheriff and he wasn't going to give anything less.

He did have a soft spot for the ladies though, especially Patti. He had an ongoing battle with River Bend Bill over the years concerning Patti. Every time Steele had Patti convinced to marry him, Bill would show up just long enough to spoil it. He couldn't understand why any woman, especially a good looking woman like Patti Nate, would ever give an old codger like River Bend Bill a second look or even the time of day. He was dirty, dressed like an old farmer and just plain smelled most of the time. Steele was sure that he was finally winning Patti over and he wasn't about to let old Bill mess it up this time. He was on the lookout for him. He even put the word out on the street with the other men in town to let him know if River Bend Bill showed up anywhere in town.

Sheriff Steele had risen extra early today and went to his office to check out some paperwork that he had been avoiding for days. He hated paperwork and wished he could afford a deputy to do it. He had told Jess last night at the saloon that he hadn't found anything yet on Hank Beard. He didn't know Ben Grady and Hank Beard had been friends. Then again, he hadn't known much about Ben Grady either, except for the fact that he was a hired gun and rarely came into town. He finished his work and headed over to the saloon to get a bite of breakfast. The fact that he'd get a chance to see to Patti again was just the icing on the cake. He walked in and sat down at a table and Jed brought him a hot cup of coffee.

"Hey, Sheriff, how's your day going so far?" asked Jed.

"So far, so good," he replied.

"Want some breakfast?"

"You bet. Is Patti working this morning?"

"Of course," he said. "I dcn't find a better cook in this town. I'll let her know you're here, Sheriff. You want your usual?"

"Tell her to throw in a little extra bacon this morning, Jed," he submitted. Jed went in the back to let Patti know the sheriff was in. She came out a few minutes later with a plate of food for the sheriff.

"Good morning, Sheriff," she said with a teasing smile across her lips. "How's your day going so far? Anyone get shot or have you run anyone out of town yet this morning?" He knew that Patti was referring to River Bend Bill. She seemed to like the fact that two men were pursuing her and the sheriff knew it. What he didn't know is Patti didn't really love River Bend Bill. She was just playing one against the other. Her real love was for Mark Steele and she figured he would find that out in due time. She knew she would end up marrying Steele and the fact that the sheriff didn't know that yet was something she enjoyed. She knew most men usually had to learn things the hard way.

"No, I haven't shot anyone or run anyone out of town yet, but you can bet that I'll run that old vermin out of town if he shows up" he warned. "What in the hell do you see in that old codger anyway?"

"Oh, he's not all that bad," she offered. "And he's always so polite to me. Much like that young man Jess who kept calling me ma'am last night."

"You mean the young man who shot a man dead and then ate dinner five minutes later?"

"Well, he *was* nice," she said. "Who is he, by the way?"

"I don't know yet," replied Steele. "All I know is what he told me. He said he's looking for a man by the name of Hank Beard. Beard is one of three men who killed his family and raped his ma and little sister. What kind of man could rape and kill a little seven-year-old girl?"

"The kind who ought to be hung, but only after someone takes a knife to a particular area first," she said with certainty in her voice. The sheriff winced knowing just exactly what she meant. Just then, Jess walked in the saloon and came over and sat down with the sheriff.

"Good morning, Mr. Williams," said Patti, "can I get you some breakfast this morning?"

"Yes, ma'am, and some hot coffee if it's not too much bother," replied Jess.

"See what I mean," exclaimed Patti, looking at the sheriff. "Polite and nice, just like River Bend Bill." Sheriff Steele spit the bacon out of his mouth.

"Nice my ass!" exclaimed Sheriff Steele.

"I'm just saying," she replied, walking into the back.

"Did I miss something?" asked Jess.

"You should have missed seeing River Bend Bill," Sheriff Steele snapped back.

"Sorry, Sheriff," he replied. "I didn't know it would cause that much trouble."

"Well, it's not your fault," he admitted with a look of irritation on his face.

"Did you find out anything on Hank Beard yet?"

"Sorry, but no," replied Steele. "I looked through all my wanted posters this morning and didn't find anything on him. I don't always get every wanted poster though. I guess you want this sketch back," the sheriff said, pulling the picture out of his pocket and setting it down on the table in front of Jess. Jess glared at it for a moment, feeling the hatred for this man. Patti walked up to the table and set the plate of food for Jess down. She couldn't help but notice the picture of Hank Beard.

"I've seen that man before," she said. "He's been in here a couple of times. Is that the man you're looking for?"

"Yes," he replied quickly. "Please tell me anything you know about him. Do you know where he is now? Do you know if he works for someone in the area, one of the ranches maybe?"

"Whoa, hold your horse's young man," she replied. "I don't know a thing about him. He's only been in here a couple of times in the middle of the afternoon and he only has one or two beers. He never came in at night or hung around with any of the locals. He did have a beer with Ben Grady one of the times he was in here. They only talked a few minutes and then this guy in the picture left. Ben stayed around a few more minutes then left. Is this the guy that did those terrible things to your family?"

"Yes. He's one of the two left alive so far," replied Jess. "After I catch up with him, there will be only one left."

"Well, after hearing what he did to your little sister, I hope you do to him what you did to Ben Grady last night," she implied.

"That would be too good for this man," he said with a deadly look on his face. "He won't die so quickly. He's going to feel a lot of pain before he meets his maker."

"Sheriff, what do you think Beard and Grady were up to?" asked Jess.

"Who knows for sure?" he replied. "I didn't know the two knew each other. Besides, Ben didn't come into town all that much. They must have been planning something and I'm sure that whatever it was, it wasn't anything good."

"Well, I guess it doesn't really matter. I just need to find him and put him down for good."

"I have no doubt that you will do just that, Jess," replied Sheriff Steele. "I have no doubt at all."

Hank beard had been on the trail for several days now. He was tired, dirty, and hungry; and he didn't like to be any of those things. He wiped the sweat from his forehead with his yellow bandana. You could hardly see the color now. It looked more like a faint brown. He hadn't had a chance to take a bath since he left Timber to check on the stagecoach that ran the money from the Mason ranch to the bank in Timber. The Mason ranch was one of the largest and richest in the area and Paul Mason was a very wealthy man.

Hank Beard and Ben Grady had figured that they could score big holding up the stagecoach that carried Mason's money long before it ever got to the bank in Timber. Ben Grady had helped load the money in the box for Mason and even rode shotgun for the stagecoach a few times. Only a few people knew what day the money coach would make the run. Beard had spent the last several days checking out the route and waiting for the coach to make a run. When it finally did, he was certain that he had picked a great spot to hold it up.

There was a sharp bend in the trail, which forced the coach to slow down to a crawl. There was a rock cliff just off the right edge of the trail and a clump of trees on the other side no more than fifty feet from the trail. It was a perfect ambush spot. Hank figured they could take out the two lead guards instantly and probably take out the shotgun rider and driver before they could get off a shot.

He was heading back to Timber to meet with Ben Grady and firm up when they would hit the stagecoach. He had no idea that Grady was dead yet, and no idea that someone was hunting him. He stopped along a creek and rinsed out his bandana and washed his face off. It felt good. He climbed back in the saddle and placed his shotgun back across his lap as he always did. He figured that he was about three hours from Timber and decided to keep riding until he got there. His thoughts turned to his pals. He pictured Hastings chasing a skirt back in Tarkenton and Blake Taggert murdering another family and raping and killing another young girl.

≈ ≈

Frank Reedy and Todd Spicer rode into Tarkenton in the morning. They stopped at the livery and stabled their horses. Then, they headed down to the sheriff's office. Sheriff Manley was just coming out of his office when they got there.

"Hi, Sheriff," said Reedy, "got a minute?"

"Maybe," replied Sheriff Manley. "Depends on what this is about? I haven't had my breakfast yet."

"It's about a man we're looking for," replied Reedy. "Well, a kid really by the name of Jess Williams." That got Manley's attention immediately.

"Well, come on in then," he said, as he walked back into his office followed by the two men. "What business do you have with Jess Williams?"

"To be honest, Sheriff," answered Reedy, "we've been hired to bring him back to Black Creek, Kansas, to answer for the murder of a man there."

"Really?" asked Sheriff Manley. "He didn't seem like a murderer to me. Who'd he kill?"

"A man by the name of Red Carter," interjected Spicer.

"And who hired you?" asked Manley.

"Red's father, Dick Carter," replied Reedy.

"Well, it doesn't matter anyway," said Manley. "He left town a couple of days ago. He was involved in a few gunfights while he was in town, but they were both fair fights; although it didn't really seem like it."

"Really, what do you mean by that?" asked Reedy.

"The two men he killed never had a chance from what I hear," replied Manley. "Those that saw the shooting said the kid was so fast the other men never got their lead pushers out of their holsters."

"Well, that don't matter, Sheriff," Spicer snapped back. "He's a murderer and we plan to take him back to Black Creek when we find him."

"Suit yourself, but I wouldn't go up against that young man. He's just too damn fast. You boys will find yourself planted in the ground if you plan to brace that boy," said the sheriff, almost proudly. The sheriff's stomach growled and he walked out and left Reedy and Spicer in his office. Reedy looked at his partner.

"That bad feeling I had about this whole thing just got worse," Reedy said apprehensively.

"Hey, like I keep telling you, ride out anytime you like. Just don't forget to leave your share of the money," groused Spicer. They walked out of the sheriff's office and hollered out to the sheriff who was almost across the street. "Hey, Sheriff," asked Reedy, "did Williams say where he was headed?"

"No, he didn't say. He just rode out. Sorry I can't be any more help." Manley lied about it, not wanting these men to have any more information about Jess's whereabouts.

They headed for the stables to get their horses and try to decide what to do next. The stable boy, Billy, got their horses saddled and brought them out to Reedy and Spicer who had been talking about Jess. Billy had overheard Jess's name.

"You know Jess Williams?" asked Billy as Reedy and Spicer quickly exchanged glances.

"Yeah, we know him," replied Spicer. "He's a good friend of ours and we're looking for him. We did some work together and we owe him his share of the money."

"You guys bounty hunters, too?" asked Billy keenly.

"Yes. You could say that," replied Reedy. "Do you know where he was headed when he left town?"

"Sure, he said he was headed for Timber, Texas. He heard that one of the other men he's looking for was down there. Did you hear about the gunfight?" Billy replied excitedly.

"No, why don't you tell us about it," replied Reedy.

"Jess squared off with two men at the same time in a gunfight and they never had a chance," exclaimed Billy. "And he killed Ben Grady who was one of the fastest men on the draw and Grady didn't even clear leather. Jess was so fast you could hardly see him draw. Ain't no one faster than Jess Williams, that's for sure. When you guys see him, tell him Billy and his ma said hi. He gave me money to get my ma's bum leg fixed up. He sure is a good friend to have."

"Thanks, kid," replied Reedy. "We'll tell him you said hi."

Reedy and Spicer rode out of town heading for Timber. They rode for a while in silence. Reedy was thinking about this young man, Jess Williams; Spicer was thinking about the money he was about to make. Reedy finally broke the long silence.

"You know what, Todd," said Reedy. "The more I learn about his kid, the more I like him. I mean, how bad can this kid be when he gives some stable boy enough money to get his ma's leg fixed? That doesn't sound like a cold-blooded killer to me."

"Hey, I've known cold-blooded killers that would buy kids candy," retorted Spicer. "Even the worst of men have a heart sometimes. But that don't make them nice men. Besides, it just doesn't matter. We're getting paid to kill him or bring him back. We're not getting paid to judge him."

"Well, I'll go along until we finally meet up with him. When we do, I want to talk to him first," replied Reedy. Spicer just shook his head wondering if his partner was going soft on him.

☙❧

Jess spent the remainder of the day walking around town. He had some dinner and turned in early. He decided not to go to the saloon for a drink; opting instead to go to his room and get a good night's sleep.

Hank Beard finally arrived in Timber late that same night. He didn't stop in the saloon for a drink either. He was tired and went straight to the hotel and got a room for the night. He had no idea that Ben Grady had been shot dead. He also had no idea that his room was just two doors down from the young man that killed Grady. Fate has a funny way of arranging things sometimes.

CHAPTER THIRTEEN

Timber was a quiet town in the morning. Jess got up at daybreak, saddled Gray and took an early ride around the area checking things out. It was early afternoon when he stopped in at River Bend Bill's and had a cup of coffee with Bill. He took two pounds of fresh coffee to his new friend and Bill couldn't say enough about how nice it was for Jess to do that for him. Bill didn't have much money and sometimes he couldn't afford to even buy coffee.

"Well," said Jess, "I gave the sheriff and Patti your messages."

"I would have loved to be there when you did," laughed Bill. "What did Patti say when you told her?"

Something like; "Oh no, not this again!"

"Hah! I'll bet the sheriff was pissed as hell, wasn't he?" asked Bill.

"I thought he was going to spit blood," Jess said with a smile. "I hope you're not thinking about going into town any time soon. The sheriff has men watching for you and he'll throw you in the hoosegow for sure if you show up. I think I'd wait awhile if I were you."

"Maybe. Hell, I got nothin' but time anyway," he said.

Bill lifted his cup to his lips for another sip of fine coffee when he noticed a small cloud of dust over the other side of the river. He stood up and so did Jess. They spotted four riders following a large man wearing a hat that looked too big for him. They were heading into Timber. Bill recognized the lead rider as Paul Mason.

"That's Paul Mason," said Bill. "I wonder what he's heading into town for. He never comes to town unless there's some kind of trouble."

"Actually there was a little trouble day before yesterday," replied Jess. "I killed a man by the name of Ben Grady." River Bend Bill gave him a disconcerted look.

"You drew down on Ben Grady and lived to tell about it?" he asked excitedly.

"He drew first," he replied flatly. "I didn't start the fight. I only finished it."

"*You* beat Ben Grady to the draw?" he asked again.

"How many times do you want me to tell you?"

"Well, it ain't finished," River Bend Bill said as he sat back down. "It ain't finished until Paul Mason says it's finished. He was paying Ben Grady a lot of money to be his lead hired gun. He's gonna be mighty pissed off. He ain't bringing those four riders into town for no Sunday meetin'."

"Maybe I should head back to town and see if the sheriff needs any help," implied Jess, a worried look on his face.

"Hell, it ain't your job," said Bill. "Have another cup of this fine coffee."

"It might not be my job, but I caused it," he replied. "Actually, Grady caused it, but I don't like anyone paying for my doings." Jess gulped down his coffee and got on his horse and headed straight back to town.

Paul Mason was mad as hell. He was paying Ben Grady ten times what he was paying any of his other hired guns. Of course, Grady was ten times as good as any of them. Mason lived by a few hard and fast rules in his life. One of them was you get what you pay for. If you want the best, you have to pay for the best; and Grady was the best. At least, he had been the best he could find, up until now. Mason had a temper hotter than most branding irons. When one of his hands came back to the ranch after hearing how a young kid shot Ben Grady dead in a fair gunfight, Mason got so mad he punched the ranch hand who told him about it and stormed outside and shot the first thing he saw, which happened to be the man's horse. He shot the horse three times and then threw his gun as far as he could. He spent the remainder of the day cursing and giving everyone a hard time while he gathered up a group of men to ride with him to Timber. They arrived in Timber in the early afternoon. Mason was leading the group by a few feet. Not because he ordered the men to stay behind him, but because they were all afraid of what he might do if they took the lead. They rode up to the sheriff's office, but didn't dismount. Mason yelled out from his horse.

"Sheriff Steele, I know you're in there," growled Mason. "Come on out. I want to talk to you." The other four men just sat on their horses.

The door of the sheriff's office opened up, but Steele didn't appear right away. He stayed back a little for a moment to see if things would explode right away. When they didn't, he slowly walked out of the doorway. He was holding a double-barreled sawed-off shotgun. He was wearing his pistol and he also had another Colt .45 stuck in his belt. He believed in being prepared.

"What can I do for you, Mr. Mason?" Sheriff Steele calmly asked.

"You can start by telling me who killed Ben Grady," directed Mason. "Then, you can point him out to me so I can kill the bastard."

"You know I won't stand for that, Mason," countered Sheriff Steele. "Ben Grady was killed in a fair fight. As a matter of fact, he drew on the kid first."

"You're crazy, Sheriff," Mason bit back. "You know there ain't no one fast enough to take down Grady, especially some wet behind the ears young kid. Hell, you were afraid of going up against Grady yourself! If I have to, I'll have each one of these men challenge this kid one at a time in a fair fight. You can't do anything about that now, can you?"

"Well, no, but if you do that, Ralph the undertaker will be a happy man," replied Sheriff Steele.

"Really! Why is that?" Mason asked infuriated, still clutching the reins on his horse so tight the horse was jerking his head up and down.

"Because he'll be making four new wooden boxes to put your men in and maybe even one for you," replied Steele matter-of-factly. "Hell, Mason, you know as well as I do that Grady could take any two of your men at the same time and not even break a sweat. This kid took Grady down and Grady never got his pistol out of his holster. Add to that, the fact Ben Grady went for his gun first."

"Sheriff, I don't give a damn about any of that," snapped Mason. "Now, I'm not asking you again. Where is this dirtball of a kid?"

"First off, don't threaten me, Mason," retorted Steele angrily. "You should know by now that I don't react too kindly to threats. Besides, he's not here right now. Seems he took an early ride this morning. He'll probably be back sometime later this afternoon." Mason glared at Sheriff Steele.

"Sheriff, we'll be over in the saloon having a drink. We can wait, but when I leave today, that kid will be in a box and I'll even pay for it!" hollered Mason, as if he wanted the whole town to hear.

"I'm afraid you just might pay for it," said Steele, meaning something altogether different; but Mason and his group didn't hear him. They had already turned their horses around and headed across the street to the saloon. They dismounted and walked into the saloon and bellied up to the bar.

"Jed, get us a bottle of your best whiskey and four glasses," barked Mason, "and make it fast."

"Yes, sir, Mr. Mason, right away," replied Jed, as he went into the back room and brought out two bottles of his best whiskey. He knew from experience that one bottle was not going to be enough. Ray, one of the four men that Mason brought with him, and the fastest of the four with a pistol, poured a shot for Mason and himself.

"I'd sure like to get the first crack at that kid, Mr. Mason," Ray said enthusiastically.

"That's fine by me, Ray," replied Mason. "I know you and Ben were good friends. That's why I brought you along. The fact you're the next best man I have with a pistol wasn't lost on me when I picked you."

"Hey, what about us?" asked one of the other men.

"You'll all get your chance after Ray here," an enraged Mason replied. "And whoever plugs him gets a hundred dollar bonus in his pay envelope next month." They all smiled at that, but Ray was smiling the most. He was going to get the first crack at this kid everyone claimed was fast and he was sure he could take him. He had no way of knowing just how wrong he was. Mason and his men settled in for the wait and Sheriff Steele watched the saloon from his office window. He knew today was going to be a day he would more than earn the small salary the town paid him. Hopefully, at the end of the day, he could spend some of it on a drink; which he was sure he was going to need by then.

❦

There were bad men and then there were really bad men. These were men who would kill without remorse or rob people of their life's work and sleep like a baby with no regret for their actions. However, Blake Taggert didn't belong to that class of men. He was in a class all by himself. He was just plain evil to the bone. If ever God made mistakes, Blake Taggert was surely one of them. There was absolutely nothing good about Taggert. He had killed his first man when he was just twelve. That man was his father. His father was a mean ornery cuss who beat Blake's mother; and whenever he felt like it, he'd beat on Blake. One night, he took a bottle and broke it over Blake's head. It cut Blake's head so bad that the blood just kept running in his eyes and he could hardly see. Blake was used to the violence, but for some reason something snapped inside him that night. Maybe the knock on his head did something to change him or maybe he was just a bad seed and he had finally had all he could take from his father. Blake went over to the fireplace and took down the Winchester rifle that his father always kept there and shot his father four times. When his mother screamed at him, he shot her three times. He saddled up the best horse, took all the money his parents had stashed in the house and never looked back. Truth be known, no one ever figured out Blake was the one who killed his parents. Everyone thought Blake had been kidnapped and killed or had run off after finding his parents murdered. No one really cared so the matter was just considered another unsolved murder.

While Beard was on his way to Timber, Blake had done what he said he had planned. He rode out to the homestead outside of Red Rock and murdered the family he told Frank about. He walked into the house about midnight and used the pillow to shoot the couple and then he raped the young daughter. The worst part about it was he dragged the daughter into her parents' bedroom and raped her right there on the bloody bed between her now dead parents' bodies. Before he was finished with her, she was covered in her parents' blood and she was almost in a catatonic state from the shock of what was happening to her.

Then, when he was finished with her, he took his pistol, stuck it between her legs, and fired one shot. The shot was somewhat muffled and the bullet passed out of her stomach, along with some of her insides. He watched the life drain out of the girl and then he smiled at his work. He ransacked the house until he found the money. They had over six hundred dollars stashed in several different places and when Blake was satisfied he found all the money, he headed back to Red Rock; making sure no one saw him return. It was several days before the bodies were discovered, but no one had a clue as to who would do such a horrible thing. Blake just smiled to himself when he heard the men talk about it at the saloon. "Blew the girl's innards right out!" he had heard one of the old men say.

Jess arrived back in town shortly after Mason and his hired guns went to the saloon. He took the back way into town and slid up to the side window of Steele's office. He could see Steele sitting in a chair and looking out the window.

"Afternoon Sheriff, you having a bad day?" asked Jess.

"Christ, Jess!" exclaimed a surprise Sheriff Steele. "Don't ever sneak up on a man like that unless you plan on getting shot!" Steele relaxed a little. "Actually, I'm watching trouble right now over there at the saloon. Why don't you come on in? I can see all five of them and they're all bellied up to the bar and not looking this way." Jess quickly walked into the sheriff's office.

"So, is this a result of what happened with me and Grady the other day?" asked Jess.

"You have a keen sense of perception for as young as you are," replied Sheriff Steele. "Yeah, old Mason and his group are over there waiting for you to come back to town. Then, they plan on making sure you're dead before they leave."

"Not very friendly people hey, Sheriff?" Jess asked sarcastically.

"Paul Mason is a lot of things," replied Steele. "Rich, tough, married to a beautiful young woman, but definitely not friendly."

"Did you explain it was a fair fight and that Grady drew first?" asked Jess.

"No, and I didn't tell him about the time my father gave me my first horse either since I didn't think he was interested in either of those stories," the sheriff said mockingly. "Of course I told him. He just didn't give a shit."

"Well, what do you suggest, Sheriff?"

"Well, it seems to me you've got two choices," he replied. "Head out of town and put some distance between you and Mason or go over there and probably get shot. I'll be glad to stall them for as long as I can."

Jess thought about it for a minute. "I haven't finished what I came here to do. So, I guess I'll just have to go over there and have a little talk with Mason."

"Damn it," he complained. "I just knew you were going to say that. Listen Jess, I've known Mason for a long time and he's not a man to be messing with. He said he plans on seeing you dead for killing Grady and he'll damn sure try. You won't talk him out of it, if that's what you're thinking."

"We won't know until I try now, will we? Besides, if I start running from trouble now, I'll be running forever and that's not going to happen. You can join me if you want, it's your choice. It's not your fight and I won't ask you to involve yourself in the matter. I believe in a man taking care of his own problems," he stated it as plainly as he could.

"Maybe, but I'm still the sheriff in town and I won't stand for any gunplay unless it's fair. That's what I get paid for. So, I guess I'll just tag along for the hell of it. It's either that or do more paperwork."

Jess knew Sheriff Steele would involve himself, it was just in the nature of a man like him to never shy away from a problem. Steele grabbed a few more shotgun shells and put them in his front pocket. He noticed Jess had two pockets sewed into his shirt that held two shells in just the right place.

"Kind of handy," said Steele, as he nodded at Jess's shirt as Steele was putting the twelve gauge shotgun shells into his pocket.

"I like to be prepared, Sheriff," he replied.

They both seemed ready and they looked at each other for a moment as if to wonder how their two lives had seemed to cross paths at this moment in time. Then they nodded at each other and walked out onto the front porch of the sheriff's office. They took a look around the street and up at the rooftops to make sure no one was ready to take a shot at them. As they walked across the street, and without taking his eyes off the front doors of the saloon, Steele said, "I sure hope you're as good as Jed said you was." There was no answer from Jess. He had other things to concentrate on.

As they walked up the two steps to the porch in front of the saloon, Steele could see that the four men who rode in with Mason had turned around with their backs to the bar. As Jess and Steele walked into the bar, the two of them split up. Jess went to the right and Steele to the left. Steele could hardly hear it when Jess said to him in a whisper, "the two on the left are yours, if you want in." The room was so quiet you could hear a cockroach fart. Finally, Mason finished up his drink and slowly turned around to face Jess and Sheriff Steele.

"Sheriff," said Mason, as he shot a look at Jess. "Is that the young man responsible for killing Ben Grady?"

"As a matter of fact, yes it is," answered Steele, setting the twelve-gauge on a table, but still within his reach. Mason looked Jess over for a moment. He was looking at a young man who looked to be not more than seventeen years old; however, Mason could sense there was more to this young man than a cursory glance could tell.

"So, you're the kid who outdrew Ben Grady?" asked Mason.

"Yep, that would be me," said Jess, not taking his eyes off Paul Mason. Jess realized right off Mason was the man who controlled his other four hired guns in the saloon, who were all staring at Jess. Jess knew they would do nothing without Mason's approval.

"You know what son, Ben Grady was my best man. You have to realize just how hard it is for me to believe that a young kid like you outdrew him. Hell, boy, you ain't lived as long as Ben Grady was hiring his gun out. The Sheriff here claims it was a fair fight?" an angry Mason spoke. Sheriff Steele didn't move or say one word, but a voice from behind the bar spoke up. It was Jed, the barkeep.

"Mr. Mason," interjected Jed. "I saw the fight and it was a fair one. Ben drew on Jess first. Jess here drew that gun so fast I could hardly see it. Grady never even had a chance. His gun damn near fell back inside the holster. The only reason it didn't was Grady fell back and his pistol fell out of his hand and on the floor. I'm telling you, I saw it; but I still don't believe it."

Mason listened to Jed's recount of the gunfight, but it only made him angrier. There was no way he could replace Ben Grady unless he could hire this young man who had killed him. He didn't think that was possible and he wasn't sure in his mind this kid was all that good. Maybe he just got off a lucky shot. He didn't know and he didn't really care. All he cared about was that he had lost his best man and because of that he would lose a lot of money over the next year or so it would take to replace him.

"Well, son," groused Mason. "It seems like we have a problem." Jess cocked his head a little and smiled at Mason, which only made him angrier.

"I don't seem to have a problem," replied Jess. Mason took a step forward.

"You don't see that you have a problem?" he asked. Jess thought about if for another moment. He looked at the other four men standing at the bar and then back to Mason.

"No, not really," replied Jess calmly. Mason started peeling his leather gloves off one finger at a time while trying to stare Jess down. Jess didn't flinch or show the slightest sign of being nervous.

"How old are you son?" asked Mason.

"Sixteen."

"Only sixteen?"

"Yes, sir."

"How long have you been using that pistol?"

"Long enough, I guess."

"You guess?" An annoyed Mason questioned.

"That's what I said," said Jess casually.

"Where'd you get a gun like that?"

"Found it."

"Well, son, how the hell did you make it to sixteen with an attitude like that?"

"I didn't know I had an attitude."

Steel was trying to hold in a laugh although he didn't know how he could laugh at a time like this. Here he was listening to this young man facing up to an old, tough, rich ranch baron and the kid was either toying with Mason or just didn't care about answering his questions. Steele had never seen anyone talk to Mason like this before and he kind of liked it. Mason, however, didn't like it one bit and his ears were beginning to turn red. He was losing what little patience he had left with Jess.

"Damn it kid," yelled Mason. "You're really starting to piss me off. Now, here's the deal. I believe in an eye for an eye. Now, the sheriff here says he won't stand for anything but a fair fight. If it was up to me and the sheriff wasn't here, I'd have just shot you on sight when I found out who you were. As you can plainly see, I brought out four of my best men. Ray here is the best of the four. Grady was a good friend of Ray's, and Ray here wants to make you answer for killing Grady. You understand what I'm saying?"

Jess never took his eyes off Mason. He could see Ray, who was to Mason's right and he watched him out of the corner of his eye. But his main focus was on Paul Mason, and he stared deep into Mason's eyes. It was the kind of stare that looked through a man, yet still allowed you to see everything else in the room. Then, after a moment of tense silence following Mason's little speech, Jess spoke in a very low, soft and deliberate tone with no telltale signs of fear.

"Mr. Mason, I guess you've had your say and now I'll have mine," he said slowly. "I didn't know Ben Grady and I sure didn't pick a fight with him. He drew on me first and for no reason, so that meant he was nothing short of a murderer. Now, you paid him to be a hired gun, which is no different than a murderer. That, Mr. Mason, makes you a murderer too, which in my book, puts you on the wrong side of right. Now, to make matters even worse, you come to town hell bent to kill me just for defending myself. Was I supposed to just let him shoot me so you could be in a better mood today? Maybe no one ever taught you right from wrong, but more likely than that, I figure you just don't give a shit. So, now here's *my* deal and you listen real close because I don't have a habit of repeating myself. You see, Mr. Mason, it really doesn't matter if you have Ray challenge me first or if you have one of the others do it. It doesn't even matter if you have all four of your men take me on at one time.

You see, the only thing that really matters here, is I'm going to put the first bullet square in your chest about a split second after anyone moves in this room including Jed behind the bar there. Do you understand *that*? No matter what happens today, you die. Maybe me, maybe the sheriff here and maybe everyone in this room will die, but make no mistake about this, *you* are going to be the first one to die here today. Now, that's the deal. I don't have another thing to say about it so don't ask me any more questions. I've wasted enough of my time with you already." Jess had now altered Mason's entire game plan and Mason was not happy about it.

Mason was a man who hadn't been talked to in this manner for more years than he could remember. That, along with his temper, was the only explanation for what happened next. The only thing you could hear before Mason went for his gun was; "you bastard…"

Mason's hand was moving. Jess stole a glance at Ray and determined that Ray was going for Steele. Jess figured that Steele was in now like it or not and Jess would let him handle Ray and the other man. Mason's hand never got a grip on the pearl handle of his Colt .45. Jess's shot caught him square in the chest. The other four men were all going for their guns. Jess' second shot hit the man to Mason's immediate right and his third shot hit the man next to him. He had fanned the second and third shots with his left hand. Steele had caught his first man, Ray, before he got his gun leveled at Steele, but he took a shot in the left shoulder before he caught the second man. Within a few seconds, five men lay dead on the floor and the smoke was heavy in the air from the gunpowder. Steele couldn't help but notice Jess had shot Mason and the man next to him before he got his first shot off. Jed just stood behind the bar at one end like a statue.

"Jesus Goddamn Christ," he said, almost in a whisper.

Steele was somewhat in shock himself, partially because he had been shot, but mostly because he couldn't believe the speed of Jess's gun hand. He knew a lot of men that were considered fast at skinning leather; but the truth was it was mostly that they were cool headed and didn't miss with their first shot. The ones that were considered fast were the ones who stayed cool under pressure and made their first shot count, but this was different. Jess was not only cool under pressure; he was blazingly fast and accurate. Jess had pulled off all three shots in less than a second and he made every one of them count. Jed threw the sheriff a bar towel after he finally broke himself from his trance and Steele tucked it under his shirt where the bullet had passed through his shoulder. He winced a little at the pain it caused.

"Jess, I thought Jed here was exaggerating a little when he told me how fast you were, but now that I've seen it for myself, even *I* can't believe it," exclaimed Sheriff Steele. "How in the hell did you ever learn to shoot that fast?"

"Practice, Sheriff, lots and lots of practice," he replied as he replaced the spent cartridges and holstered his pistol. Sheriff Steele shot Jess a strange look. Jess noticed the fine bottles of whiskey on the bar. "Sheriff, how about I buy you a drink. It doesn't look like these boys are going to finish that bottle and it sure looks like a good one at that."

"That's one of my best bottles," offered Jed. "Mr. Mason only drinks the best and he had me order it special. It's really good whiskey."

"Well, I guess I can have a drink or maybe two before I go to the Doc's. Hell, this doesn't look too bad," said Steele, as he checked his shoulder where he had taken a bullet.

Sheriff Steele and Jess finished the bottle without another word and Jed just looked at the both of them thinking that he had just witnessed something not too many people would ever get to see. When the bottle was empty, the sheriff went to see the Doctor and Jess sat down at a table and looked at the five dead bodies lying on the floor. He wondered if Sheriff Steele hadn't thrown in with him if he would be lying on the floor dead right now. The sheriff had sent the undertaker and some men over to clean up and carry the bodies out. Jess watched, showing no emotion. He finally spotted Patti looking out of the back door of the saloon. He looked at her and smiled a little. So little, you could hardly tell. After the bodies were all removed and Jed had mopped up most of the blood, Patti came out and sat down next to Jess.

"I've seen a lot of shooting in my days, but nothing like that," said Patti, a bewildered look on her face. "You're not just any young man, are you Jess Williams? There is something very special about you. Maybe you were born to it or maybe destiny has just singled you out for something special, but you're not like other men. I'm glad I had the chance to meet someone like you."

"Thanks, Patti," he said. "I wonder about it myself sometimes. I figure that you're a special woman, too, and I'm glad I got to meet you." Patti stood up and smiled down at Jess.

"How about something to eat?" she asked.

"That sounds like a great idea."

Patti nodded and went back in the kitchen and fixed Jess a plate of the day's special. A few men were starting to filter into the saloon now. They had heard about the gunfight and they were quiet and just sat around and talked amongst themselves, every once in a while they would glance over at Jess. He heard them, but he didn't listen. He knew what they were talking about and they'd be talking about it for the rest of their lives. They'd be telling the story about how they were there the day that Jess Williams took down three men in one gunfight. Jess continued to eat his food and when he finished, he went to his room and stayed there for the remainder of the day.

CHAPTER FOURTEEN

Hank Beard left Timber about an hour after Jess had ridden out to have some coffee with River Bend Bill. Their paths never crossed even though they had just spent the night in the same hotel with only one room separating them. Here was the man Jess was looking for and he had been in a bed less than thirty feet away. Beard hadn't talked with anyone and had no idea Jess was in town or that he was looking for him. He had other things on his mind. He was focused on the planned robbery of Mason's money coach and he wanted to talk to Grady and finish up their plans. He knew Grady wasn't in town because when he was, Grady's horse was always in the same place at the stable and it hadn't been there when Beard had arrived. And because Grady didn't often come to town, he didn't think this unusual. Beard knew that Grady usually stayed out at the Mason ranch and close to Mason himself since Mason had his share of enemies.

Hank spent most of his day checking out some hiding places within a mile or so out of town just in case. Little did he know he was at one point within half a mile from River Bend Bill's place while Jess was having coffee with Bill. He knew about Bill's place and he avoided it because he didn't want anyone to know what he was up to. Hank figured the less people knew the better. He eventually arrived at the Mason ranch just about sundown. The shootout in the saloon between Steele, Jess and Mason and his four hired guns was already history and people were talking about it.

Word had already reached the Mason ranch and Mason's widow was already finished with her grieving. She shed a few tears, but the truth was she had fallen out of love with Paul Mason a long time ago. He cheated on her and treated her like a tool that he had to keep around when the need struck him. She wouldn't miss him. She would miss the young Paul Mason she fell in love with years ago, but not the Paul Mason who had become so wealthy that he paid more attention to his money than his wife. Before the end of the day, she had already started to rearrange the ranch to fit her desires and she even threw some of his things out. After Hank stabled his horse, hoping he could bed down for the night and visit with Ben Grady, he walked up to the bunkhouse and asked for a cup of coffee and if anyone knew where Ben Grady was?

"Didn't you hear? Ben's dead and so is Mr. Mason," said a tall lanky cowhand by the name of Luke. "Hell we don't even know if we have a job anymore."

Several of the men in the bunkhouse told the story to Hank about this young bounty hunter killing Ben and then facing down Mason and four other hired guns. They talked about how Ben never cleared his gun from its holster and how Sheriff Steele had thrown in with the kid against Mason. Beard listened to the story intently, taking it all in and having a hard time believing it. He was listening especially hard when one of the men told of Jess asking Grady if he knew a man by the name of Hank Beard and that he was looking for him.

"Did this Williams kid say why he was looking for me?" asked Hank.

"Said something about you killing his family and all," replied one of the hands.

"Said you killed and raped his little sister. You didn't do none of that, did ya, Hank?" asked one of the other hands.

"Hell, he's talking out his ass," lied Grady. "I ain't raped any women and I sure ain't raped no little girls. I can get all the women I want, anytime I want." Beard took another swallow of his coffee. The hands were all watching him and wondering what he was going to do about the kid who was gunning for him.

"You boys mind me bunking down here tonight?" asked Grady. "I don't need much, just a spot to lay my bedroll."

"Sure, that's fine, I guess," said one of them. "But if that kid comes gunnin' for ya here, you're on your own. None of us are tangling with the guy that took down Ben Grady."

"Don't worry, boys," said Grady. "I take care of my own business. I ain't scared of no boy even if he did take down Grady. He comes in here looking for me you just let me handle him."

Hank sounded pretty convincing, but the hands could tell he was worried. He knew how fast Grady was and anyone who could take him in a fair fight, had to be pretty damn good. Hank figured right then and there he would try to find the kid and ambush him. Hell, he'd blow a hole in him with his shotgun before the kid even knew what hit him. He'd do it while the kid was asleep.

He finished his coffee and lay down on his bedroll. He was trying to figure out who he would ask to go in with him on the stage robbery now that Grady was dead. Even with Paul Mason dead, his widow would still run the ranch and still run the money into the bank in Timber. He already had it all planned out so maybe he would cut himself in for sixty percent instead of fifty. That would leave him with enough money to last him for years.

His thoughts turned to the kid that was gunning for him. He figured it must be someone related to the family he and his other two partners had murdered. That wasn't the first family they had murdered, and it wasn't the first time Blake Taggert had raped a woman, but it *was* the first time Blake Taggert had raped a little girl. He and Hank had gotten into a real bad argument about it and Hank told him if he ever did that again it would be the last job they would do together. He didn't care what Taggert did on his own; he just didn't want anything like that tied to him. Hank had no problem with robbing and killing people though. He was the one who took the kitchen knife to Jess's ma. He stabbed her while she was screaming and he kept stabbing her, over and over again. Hank dozed off to a light sleep. He had his twelve-gauge lying next to him under his blanket with his hand on it. He knew someone was hunting him and he wasn't going down easy.

≈≈

Frank Reedy and Todd Spicer finally reached Timber about noon the next day. They rode hard to try to reach Timber before Jess left. They argued all morning about what they would do when they finally caught up to Jess. The only thing they agreed on was that Spicer would let Reedy talk to Jess first. After that, if reedy didn't want any part of it, he would just leave and let Spicer do what he was hired to do. Reedy agreed with that only because of professional courtesy, one bounty hunter to another.

Jess was having some lunch at the saloon and watched Reedy and Spicer ride into town. He didn't know either of the two men, but he knew they were up to something. He watched the two men through the saloon window as they rode up to the sheriff's office and dismounted. They stopped on the porch again and spoke to one another for a minute and then went inside the sheriff's office. Steele was doing what he loathed more than anything, paperwork.

There were five new corpses and that always meant paperwork. He looked up from his desk. He knew in an instant he was looking at two bounty hunters. You could always tell. Hunters were always heavily armed and had a look in their eyes that most men didn't, and these two were no exception.

"Can I help you gentlemen?" asked Sheriff Steele.

"Well, I'll be damned," said Reedy. "Mark Steele, when did you pin on a badge?" Steele stood up to get a closer look at Reedy.

"I'll be damned if it ain't Frank Reedy," exclaimed Steele. "How in the hell have you been? It must be ten, no fifteen years since I last saw you. It's been ten years since I pinned on a badge myself. What happened to yours? Last time I saw you, you were wearing a United States Marshall's badge."

"Hell, being a Marshall doesn't pay enough," explained Reedy. "Bounty hunting pays a lot more and the risk is the same or sometimes less. Plus, we're both doing the same job except I get paid better. You ought to try it. We could use another hand. There are lots of bad guys out there that need catching, Sheriff."

"It's not for me; at least not yet," replied Steele. "Being sheriff ain't all bad. I get an office and I don't have to spend my nights on the trail sleeping on hard ground. I sleep in a nice warm comfy bed every night."

"That ain't all bad either, I guess," admitted Reedy. "Sheriff, this is my partner, Todd Spicer." Steele shook Spicer's hand.

"Sheriff," Reedy continued, "we're looking for a young man, about sixteen or seventeen years old. His name is Jess Williams." Frank noticed a change in Steele immediately. "You know him, Sheriff?"

"Yes, I do," replied Steele cautiously. "What's your business with him?"

"We've been hired to bring him back to Black Creek, Kansas, for the murder of a man there," replied Reedy.

"Who'd he murder?"

"A man by the name of Red Carter."

"And who hired you two to bring him back?"

"His father, Dick Carter," replied Reedy, knowing what Sheriff Steele would think. "Red Carter was his only son."

"Murdered? You sure about that?" asked Sheriff Steele. "Jess doesn't seem like a young man who would murder someone. Kill for sure, but not murder."

"I guess you must know him then," said Reedy. "Sounds like you've taken a liking to the kid."

"I guess you might say that," he replied. "You get to know someone who comes to your town and ends up killing four men in a few days. All fair fights, I might add. That's why I'm having a hard time believing he would murder someone. Hell, he wouldn't have to murder anybody."

"What do you mean by that?" asked Spicer.

"The kid's so damn fast with that gun of his, all he'd have to do is call a man out," replied Steele. "I've got to tell you that kid's got an unnatural ability to draw and shoot a pistol and hit what he's aiming at. Have you got a legal warrant on him?"

"We don't need any warrant, Sheriff," interjected Spicer. "We've been paid to bring him back and that's what we aim to do, one way or another. It'll be up to him if it has to go down bad. We've been paid to bring him back, dead or alive, no matter what," said Spicer. Steele shook his head.

"This ain't right and you boys know it," complained Steele. "I ain't letting you men just take this kid because some rich rancher hired you to do it. You have no warrant or legal paperwork on him. I'm sorry, but if you attempt to take him, you'll have to deal with me along with the kid. Otherwise, go back to Kansas and get a warrant. Frank, you should know better." Spicer was losing patience and Reedy knew he had to offer up something else.

"Sheriff, we just want to talk with him first," pleaded Reedy. "At least give us that and then we'll see how it goes. How's that sound?"

"Sounds like the first sensible thing you've said up to now," Steele replied. "I think he's over at the saloon getting a bite to eat. You boys need to understand something though. This kid ain't one to be messed with. And I'm not kidding about his shooting ability. You boys better think twice about what you're doing."

Steele walked them both over to the saloon. Jess watched the sheriff come out of his office with the two men in tow. He slipped the hammer strap off his gun and straightened himself in his chair and slid it back enough for his gun to clear the table if he had the need to use it. He trusted the sheriff, but not these other two men. There were half a dozen men in the saloon and they noticed the change in Jess and seen him remove the hammer strap. He watched the sheriff come through the door first and kept his eyes on the two men, one on each side of the sheriff.

"Afternoon, Jess," said Sheriff Steele. "These two men say they have business with you. They say you murdered a man back in Black Creek, Kansas, by the name of Red Carter and they've been paid to take you back there for questioning. They don't have a warrant or any legal papers on you, so you don't have to go back with them or even talk with them if you don't want to. I know one of these men, Jess. He's always been a fair man and he says he just wants to talk to you first. So, what do you think?" Jess didn't look at the sheriff yet, he kept his gaze on the two men standing behind him.

"Sheriff, I don't mind talking with them, but first there are a few things you need to know. Red Carter shot the sheriff of our town and for no good reason. The sheriff was just trying to take him into custody again. Sheriff Diggs was a good man and a good friend to my family. That's probably why they don't have a warrant for my arrest. Red Carter was a murderer and I called him out fair and killed him fair. Now, that being said, what do you two want with me?" Spicer was getting frustrated at all the talking.

"I'm going over to the bar and get a drink, Frank," said Spicer impaintently. "Let me know when you're done *talking* to the kid. And don't forget; leave your five hundred on the bar if you walk away from this." Reedy nodded at Spicer and then turned his attention to Jess.

"Listen kid," said Reedy, as he sat down in front of Jess. "We've been chasing your tail for a while now and everywhere you go, people end up dying. And yet, everyone says you're an okay fellow. I haven't run into one person yet who said you started any fight except the ones with Red Carter and another guy you shot by the name of Randy Hastings. So, I gotta ask you kid, did you shoot Red Carter fair and square, just like you said?"

"Yes, sir," he replied bluntly. "I started that fight with Red Carter and I called him out, but only because he killed the sheriff in cold blood. I also let him draw first. Then, I shot him dead. That's the truth." Reedy sat back in his chair and thought for a moment.

"Okay, I believe you're telling me the truth," said Reedy. "Answer me one more question just for my own satisfaction. The man you shot, repeatedly I might add, back in Tarkenton, Kansas, by the name of Randy Hastings. Was he one of the men who murdered your family?"

"Yes, sir, he was, and I ain't sorry I killed him," he replied coldly. "I'm here looking for one of the other two, a man by the name of Hank Beard. When I find him, I plan to kill him like the dog he is."

Reedy looked into Jess's eyes and he saw the look of a young man who was already a hardened killer and a hunter of men. Reedy knew he could not take this young man back to Black Creek and hand him over to Dick Carter. Of course, Reedy saw something else in Jess's eyes and his self-preservation was also a large part of his decision. He knew Jess wasn't going to let two men or even an army of men take him anywhere. Reedy wanted to live another day to do another job. He knew if he tried to take Jess back, that wouldn't happen. Reedy stood up and walked over to the bar next to Spicer and dug into his pocket and placed the five hundred dollars that Carter paid him in advance on the bar.

"This young man ain't a murderer and I won't have anything else to do with taking him back to Carter," Reedy stated firmly. "It ain't right and I've been trying to tell you that all along. Why don't we both go back to Kansas and tell Carter we couldn't find him?"

"You're going soft in your old age, Frank," said Spicer, as he put the money in his front pocket. "A job is a job. We don't ask questions or make judgments about the men we hunt. Hell, you'd better go back to wearing a badge and leave bounty hunting to guys like me who don't give a rat's ass whether or not a man is good, bad, guilty or innocent. We just bring them in and collect our money." Todd finished his drink and turned to face Jess sitting at the table.

Reedy said in a low voice that only Spicer could hear, "Don't do it, Todd. I'm telling you, this kid will drop you dead. You can't outdraw him. It ain't worth it."

"Bullshit, Frank. I'm gonna make a total of three thousand dollars when this job is finished. I ain't walking away from that much money," snapped Spicer.

Spicer stepped away from the bar and looked straight at Jess. Sheriff Steele had sat down at a table next to Jess. If this was going to be a confrontation between two men, he wouldn't interfere. His job now was to keep the odds even and to make sure Reedy didn't change his mind and throw in with Spicer at the last minute. He started to think about more paperwork. He moaned, but it wasn't from his shoulder wound he had gotten yesterday, it was from the thought of more paperwork he was now sure he would have to do; and soon.

CHAPTER FIFTEEN

"Son, stand up so I can talk to you, face to face," demanded Spicer. Jess slowly stood up, glancing at Steele. It was a look that told Steele he need not get involved in this. Then his eyes locked on Spicer. The look in Jess's eyes unnerved Spicer momentarily, but Spicer was a hardened man who had faced death many times and survived.

"I only got one question, boy," said Spicer. "You going back willingly or do I have to drag you back there behind my horse?"

"No." Jess stated flatly.

"No, what?" asked Spicer. "No, you ain't going back or no, you ain't going back dragged behind my horse? Which is it?"

"Neither."

"Well, then just what do you think you're going to do?"

"Probably shoot you, unless you suddenly come to your senses," replied Jess.

Reedy looked at Steele who almost let out a little chuckle at that comment.

"You think you can take me, kid?" Spicer spat.

"Yes."

"You're that certain?"

"Nothing is certain in life," replied Jess.

"But you think you're that fast, eh?"

"Yes."

"Frank, you sure you don't want in on this?" Spicer asked Reedy, glancing back at him, now seeming just a little unsure that he wanted to take Jess on alone after seeing Jess's demeanor.

"Like I told you, Todd, I don't agree with this job. It stunk right from the beginning. Leave it alone and let's go back to Kansas. I'm telling you, this kid will drop you before you even know it happened. I feel it in my gut," urged Reedy. Spicer turned his stare back to Jess who hadn't moved except to move his gun hand into position.

"Well, kid. This is your last chance," prodded Spicer. "Either you go back to Kansas with me willingly or I'll have to pack you on a mule bent over. What do you say?"

"That's just not going to happen," he answered plainly.

Bounty hunters were a tough lot. They would face odds that most men wouldn't. Most bounty hunters were pretty good with a gun and Todd Spicer was better than most. Bounty hunters were the type of men who stayed cool while facing death and Spicer was better than most at that, too. But most men just couldn't walk away from a gunfight once they were in. It was a matter of honor. Most men would rather die and have people talk about how tough they were instead of walking away from it and having people talk about how they had turned tail and ran like a yellow dog. That kind of thing would follow a man around forever. These things, along with the thought of three thousand dollars, made Todd Spicer do what at any other moment in his life know he shouldn't do. He had as good a sense about people as Frank Reedy did and he knew he was about to bite off more than he could chew, but he just couldn't stop himself now.

Spicer went for his gun and it was a strange thing from his perspective. He felt himself reaching for his gun and even felt his thumb touch the hammer. Then, he felt a hard thump on his chest, heard a loud noise and saw a flash in front of him. He never blinked. He couldn't understand how it happened so fast. He never even saw Jess draw his gun, yet here he was with a hole in his chest and the kid standing there with his gun pointed at him, and it was all over and he didn't see any of it. He let go of his gun, which never even moved out of the holster. He glanced over at Steele who had a look of disbelief on his face and then he dropped to his knees, both of his hands trying to stop the blood that was now gushing from his chest. Todd Spicer finally fell face first onto the floor, dead before he hit it. Sheriff Steele, who had stood up after Spicer had been shot, sat back down again.

"Damn it, Jess, you ain't natural," said Steele, shaking his head. Reedy walked over to Spicer's body, turned him over, and began to talk to him as if somehow he could hear him from the great beyond.

"I told you not to take him on, but would you listen? Hell no, you stubborn son-of-a-bitch. And now, there you are lying in your own blood, deader than dead. Damn it!" Reedy kept shaking his head in disgust as he reached into Spicer's front pocket where he had tucked the five hundred dollars Reedy had put down on the bar. He pulled out the money along with Spicer's five hundred and put the thousand dollars in his front pocket. He would take the money back to Carter and tell him what happened. He wanted no part of the money or Dick Carter. Then he sat down in a chair next to Spicer's body.

"Sorry Sheriff, seems like you got more paperwork to do," said Jess, as he sat down at the table. "It wasn't my call. I didn't want it."

"I know," replied Steele. "It seems like men just keep coming to you to get themselves killed. Hell, maybe you should become a preacher?"

"Now, why would I want to go and do something like that, Sheriff?"

"So you could read them their last rites before you kill them," replied Steele. Jess almost smiled at that.

"Mr. Reedy, do you want him buried here or are you taking him back to Kansas?" asked Sheriff Steele.

"Hell, might as well bury him here. You *do* have a cemetery for idiots, don't you?" he asked.

"Sure do," replied Steele. "Most of the men buried there were idiots the day they died. The rest of them were drunk and stupid."

"Well, just add one more to it," said Reedy. "I'll pay the undertaker on my way out of town. I'll take it out of his share of the money, I think Dick Carter would say okay, not that I give a shit anyway."

Jess and Steele walked out together. Jess spent the remainder of the day walking around town and asking a few townspeople if they knew anything about Beard. No one did. He had supper and checked on Gray. He went up to his room early, forgoing the saloon. Tomorrow he planned to ride out to some of the ranches to ask about Beard. He fell asleep and dreamed of little Samantha. She was throwing hay around the yard and throwing chicken eggs on the ground. Agitating Jess like usual; except she had a bullet hole in her head.

≈≋

Beard spent the day hanging around the Mason ranch. He had decided to go into town at night and try to ambush Jess. He even spoke with Mason's widow to see if she would hire him on. He didn't really want a job. It was just a ploy to show he had a reason for hanging around. He left the Mason ranch before dark and rode within a mile of Timber. He made a fire and some coffee and waited until late before he snuck into town. He wanted to make sure that most of the townspeople were in bed and out of the saloon. He planned to sneak into Jess' room and ambush him. He would shoot him while he was sleeping and head out of town in the dark; hoping that by the time people woke and found out what had happened he would have a good head start. He hoped it would be enough time for him to hide in the hills near the small ravine he had spotted the other day.

It was three in the morning when Beard tied his horse up to the pole on the back porch of the hotel. Sheriff Steele had already made his last rounds and was turned in for the night. Jed was still cleaning up the saloon, but there were no paying customers in there. The last of them left over an hour ago. The desk clerk in the hotel was up in his room, asleep. Beard tried to be as quiet as he could. He went into the lobby behind the counter and checked out the names on the register. He found the name he was looking for. Jess Williams was the name next to room #201. Beard thought that almost funny since he had stayed in room #203 just the other night.

This hotel was like most small hotels in many small towns. Drafty, in dire need of a coat of paint and creaky, especially the floorboards. That fact had not gone unnoticed by Jess. He paid attention to many of the smallest details concerning his surroundings. He noticed that the third step going to the second floor had a squeak to it. He was also aware that the floor just five feet from his door squeaked ever so lightly when you stepped there, and he had made a mental note of the fact that the top of the door to his room stuck a little. Not enough to stop you from opening the door, but just enough that when the door was opened, the top would hold slightly so when you continued to push on the door, the top would pop open and cause the all too flimsy door to shake a little.

Jess never heard that third step, although Beard paused for a full minute when he hit it and it squeaked. And Jess never *consciously* heard the slight squeak of the floor by his door, although it broke a bead of sweat on Beard's forehead. He waited for another minute or two after that one. He was standing just outside of Jess' room, trying to hold his breath and not move. He was waiting to see if anyone heard the floor squeak before he made his move into Jess's room. He also took this time to gather up enough courage to make his move.

Sometimes when one was asleep, a sound out of the ordinary sometimes wakes a person up even when you never really consciously heard the sound? That's what the squeak outside Jess's door was like. Jess didn't consciously hear it, but his *subconscious* did, and his brain began giving out signals to let him know that something was awry. It didn't wake him. It just put him on the edge of awake.

Now, when the door did that little shaky thing when Beard finally got the nerve to push it open, well, that was another thing. Jess was always prepared for an ambush. When he slept, he slept with his shotgun by his bed within easy reach and his pistol was right next to his right hip. He always slept on his back and he always moved the bed so that he had a clear view of the door when he opened his eyes. Those things, along with the squeaky floor and the shaky door, were what spelled bad news for Hank Beard, although Hank didn't realize it yet.

Beard pushed the door and noticed that it was stuck a little at the top. He had already made the decision to open the door and even though his brain was telling his body he should stop, his body weight was already in motion and it was one of those things that you just can't stop in time, even though you know you should. Beard threw open the door and raised his shotgun to put a load of buckshot into Jess, but things didn't quite go the way Beard had planned.

Jess was awake and had his pistol trained on the door before it was open enough to see who was coming in. The next thing Jess's eyes saw in the dim light was a shotgun barrel. That was all he needed to know. Jess' first shot was right through that flimsy door just as it flew open and it hit Beard in his left side knocking him off balance. By then, the door was fully open and Beard was totally exposed. Jess's second shot hit Beard in his right shoulder, which caused him to drop the shotgun as he fell against the wall a second time, this time falling on his ass. By now, Jess was standing up and hovering over Beard, trying to see in the dim light. The noise had awoken just about everybody in the hotel, including the desk clerk who was quickly coming down the hall with an oil lamp. He stopped outside of Jess's room and called into the room.

"Mr. Williams," he said, "are you okay?"

"Yes, I'm fine," replied Jess. "Bring that lamp a little closer and be careful stepping over the trash."

The clerk stepped inside Jess's room and held the light up high to see the room better and gasped when he saw a large man sitting against the wall bleeding from both sides.

"Hold the light a little closer to his face," asked Jess.

The desk clerk put the lamp as close as his shaking arm would allow him. Jess recognized the man as Hank Beard, the man he had been looking for. Jess never took his eyes off Beard and he never looked at the desk clerk. He simply said to the clerk, "Leave that lamp on the table there, and shut the door on your way out." The desk clerk, not one to argue, especially with the young man who had already killed several men over the last few days, did what he was told and left. Hank Beard was bleeding pretty badly. His pistol was still in its holster and he thought about trying to go for it, even with a bad shoulder. He looked up at Jess.

"Do I know you, son?" asked Beard, lying about it.

"You should."

"Well, I don't," replied Beard, still lying.

"So, you're going to lie about it, too?"

"I ain't lying," spat Beard.

"Why'd you come in my room with a damn shotgun?"

"I got lost."

"Lost?"

"Yeah, I stayed in the room two doors down from here the other day," said Beard. "I thought I was going into my room."

"There's an old woman staying in that room tonight."

"How do you know that?"

"I pay attention."

"Well, what now?"

"You don't remember me?"

"Remember what?"

"Meeting a young boy in a wagon back in Black Creek, Kansas?" Jess reminded him.

"Maybe," Beard responded.

"Maybe right before you went to that young man's home and murdered his family," exclaimed Jess angrily.

"I don't know if I remember that," Beard lied. He knew what Jess was talking about. He just didn't want to admit it.

"You're one of the men who murdered my family."

"So, who are you?"

"I'm that young boy in the wagon you met that day, by the creek."

"Well, if you're hunting me for the bounty, I'll pay you twice what I'm worth," pleaded Beard, trying to buy his way out of a bad situation.

"You don't seem to be listening to me," replied Jess. "That family you murdered. That was *my* family. The man you shot down was my pa. The woman you butchered in the house was my ma and the little girl you beat, raped and shot was my little seven-year-old sister, Samantha." Beard knew he was done for.

"I never touched your little sister. That was Taggert's doing and I didn't like it none and I told him so." Beard said still pleading.

"And you think that makes you innocent?" asked an infuriated Jess. "You didn't stop him. You were there. Even if you didn't do any of the killings, you're just as guilty as the other two men."

"Listen, you can't talk Taggert out of anything once he's made up his mind about something," implored Beard.

"Well, I guess that's just a bad break for you," replied Jess. "Now, you wanted to buy your way out of this, so I'm going to give you that chance."

"How much?" asked Beard thinking he might get out of this thing yet.

"Money ain't what I'm here to collect."

"Then what is it if it ain't money?" asked Beard.

"I'm here to collect your soul and your life along with it," he replied menacingly. "And it's not going to feel good either."

"You'd shoot an unarmed man?" asked Beard. "That just ain't legal, no matter what I've done."

"You weren't unarmed when you came in here with that shotgun," he countered. "You weren't unarmed when you shot my pa and killed my ma and little sister."

"But you can't just shoot me while I'm sitting here," pleaded Beard. "Hell, you've done shot me twice already. I can't draw. I can hardly move my gun hand. That just ain't fair."

"You want a fair fight after sneaking into my room in the middle of the night and trying to plug me with that shotgun there?" he asked. "You think that was fair?"

"I heard how fast you were," replied Beard. "I needed an edge."

"You want fair?" asked Jess. "Hell, I'll give you fair. You don't deserve it, but I'll give it to you. It will make killing you even more satisfying." Jess holstered his pistol.

"What are you going to do?" asked a confused Beard.

"Go ahead and take your pistol out of that holster," said Jess. Beard was frenzied now. He wasn't sure what Jess was planning, but he also knew his choices were running out. He'd bleed out soon and he knew it. He slowly pulled his pistol out of his holster and laid it on his lap.

"Okay, now what?" he asked.

"Pick it up with your gun hand and point it at me," demanded Jess. "Make sure you aim real good because you're only going to get one shot if you're lucky."

"Is this some kind of trick?" asked a confused Beard. "You want me to point this pistol at you?"

"Well, at least your hearing's not gone yet," said Jess. "Come on, point the gun, but don't try to pull the trigger yet." Beard slowly raised the pistol and pointed it right at Jess's chest. His hands were a little shaky, but at this short distance he couldn't miss.

"Okay, now you've got fair," said Jess. Your gun is pointed at my chest. My gun is still in its holster. Now all you have to do is pull the hammer back and pull the trigger before I draw and plug you. That's fair, don't you think? Hell, you can even use both hands to steady yourself if you want to."

Beard knew his options were quickly running out. He was bleeding out fast now since his heart was beating rapidly and he knew he would begin to lose consciousness soon. Besides, he figured he had at least a pretty good chance now. He had his gun pointed straight at Jess and had both hands holding the gun steady. No matter how fast Jess was, Beard figured he had at least a fifty-fifty chance of living through this. He thought Jess stupid for giving him this much of a chance. Beard looked into Jess' eyes. For a split second, just before his thumb began to pull back on the hammer of his pistol, Beard realized he was doomed. Some unconscious thought told him this was the end. A split second was all it took. Before Beard had the hammer back far enough to cock, Jess slicked his pistol out and shot Beard right where he had planned to, straight in the groin. Beard let out a loud scream and dropped the gun in his lap, which only added to the pain.

"Damn it!" he shrieked. "You ain't supposed to shoot a man in his privates! It ain't right!"

"You're no man," he retorted angrily. "You're a cold-blooded killer and you don't deserve right. You deserve what you got and you deserve what you've got coming next."

"Just finish it!" bawled Beard. "I've had enough. I don't give two shits about you and your dead family. I enjoyed killing them! How do you like that?"

"I'll finish you when you tell me where Taggert is," warned Jess.

"Go screw yourself!" hollered Beard. Jess took a step closer to Beard and put a slug into Beard's left kneecap. Beard screamed with excruciating pain.

"Tell me where Taggert is or I'll gut shoot you and watch you die slowly," he threatened with an ominous look.

"He's in Red Rock, Texas, south of here, you bastard! Now finish it!" begged Beard.

Jess walked up to Beard who was starting to lose consciousness. Jess put his pistol on Beard's forehead and looked into his eyes. There was no look of fear, just a pleading look that said to finish it. Jess pulled the trigger and Beard's brain matter splattered onto the wall behind him. Jess wiped his gun off on Beard's shirt and placed it back in his holster after replacing the spent cartridges. He felt no remorse. He felt good that another part of his mission was finished. He had only one more to go.

CHAPTER SIXTEEN

Jess stared at Beard slumped against the wall all shot to hell. He knew what he had just done would be thought of as terrible, unless people knew the whole story. He couldn't worry about that now. He still had one more task. Find Blake Taggert and kill him. And now he had a lead, a town called Red Rock. Jess would head out first thing in the morning. He heard footsteps coming up the stairs and he knew the first one to come in the room would be Sheriff Steele. Steele had his gun drawn, but down at his side. Steele was certain that if anyone was dead in this room, it wasn't going to be Jess Williams. Steele glanced at Jess and then took a long look at Beard. He had seen men shot up before, but this was the worst he had ever seen. He looked back at Jess.

"Son, I believe you've got a mean streak in you," said Steele. "I'm going to go out on a limb and assume the head shot was last?" Jess nodded affirmatively.

"Good, otherwise, I'd have to start wondering about your sanity," said Steele.

"Well, maybe I am a little crazy, but at least I got a reason," he said defensively.

"I can't argue with that," he agreed. "Did you get what you wanted?"

"I sure did."

"Did he tell you anything about the other man you're looking for?"

"Yes, as a matter of fact, he told me he was in Red Rock, Texas," replied Jess. "Do you know where that is, Sheriff?"

"It's about a ten day ride south of here. How'd you drag that out of him?"

"I traded him."

"Traded him? For what?" he asked dubiously.

"A bullet in the head."

"Maybe we should talk about that crazy thing again."

"Maybe," he agreed.

"Suppose you're heading to Red Rock, huh?"

"First thing in the morning, Sheriff," replied Jess. "Besides, I figure that I'm beginning to wear out my welcome here."

"I have to admit I am tired of burying people lately," he replied. "I could use a break from all that paperwork."

"Well, Sheriff, I am sorry for putting you out, but this was going to happen somewhere and your town just happened to be it," said Jess. "I suppose you could blame Beard for coming to your town."

"Hell, I'm not blaming anyone, Jess," he explained. "I don't blame you for doing what you did. I would have done the same thing. Maybe not quite as violent as you, but I would've plugged this one for sure. I'd also hunt down that guy Taggert and put a bullet in his sorry ass too. Don't feel like you've done anything wrong. Actually, you probably saved a few lives today by killing this one here. I have a hunch he wasn't going to start attending church on a regular basis anytime soon."

"Thanks, Sheriff. I'll tell you this, you've made a friend for life," Jess said sincerely. "If you ever need anything, you can call on me. I'll be here as fast as a horse can carry me."

"I'll remember that," he replied keenly. "I can't think of anyone I'd rather have in a pinch backing me up. I won't hesitate to call on you and that's a fact."

⚐ ⚑

Jess saddled up and rode out of town at first light. He had never gotten back to sleep after killing Beard. As he rode by the sheriff's office, he noticed Steele at his desk. Steele looked up and Jess nodded at the sheriff. Steele thought to himself, as he watched this young man who had become a hardened killer at such a young age, he was surely glad that he wasn't this Blake Taggert fellow. He also wondered how many more men would fall into their own pool of blood for getting in his way. He knew one thing for sure. Jess wasn't ever going to quit killing men. There were too many gunslingers out there who would like to take out someone with a reputation and Jess was gaining one rapidly. Steele laughed to himself when he thought about men who cut notches in their gun handle for every man they killed. Hell, if Jess did that, it sure would mess up that beautiful pistol he had.

꿕 ꛅ

There was a lot of talk about the savage murder of the family outside of Red Rock. It was the daily talk at just about every place the townsfolk gathered. Taggert stood at the bar and listened to all the threats.

"If I caught that bastard, I'd cut his balls off and watch him bleed to death," said one man.

"Hell, not me," said another, "I'd ram my rifle right up his ass and let one go!"

The talk didn't bother Taggert. Hell, nothing bothered Taggert. He quit caring about life a long time ago. He wasn't really afraid of dying. He simply wasn't going to do anything that would hasten it. He figured that every time he cheated death it gave him one more chance to kill someone else or have his way with another young girl, and the younger, the better in his mind.

No one suspected Taggert as the one who did the killings. His family had lived around Red Rock all their lives and Blake had been in and out of town every few years. Red Rock was where he went between his crimes. It was kind of a hide out for him. Actually, this was the first time he had done any killing around Red Rock, except for the time he had killed his own family.

The first time he had returned to town after killing his family, everyone was still telling him how sorry they were for what had happened to his family and that they had never caught the culprits who had done it. Blake always found that somewhat funny, although he wasn't sure why. So, whenever he came home, he was welcomed and no one ever thought anything bad of him. Little did he know things were about to change. His final destiny was heading for him and it had a name; Jess Williams.

※ ※

Jess enjoyed being out on the trail. He wasn't in any hurry since he had a long way to go before he got to Red Rock. He wasn't worried about Taggert leaving Red Rock before he got there. He'd just get a lead on him and follow him for the rest of his life until he found him or died trying.

He knew that he was gaining a reputation with a gun and that soon, someone would challenge him just for the reputation of beating him to the draw. Maybe one day, there would be a bounty on his head, and men would hunt him down for the money. Either way, he realized then and there that his life's path had been chosen for him. He would hunt down the worst of men for the bounty on their heads.

Jess worked his way south into Texas going around towns unless he needed supplies. On the fourth day, he camped a few miles outside what looked like a fairly large town. He ate a simple meal and kept a low fire. He rode into Largo, Texas, about an hour after daylight. There were plenty of hotels and eating establishments and what looked like a new livery. Jess stabled his horse and paid the man working the livery an extra dollar per day to get Gray some extra care and the best grain the man had. The livery worker, a small black man by the name of Earl, had a huge smile on his face when Jess gave him the extra dollar.

"Thank you, sir," exclaimed Earl. "I'll make sure I take real good care of your horse. He'll get a good brushing and a bucket of my best grain."

"You're a good man, Earl," he said smiling. "Maybe you could tell me the best place to get a good meal and to bunk down for the night."

"I sure can," he said. "Bridger Café is the best place for food, course that's 'cause my wife does most the cookin' there."

"Can she make good biscuits?"

"Oh my Lord, she can make the best biscuits in the whole state of Texas and I ain't just saying that 'cause she's my woman," he said proudly.

"How about the best hotel?"

"They are all about the same," he observed. "Bridger's Hotel is probably the cleanest, but any of them are okay. You staying awhile or just passing through?"

"Probably just passing through, but I never know for sure. Can you point me in the direction of the sheriff's office?" Earl looked down at the ground and cleared his throat.

"Well, his office is right over there," said Earl, pointing in the direction of the sheriff's office. "If you're only staying overnight, maybe it's best not to bother him."

"Really?" he asked. "Why is that?"

"Well," he replied nervously, "don't say I said so, but he can get pretty ornery pretty fast. I once saw him shoot a man just for calling him a jackass."

"Really?" Jess replied.

"Sure did. I watched him do it," he said. "Right over at the Mustang Bar there."

"I'll keep that in mind," replied Jess. "I'm not here looking for any trouble. I just need to ask him a few questions about a man I'm looking for."

"Good luck, and make sure you smile when you talk to him," exclaimed Earl. "It just might keep him from getting pissed off."

Jess headed over to the sheriff's office. It wasn't far from the livery and while he was walking down the street, he thought about his decision to be a bounty hunter. He figured he would ask the sheriff for any bounty information on wanted men. A deputy was sitting in a chair just outside the door to the sheriff's office. Jess walked up slowly and stopped short of going up the one step to the sidewalk in front. He sized the deputy up in a second and he could see the attitude on the deputy's face.

"Whatcha need, mister?" the deputy asked in a slow sarcastic drawl.

"I'd like to talk to the sheriff for a minute if that's possible," he replied. "If he's busy, I can come back later."

"What's your name?" the deputy asked, in that same smart-alecky drawl.

"Jess Williams."

Jess could see an immediate change in the deputy's eyes. The deputy sat straight up and his eyes strangely went first to Jess's gun and then to Jess's eyes. Jess could see fear in the deputy's eyes, but along with that, a look of respect. It was obvious to Jess his reputation had already spread deeper into Texas.

"Hell, I know who you are," said the deputy, dropping the smart tone now. So does the sheriff and I'm sure he'll want to see you. Hold on just a minute while I get him." The deputy went inside where the sheriff was having a conversation with the two other deputies.

"Uh...Sheriff?" asked the deputy.

"What the hell do you want?" hollered the sheriff. "Can't you see I'm trying to talk to these other two idiots who are supposed to be doing something for their pay?"

"Sorry, Sheriff, but there's a young man outside who wants to talk to you," pleaded the deputy.

"Like I give a shit," retorted the sheriff. "Tell him to go tell his mama about his problems."

"But Sheriff...he says his name is Jess Williams," said the nervous deputy. "You know, that kid we heard about? The one who took down Ben Grady up in Timber?"

"Well, that's different," the sheriff said, his attitude changing completely. "I'd sure like to meet that boy. Send him on in here and as for you two dumb-asses, we'll finish this later!"

Jess could hear loud talking and then the deputy was at the door again and waving Jess in. Jess looked at each of the three deputies and they all seemed nervous and they had a look of respect in their eyes. Jess' gaze settled on the man sitting behind a large desk. On top of the desk lay a shotgun and a .45 pistol. Jess remembered what Earl the stable man had said and Jess could tell that Earl had told the truth. This man was just plain ornery right down to the bone. Jess knew from the moment he locked eyes with the sheriff, he would have to tread carefully. Then the sheriff did something he rarely did, he smiled at Jess. This did not unnerve Jess, but it sure startled the deputies. Each one of them could count on one hand the number of times the sheriff had smiled and it was usually when he had run someone out of town or shot someone; and even then, he rarely smiled.

"So, you're the Jess Williams we keep hearing so much about. You've got quite a reputation already for such a young man. I hear you've killed a dozen men and you don't look like you've made seventeen years old yet. Now, that's pretty impressive, even in these here parts." The sheriff stood up and reached out and shook Jess's hand. "Welcome to Largo, Texas, Mr. Williams. My name is A. J. Rubel. I'm the sheriff here in this godforsaken town. What can I do for you?"

"I'm looking for a man by the name of Blake Taggert," replied Jess. "He's one of three men who murdered my family back in Black Creek, Kansas. Here is a sketch of him. My last lead said he was still in Red Rock, but I thought I'd check in and see if you knew anything about him while I was here." The sheriff took the sketch and shook his head no and then handed the sketch to the deputies and they passed it around to each other. None of them recognized Taggert.

"If he had been around here, we would have known about it," the sheriff said. "Murdered your family, you say?"

"Both my parents," he replied. "Then they raped and shot my little seven-year-old sister."

"Bastards ought to be shot down like dogs," replied the sheriff, shaking his head in disgust.

"Two of them have been already, replied Jess. "I just need to find the last of them and finish the job."

"Good for you, son," exclaimed Sheriff Rubel. "I've always believed in an eye-for-an-eye." One of the three deputies who had been standing quietly walked over closer to the sheriff's desk.

"Sheriff, I just was reading over some papers and there was a murder real similar in Red Rock recently. Seems some son-of-a-bitch robbed and murdered a family there. I remember it 'cause it sounded so bad. The young girl was raped on the bed between her dead parents and laying in their blood. Then the bastard who did it stuck his pistol up her...well, you know. They say it was awful, but they don't have any suspects yet. If your man is supposed to be in Red Rock, then maybe he did it."

"Well," said the sheriff sharply, "I'm going to send a wire to the sheriff of Red Rock and let him know about this Taggert fellow. It sounds like he could be the guy who did the killings over there too."

"Sheriff, could I ask you a favor?" asked Jess.

"Sure," he replied.

"When you send the message to the sheriff of Red Rock, could you just inquire about Taggert's whereabouts?" he asked. "I'd like to deal with him myself. If they catch on to him, he will probably be hanging from a tree before I get there and that would be too good of a way for Taggert to die."

"I agree," he replied. "Alright, I'll just make an inquiry as if an old friend was looking for him. Anything else I can do?"

"Yes, one more thing if you could," Jess replied. "Can I look through your wanted posters? I'm looking for men who have a bounty on their heads, but only the worst of the lot. I'm not looking for horse thieves or bank robbers; only the ones guilty of murder or rape and wanted dead or alive."

"So you're going into the bounty hunting business, huh?" asked the sheriff.

"I guess I came by it came naturally. Seems like it's what I was born to do, Sheriff," Jess stated plainly.

"Sure. But I don't think you'll find any of what you're looking for here," replied Sheriff Rubel. "Most of my posters are for small offenses."

"Thanks, Sheriff," he said. "I'll stick around a few days until you get a response from Red Rock, if that's okay with you?"

"You're welcome to stay as long as you want, but you watch you back," warned the sheriff.

"Why's that, Sheriff?"

"Your reputation with that gun of yours is spreading like a wild fire and there are some real tough guys that come into town from time to time," he implied. "They'd like nothing better than to be the one to take you down, if you get my meaning."

"Thanks for the warning, Sheriff, and I know exactly what you mean," he replied.

Jess left the sheriff's office and stopped in at the first hotel he found. Then, he found Bridger's Café and Earl was right. The food was excellent and the biscuits were even better. Jess sent a dollar back to Earl's wife, Becca, who baked the biscuits. After a great dinner, Jess decided to turn in for the night early. He found the room quite comfortable and clean. He dozed off thinking about Blake Taggert. He wondered if he was the one responsible for the murders in Red Rock the deputy had spoken about. It sounded so similar. Especially about the young girl being raped and then shot. Jess decided that even if Taggert didn't do the killings in Red Rock, he would hunt down the man responsible for it, but not before he got Taggert. Nothing would stand in his way or distract him; or so he thought.

CHAPTER SEVENTEEN

Jess rose early, ate a good breakfast and took a leisurely walk around town to check things out. Things like back alleys, escape routes and ambush points. After he finished, he stopped in to see Gray and then decided to take a seat outside the hotel and just watch the town.

Largo was busier than most towns he had been in. People were all around, talking to one another. He caught many of them glancing at him and even a few of the men stared. One thing was constant though, whenever he looked back, they quickly looked away; except for the women. The young ones smiled and the old ones glared. This was something he figured he was going to have to get used to now that he was quickly gaining a reputation with a gun. He had been sitting there for about an hour when he noticed something different about the towns-folk's expressions. Many of them began to break up conversations and go into stores and buildings. He thought that odd and wondered if it had something to do with him. Then, out of the corner of his eye, he saw Sheriff Rubel walking toward him.

"Morning, Sheriff," said Jess, as the sheriff sat down next to him. The sheriff didn't return the greeting. He just watched everyone quickly scatter into shops. Within minutes there weren't many townsfolk left on the street. Except for some of the older women and they just glared at the sheriff.

"Yep," the sheriff stated plainly, "these people hate my guts. They want a safe town and a tough sheriff, but they can't put up with anyone mean enough like me to get the job done."

"Well, Sheriff, each of us carries our own burdens in life," he offered. "I suppose some are worse than others."

"One of my burdens is I worry that one day these people will have me shot and it will probably be in the back since not one of them would face me straight on," he said. "But hell, that's my problem. Yesterday you asked about any men with a bounty on them. Well, I just got a message from a little town about thirty miles from here. It seems a drifter stole a horse from some rancher there."

"Sheriff, I appreciate you bringing me this, but as I told you, I'm not interested in chasing horse thieves," refuted Jess.

"What if I told you that this rancher wasn't about to give up a good horse so willingly and the drifter shot him dead?" the sheriff responded.

"Okay. Now you have my attention."

"And then, what if I told you that his twelve-year-old son went in the house and got his pa's rifle and took a shot at the drifter and the drifter plugged that poor kid right in the chest?"

"Now I'm definitely interested. Tell me more," he said leaning forward in his chair.

"Now, there ain't any law in this little shit-hole of a town, so the Texas Rangers have been assigned to go get the bastard," he said. "The only problem is there are no Rangers within at least a week's ride of the town. You could get there easily in two days. Since there's no law in town, he might stay for a day or so. Plus, there is a reward of five hundred dollars for his return, dead or alive. So, you want the job?"

"Sheriff, why not send one of your deputies?"

"Hell, they'd probably get lost and never come back. Besides, I hear this drifter is pretty fast with a leg iron. My deputies are tough as nails, but none of them are that fast with a pistol. From what you told me, this is exactly what you've been looking for," he said smiling and raising his eyebrows.

Jess sat up straight and thought a second or two about Blake Taggert. He'd never been this close to catching him, but he'd been waiting to catch him for two years now. What were another few days? Besides, it might take that long before Sheriff Rubel got any information on Taggert. Jess looked at Sheriff Rubel and asked, "You said the boy was twelve?"

"Yep," he replied.

"Sheriff, tell me where this town is."

"So, am I to assume that you will be bringing him in dead?" asked the sheriff.

"Yes, but not on the horse he stole," he replied. "That will be returned to the rancher's wife. I'll drag him here with my horse if I need to."

"The more I get to know you, the more I like you," said the sheriff perceptively. "And I don't like most people." Jess headed straight for the stable and told Earl to saddle up Gray.

"Boy, I thought I'd never stop hearing about this nice young man who gave my wife a dollar tip last night," said a happy Earl. "She must've talked about you for an hour. Couldn't hardly get a word in edgewise, not that I usually get one in anyway. That was mighty nice of you, Mr. Williams. Yes, sir, mighty nice."

"Her biscuits were worth the dollar all by themselves," he said. "Of course, I did take into account that she's a whole lot better looking than you are Earl." Earl let out one of those huge belly laughs.

"Man, you're right about that, too!" he laughed.

"I'll be gone for about four or five days, Earl," he said. "Save me a good spot for Gray when I get back and you'll still get a dollar a day just for holding it."

"You a damn right nice feller, Mr. Williams," he boasted. "Yes sir. Where you headed?"

"Some little town called Jonesville just east of here," he replied. "Got a man there with a bounty on his head. He killed a rancher and his twelve-year-old son."

"Sounds like a man who needs to see a hanging rope."

"I don't think he'll make it that far," he said boldly, as he swung into the saddle.

"Well, you make sure you come back now," said Earl. "I'll need that money for sure. Got three kids of my own to feed and they never seem to stop eating."

"Don't worry, I'll be back," replied Jess. "Most likely with some dead weight."

Sheriff A. J. Rubel was sitting behind his desk reading a newspaper when one of his deputies came in and poured himself a cup of coffee. He, like the other two deputies, never knew for sure whether to bother the sheriff. Sheriff Rubel's temper was erratic as hell. They had been quite surprised by his friendly tone with Jess Williams.

"Uh…Sheriff, could I talk to you a minute?" asked the deputy. Sheriff Rubel slowly put his paper down on the desk and looked up at the deputy.

"I suppose so, as long as you can answer me one question." The sheriff said looking at the deputy.

"Sure, Sheriff, what is it?" the deputy asked, feeling pretty good that he hadn't pissed the sheriff off.

The sheriff said, "I just want to know if there is a sign on my forehead that says 'will the first dumb-ass that walks in here please interrupt me?'" The deputy hung his head realizing he had screwed up again with the sheriff, which was pretty much normal.

"Sorry, Sheriff, I guess I should've known better," he said soberly. "I know you like to read your paper in silence."

"Well, go on already," said Sheriff Rubel. "You've done interrupted me now. But the next time you see me reading my paper just turn your sorry ass back out the door, understand? Now what is it?"

"I was just wondering what you thought about that kid, Jess Williams?" asked the deputy. "You seemed awful friendly to him."

"And you, who finished all the way up to the fifth grade all by your lonesome can't seem to figure that out, eh?"

"But...if I could do that why would I be asking?"

The sheriff just shook his head thinking to himself how hard it was to get good help these days. His deputies were tough, but they weren't the brightest bunch. He got up and walked to the table where the coffeepot was and poured him a fresh cup. Then he walked back to his desk and sat down again.

"Well," the sheriff said, pausing for a moment and looking as if he was thinking real deep about what he was about to say. "I've seen a lot of different men in my lifetime; brave ones, cowards, braggarts, idiots, crazy ones, liars and a few stone cold fearless types. But this kid, Jess Williams, is something I ain't seen before. When you look into that kid's eyes you can see that there is a good side to the boy, but it's buried way back in there behind all that rage and hatred for the men that murdered his family and men like that. That boy's going to hunt men for a living and he's going to be damn good at it. Now some people are destined to be just normal average people and some are destined to be something special, something completely out of the ordinary. That kid's one of those destined to be special. I just think that it's a privilege to have a chance in our lifetime to know someone like that. It don't happen all that often." The deputy had listened to all of this and he took a minute to ponder all that the sheriff had said.

"And you could see all of that in his eyes?" asked the deputy.

"You can read a man's life history in his eyes if you know how to look for it."

"Damn. I wish I could do that."

"And I just wish I could get back to reading my damn paper!" countered the sheriff, getting back to his normal grumpy self.

"Sure thing Sheriff and thanks," replied the deputy, as he walked out and sat down in the chair outside the office and thought about Jess. He wondered what he would have done if his family was murdered like that. He suddenly felt glad that he wasn't that drifter over in Jonesville.

Jess hit the trail hard. It only took him a day and a half to reach Jonesville. The sheriff was right, there wasn't much to Jonesville. No law, no bank, just a saloon, general store and a livery, along with a few houses scattered around the town.

He stabled Gray and asked the boy working the livery to brush down Gray and give him some extra grain. He had ridden him hard the last day and a half. He headed for the only saloon in town. There was no name on the saloon and no doors either. Jess walked in and stopped just inside the door. There were four men in the place, not counting the barkeep. Jess walked up to the barkeep and asked for a beer. The barkeep brought Jess his beer and sat it down, but not before wiping up the bar in front of Jess. The barkeep was a short fellow, but he looked like the kind of man who didn't take any crap from anyone. Jess figured he might know about the drifter he was looking for.

"What's your name, barkeep?" he asked.

"Who's asking?"

"Jess Williams, and I'm looking for a drifter."

"Information costs money here, mister," implied the barkeep. "Hell, you don't think I make any money serving drinks in this hell-hole of a place, do ya?" Jess took out a five dollar gold piece and placed it on top of the bar.

The barkeep took it, smiled and said, "Whatcha wanna know?"

"I'm looking for the drifter who shot that rancher and his son. You know who that might be or where I might find him?" The barkeep's eyes turned cold and he reached into the pocket where he had put the five dollar gold piece and threw it back on the counter. The gold piece spun around and then fell flat on the top of the bar.

"Mister, that information ain't for sale," he said bluntly. "You can have it for free, especially if you're here to make him pay for what he did. Hell, I knew that rancher and his kid. They were real nice folks. Now, if you tell me you're a friend of his, you can take your ass back out of here."

"I'm no friend of his," he replied sharply. "I'm here to take him back for the bounty."

"I thought you might be a bounty hunter what with all them guns you're wearing," stated the barkeep. "Not only is the information free, but so is the beer. That sumbitch has been hanging around here and he'll most likely be back tonight. How are you with that fancy shootin' iron you got there?"

"Good enough."

"You'd better be, 'cause that drifter is slicker that shit with a pistol."

"You let me worry about that," said Jess with a knowing look in his eyes.

The barkeep brought Jess another beer. Jess hadn't realized how fast he had downed the first one. It had been a dusty and windy ride the last two days. Now that he thought about it, it seemed like it was always dusty and windy in Texas. The other four men in the saloon just sat there and drank. They listened to the conversation between Jess and the barkeep and decided they would wait and see what happened. They all knew the rancher and his son, too, but they weren't gunslingers. They were ranchers and farmers. And since there was no law in town, they had long ago learned to mind their own business. Jess didn't have long to wait. He had just put his glass down on the bar when the barkeep gave him a look and nodded toward the door. Jess moved back into the corner at the far end on the bar. The drifter slowly walked into the bar as if he owned it. He stopped at the table where the four men were sitting. He stared at them until each one of them lowered their eyes, humiliating them without even saying a word.

The drifter was about six feet tall with a little meat on his bones. Not heavy, but stocky. He wore two six-shooters low on his hips, but it wasn't a double holster; it was two separate holsters, one strapped over the other. The right hand gun was lower than the left. The left gun was backwards and slightly forward. Jess figured he used the second gun as a backup gun since it was designed to be drawn with the right hand.

"You boys gonna buy me another beer tonight?" the drifter asked.

"Sure mister, no problem," said one of the four men sitting at the table.

"Why, that's mighty nice of you fellows; mighty nice indeed," replied the drifter, as he walked up to the bar, but not before noticing Jess. He stopped at the bar and ordered a beer. He took a long, slow sip and sat his glass back down on the bar all the while never taking his eyes off Jess. He noticed the shotgun behind Jess, but he had not noticed Jess' pistol yet since Jess was still facing forward to the bar, watching the drifter carefully out of his side vision.

"Well, well, seems we have a newcomer to town," announced the drifter. "What's your name, boy?" Jess didn't respond right away. He just looked at the barkeep who had a look of foreboding in his eyes.

"Barkeep," asked Jess, "you got any grub in the back?" The barkeep was somewhat surprised by the question.

"Sure mister, we got some stew left over," he said. "I can get a plate of it for you if you want some."

"That would be mighty nice of you," said Jess. "I'd like to eat a bite before I leave town tonight." Jess finally turned to the drifter, exposing his gun and looking the drifter straight in the eyes. The drifter was obviously not used to someone treating him so casually.

"I asked you what your name was, son?" demanded the drifter.

"You're really not going to need to know that, actually."

"Really?" replied the drifter sarcastically. "I always like to know the name of the man who's going to buy me my next beer."

"I'm not buying you a beer," he said flatly. "Matter of fact, you're not having another beer. At least not if you are who I think you are." The drifter changed his stance a little.

"You tell me since you seem to know so much."

"You're the drifter who shot that rancher and his son, isn't that right?"

"What if I am?" asked the drifter. "What the hell are you gonna do about it?"

"Well, there's a bounty on your head in the amount of five hundred dollars if you're the man who did it, and I intend to collect the money."

The drifter laughed out loud. "So, I guess this means you ain't gonna buy me that beer, eh?"

"No, not likely," he replied. "I will buy those four men a beer though, to make up for all the beer they've obviously bought you."

The barkeep came back out from the back of the bar with a big plate of hot stew and sat it down in front of Jess. Jess didn't look at it, but he could smell it.

"Sure hope it tastes as good as it smells," observed Jess.

"It does," bragged the barkeep. "And the answer to your question is yes. That's the rotten bastard who shot the rancher and his son!"

"Shut the hell up, barkeep!" hollered the drifter. "I hear one more word coming out of your pie hole and I'll come back there and shove that sawed-off shotgun you want to reach for straight up your ass!" While the drifter was yelling at the barkeep, Jess had ever so slightly lowered his gun hand closer to his pistol.

"Seems like another mystery has been solved," said Jess. "Well mister, seems like there is only one thing left to do."

"And just what is that smart-ass?" demanded the drifter.

"I'm here to make you pay for what you've done, so why don't you go ahead and show these men just how tough you really are."

"You've got a real smart mouth on you, boy."

"Maybe."

"You know who the hell you're messing with?"

"Not really."

"I'm J. J. Johnson," the drifter said, as if his name should put fear into another man.

"Never heard of you."

"You should have," said Johnson. "I've got a reputation."

"For what? Making other men pay for your beer?" he asked, knowing it would piss off Johnson some more.

"Hell no!" retorted Johnson angrily. "For being quick at skinnin' leather!"

"Really?"

"Ain't that what I just said?"

"Show me."

"Show you what?"

"How fast you really are."

"I'll kill ya for sure," crowed Johnson.

"Really?"

"You're really pissing me off," retorted Johnson.

"I'll tell you what," he replied. "If you beat me, you can have my stew here."

That was the last straw for Johnson. Johnson tried a slight of hand on Jess. He moved his left hand on the bar just a few inches. It was enough to get Jess's attention for a split second. It was a trick that had worked often for Johnson and it had cost many a cowboy and gunslinger his life, but not today. Jess caught the hand movement and he thought it was pretty slick and it was something he would remember.

Johnson's right hand reached for his pistol a split second after he had moved his left hand on the bar and actually got it out of the holster completely, but not up far enough to point it at Jess when he felt a hard thump on his chest. He looked down at his chest as he dropped his pistol to the floor. He saw the blood streaming from the hole in his shirt and he looked up at Jess. He never thought the last sight he would see in his life would be of a young man taking a bite of stew while watching him slump to the floor.

"Barkeep," said Jess, "this stew is wonderful. Do you think I could get another plate of it after I finish this one?" The barkeep put the sawed-off back down under the bar.

"Damn," exclaimed the barkeep. "How the hell did you learn to shoot like that and where the hell did you get that shootin' iron?"

"My pa taught me, and I found it," he said, not really elaborating.

Jess finished the first plate of stew and while the barkeep was getting another plate for him, he walked over to the drifter and took off both his guns and checked his pockets. He found three hundred and forty dollars. Jess assumed it was probably stolen money. Jess gave the barkeep forty dollars of the drifter's money and told him it was for the clean-up and to buy the four men beer until the money ran out to make up for the money they had spent buying beer for the drifter. They all thanked him. That left Jess with three hundred dollars of the drifter's money.

"Barkeep, is that the horse that was stolen from the rancher?" asked Jess.

The barkeep looked outside at the horse. "Sure is."

"I want you to take that horse and saddle to the wife of the rancher tomorrow. I also want you to take the rest of this money and give it to her," said Jess, as he handed the money to the barkeep. "I know it won't replace her husband or her son, but it ought to help her some."

"That's mighty generous of you, mister," the barkeep said thoughtfully. "Whatcha gonna do with his guns?"

"I plan on trading them for a mule I saw at the stables to haul his carcass back to Largo for the bounty on his head," replied Jess.

Jess had the four men drag the body to the stables. The stable owner was more than happy with his trade. He could sell the two guns for twice what the mule was worth. Jess decided to leave in the morning and asked the man running the stable if he could bunk down there for the night. The owner had no problem with that.

Jess got settled in and started to nod off to sleep. His thoughts that night were thinking he was finally close to finding Blake Taggert. He just had to make this delivery back to Largo and collect his five hundred dollars. And as sleep finally found him, his last thought that night was; *Bounty hunting sure pays well.*

CHAPTER EIGHTEEN

Jess headed out of Jonesville at first light. It took two full days to get back to Largo since he was dragging a stubborn mule with two hundred pounds of dead weight on it. The weather didn't help much either. The first day was a nice sunny day, but with a strong wind hitting him straight in the face. On the second day, it started to rain just after the noon hour. Not a hard rain, just enough to make him put his slicker on and make the ride uncomfortable. It was still raining when he got to Largo just before dusk on the second day. He stopped at the sheriff's office and one of the deputies was sitting on the porch in front of the jail. Jess handed the reins from the mule to the deputy and told him he would send Earl over for the mule later and he would check in with the sheriff tomorrow about the bounty. He was tired, wet, and cold and he needed sleep. He walked Gray over to the stable and told Earl about the mule.

"He's yours to keep Earl, that is, if you want him," said Jess. "He's a stubborn cuss though. I had to drag his ass all the way here."

"Never met a mule that wasn't stubborn, Mr. Williams," replied Earl. "Sides, if I can't put him to work, I can sure put him on the table. I got hungry mouths to feed."

"You know Earl, I never thought of that; but as stubborn as he is, I can just see you cutting into a thick, tough steak," laughed Jess.

Jess was tired enough that he passed up going to Bridger's Café for some late supper. All he wanted was a good night's sleep. He got himself a hot bath and turned in for the night. He rose early and had a huge breakfast. Becca was definitely the best cook he had ever met, except his ma. He left her two dollars for a tip this time. He could tell that Becca and Earl were just simple folk working the hard life to make ends meet like most people. Yet, here he was, getting ready to collect five hundred dollars for less than one week's work. He decided that as long as he had the money, he wouldn't be greedy with it. He felt good about leaving the three hundred dollars with the rancher's wife back in Jonesville.

He finished breakfast and walked down to the sheriff's office. The usual deputy was sitting on the porch and he greeted Jess and told him to go on in. The deputy thought again about what the sheriff said about Jess and he looked at Jess with a new-found look of respect. Jess returned the greeting and found the sheriff sitting behind his desk reading a telegraph message.

"Well, good morning, son, and a good piece of work you did there," said Sheriff Rubel. "Five hundred dollars ain't bad for less than a week's work. Your money is at the bank right next to the hotel you're staying at. They can pay you cash or wire the money wherever you want. By the way, I knew that fella and he was damn fast with a gun. He's one sorry cuss who won't be missed."

"Can't argue with you about that, Sheriff," he replied. "Did you get any word about Blake Taggert while I was gone?"

"Matter of fact, I was just reading the message now. It seems Mr. Taggert has been in Red Rock for quite a while now. I have a hunch they don't suspect him of any wrongdoing."

"Well, whether he had anything to do with the killings in Red Rock or not, he sure is guilty of murder and he's going to pay for it," Jess said with intent.

"I have no doubt about that, Jess."

Jess spent the rest of the afternoon walking around town. He stopped in and talked to Earl. Earl had already sold the mule to a farmer and he offered half the money to Jess, but Jess refused to take it.

"I have all the money I need, Earl," he said. "Now, you might give a little of that money to your pretty wife. She just might want to buy a new dress or something." Earl laughed that loud belly laugh again.

"Hell, she done already got it all, Mr. Williams," laughed Earl. "Every last penny of it."

Jess grinned at Earl and said, "I'm going to have dinner tonight and when I see her, I just might suggest that dress thing, especially since she's already got your money."

"You tell her old Earl says she can have whatever she wants," replied Earl. "She deserves it just for putting up with me, not to mention all the hard work she does to help out. She's a keeper, that's for sure. You be sure to tell her I said that."

"I will, Earl. I surely will," agreed Jess.

Jess stopped in at the bank and wired half the reward money to Jameson's bank in Black Creek and took the other half in cash. He decided to have an early dinner. He headed for the café and was laughing to himself about what Earl had said about his wife. Jess figured he would throw in a real nice tip for her. The café was almost empty with only a half-dozen people eating. Becca saw him come in and nodded to him to sit at a table. She came out from the kitchen a minute later and walked over to a table behind him, delivering two heaping plates of hot food. Then, she turned around to Jess' table.

"How you doin' today, Mr. Williams?" she asked.

"I'm doing just fine, Becca. I had a nice talk with Earl today," he said with a slight grin on his face.

"Did you, now?" asked Becca.

"Yes. He told me to tell you what a wonderful wife you've been and to make sure that you reward yourself with a nice new dress with the money from the mule."

"That's a right nice thing for him to say, but we can't afford any new dresses," she said. "We still got kids to feed and lots of repairs to the house. New dresses are for those who got more money than we do."

"I still think you deserve a new dress," he countered. "Consider it found money."

"I'll think about it," she said, trying to get him off the subject. "Would you like something to eat?"

"Absolutely; I'm hungry as a bear coming out from a long winter."

Jess ordered and Becca had his meal out to him with a load of fresh biscuits in about fifteen minutes. During that time, several more people wandered into the café, including two men who looked like they had been on the trail for a while. They obviously had not stopped in for a bath before supper. They sat down at a table to Jess's left. Both of them were packing pistols, but one look-over told Jess they weren't anything to worry about. After Becca delivered his supper to him, she turned to the table where the two men sat down and asked them if they wanted to have something to eat.

"Damn right! What the hell you think we came in here for?" one of them said. The other one laughed, revealing the four teeth he had left.

The other man spoke in a sarcastic tone and said, "We came in for a drink, so why don't you go get us two whiskeys?"

"We don't serve drinks in here, just food," she replied nervously.

"If we wanted whiskey, we would have gone to the saloon. But we wanted something to eat, so we came in here; and you ask us if we came in here to get something to eat. See how dumb a question that is? That's why they shouldn't let people like you work in a public place. Now, get us two plates of grub and hurry it up, bitch!" barked the first man.

Becca was standing there speechless. She was just about to open her mouth when Jess, without looking up from his meal or even looking over at the two men said in a soft voice, "Becca, why don't you go wait on a different table, since it seems these two *men* don't seem to know what they want yet."

Becca gave the two men a look of contempt as she walked over to another table and continued to stare at the two men like everyone else in the place. Jess kept eating slowly and the two men were so surprised they were dumbfounded for a few seconds. They looked at each other and figured the odds were two against one so they felt somewhat daring.

"Mister, this ain't your business," said the first man nastily.

"Yeah, you'd be better off if you'd just keep eating your grub and keep your nose out of other people's business," said the second man. Jess still did not look up at either of the two men. He reached in his pocket and pulled out a silver dollar. He threw it over onto the men's table, still not looking up at them and continuing to eat as if nothing was happening. The silver dollar spun around for a few seconds, both of the men watching it spin, and then it fell flat on the table.

"What the hell is this for?" asked the second man.

"You said you wanted two whiskeys, didn't you?" replied Jess, still not looking up.

"No, you dumb-ass!" hollered the second man. "What we said was we wanted something to eat. Mister, you're as dumb as that woman over there."

Still not looking up at the men, Jess said in a firm, quite voice, "That very nice lady over there happens to be a friend of mine. She has a name and it's not what you've called her. Now, I suggest you pick up that dollar and go buy yourselves some whiskey at one of the local saloons while you still can. I'm not going to spoil my meal by eating in the same room as you two idiots." The two men stood up and they were pissed. Jess watched them out of the corner of his eye. He knew from the start these two were just talkers and he wasn't one bit worried.

"And just who the hell are you to tell us what we will or won't do, mister!" hollered the first man.

"The name is Jess Williams," he stated bluntly. Both men stiffened like oak trees on a windless day. They heard of Jess Williams since they had come to town this morning. Neither of them spoke for what seemed like a whole minute. Jess still never looked up from his meal.

"Uh…we're sorry Mr. Williams," said the second man. "We didn't mean no harm. We ain't looking for no trouble, especially with you." The second man picked up the silver dollar and put it in his pocket.

"Thanks for the whiskey," said the second man. Both men started to walk out when they both stopped dead in their tracks as they heard Jess speak up again. "You two forget something?" They knew exactly what Jess meant without asking. They both looked over at Becca and with their eyes down to the floor they both apologized sincerely.

"We're mighty sorry, ma'am. We won't ever bother you again," the first man said.

Becca said nothing. She simply looked at the two men with disgust. She was satisfied enough at the fact Jess had stuck up for her. No one, except her husband, had ever done that before. She walked over to Jess and put her hand on his shoulder as the two men left the café.

"I can't tell you what that meant to me, Mr. Williams," said a sincere Becca. "No one's ever done something like that for me before. Being a black woman ain't easy." Jess quickly looked up at Becca with a surprised look on his face.

"Earl is a black man?" he asked in a serious voice. Becca was startled for a moment until she saw Jess smile a big smile. Becca slapped Jess on his shoulder and laughed.

"So you do have a sense of humor under all that hatred you got bottled up inside you," laughed Becca. "You had me going for a second or two."

"Well, I don't see black or white when I look at you, Becca. What I see is a friend and a nice person. I like you and that's all that counts."

"You sure ain't like most people I ever met, Mr. Williams," Becca said.

"Judging by the likes of those two idiots who just left here, I hope not," he said, as he finished up with his plate of food. "Now, what are the chances of me getting me a second helping?"

"For you, all you want, anytime you want," she replied with a proud look. "And thank you again."

Jess finished up his second helping of food while everyone else in the place seemed to be watching him. When he finished up, he placed two ten dollar gold pieces next to his plate and left before Becca got back to his table. He knew she would refuse to accept the money from him. Jess went back to the hotel and got a pretty good night's rest. In the morning he stopped in to thank the sheriff one more time and headed for the livery to get Gray. Earl had him all saddled up and ready to go.

"Mr. Williams, I sure do want to thank you for what you did for my Becca yesterday," said earl with a thankful look on his face. "She told me all about it."

"I don't stand for any man picking on a woman," he replied. "It makes my blood boil."

"All the same, you sure made some friends here and that's a fact," he said with meaning. "You ever need something, you call on old Earl, you hear?"

"I'll certainly remember that," he said.

"Oh, and Becca said to stop by the café on your way out," he added. "She's got something she wants to show you."

Jess climbed up in the saddle and headed out of town for Red Rock. As he came up to the café, there was Becca in the most beautiful yellow, flowered dress. She was standing in front of the door of the café and just beaming at him.

"I wanted you to see what I bought with some of that money you left me yesterday," she said, a wide smile washing across her face. "You sure didn't have to do that. You already did enough for us."

"Becca, just seeing how lovely you look in that dress was worth it all," Jess said smiling. "You take care of yourself and my friend, Earl."

"I sure will, Mr. Williams, and thank you so much for everything. You are sure one person we will never forget."

Jess nodded to her and turned his horse around. As he rode past the sheriff's office, Sheriff A. J. Rubel was standing there and had a look of respect on his face that was a rare thing to see. There weren't many men he had respect for, but Jess Williams was undeniably one of them. The usual deputy was sitting in the chair next to the sheriff and Jess thought the deputy had a strange look on his face. It was as if he was trying to figure out something about Jess. He shrugged it off, not giving it any more thought.

⌐⌐

The trail along the way to Red Rock was lonely, but Jess didn't mind it at all. It gave him plenty of time to think about things and to practice his shooting skills. He stopped in a few towns to get supplies; but whenever he did, he arrived in the morning, got what he needed, and headed straight back out. Usually he spent no more than an hour or two in town, depending on whether or not he wanted a hot bath bad enough. It was a long haul to Red Rock from Largo, and after about six days of riding, he finally arrived at the outskirts. As usual, he camped outside of town, planning to go into Red Rock in the morning. He fried up some potatoes, cooked some beans and then he made some pan bread. He got his bedroll out. As he lay there, sipping hot coffee, he thought about all that had happened up to now. He thought about Taggert and hoped that he was still in Red Rock. He finally dozed off thinking just how he would kill Blake Taggert. He wanted to make him suffer for what he did to his family, especially Samantha. He was sure now that Taggert was the one who raped and killed her. He was sure in his mind that Taggert was the one who committed the murders in Red Rock. Taggert was about to finally pay for his crimes and the cost would be a slow, painful death. Jess fell asleep with a slight smile on his face.

CHAPTER NINETEEN

Jess woke a little before daybreak. He was anxious to get to town so all he had was coffee and a piece of leftover pan bread. He figured he could get a good meal once he arrived in Red Rock. He arrived in town about an hour after daybreak and the town was already bustling with activity. He found the first livery and met the stable owner, a young man who seemed to always have a smile on his face.

"Morning, mister, need to stable your horse?" asked the man. "I got plenty of room and you won't find a cheaper price in town. I brush each horse down once a day and they get good feed here, not that cheap crap you find at some of the other liveries in town." Jess noticed that the man was wearing a pistol, which was kind of odd for a stable man.

"Sounds like this is the place for my horse to be," implied Jess. "I like to make sure he gets the best feed and if you make sure he gets a little extra feed each day, I'll throw in an extra dollar tip every day."

"You've got yourself a deal, mister, and I can sure use the extra money," the man said. "I just bought this place last month and trying to build up the business isn't as easy as I thought it was going to be."

"I've never seen a stable man wear a six-shooter before. You use that thing often?" asked Jess.

"No, not really," he replied. "You need to carry a gun around here though, what with all the outlaws and drifters coming in and out of town every day. This place just seems to attract the worst of the lot. Hell, we have a shoot-out just about every night in one of the saloons. I'm pretty good with a pistol 'cause I practice and all, but I'm no gunslinger. Just figure it might save my life one day as long as I don't have to go up against someone really fast. Are you a gunslinger? Because if you're not, you sure got a nice pistol," the stable owner said, as he looked closer at Jess's odd looking pistol and holster.

"What's your name?" asked Jess.

"Name is Ted Watkins," replied the man. "Nice to meet you," he said as he stuck out his hand out to shake.

"Nice to meet you, Ted," he said. "My name is Jess Williams."

"You don't say?" asked Ted. "Why hell, I've heard of you. They say you're like greased lightning with that pistol of yours. Are you one of them bounty hunters?"

"I guess that's what I seem to be doing so far," he replied, with somewhat of a puzzled look on his face.

"Man, I sure wouldn't want you hunting me," said Ted. "Who are you looking for here in Red Rock?"

"The man I'm hunting is the last of three men who killed my family," he replied in a serious tone. "The man's name is Blake Taggert." Ted had a look of surprise on his face.

"Hell, I know Blake Taggert," replied Ted. "He stables his horse here sometimes. He always seemed like a pretty nice fellow. His family was murdered when he was just a kid and he took off scared to death when it happened. Now, *he's* damn fast with a leg iron. If you plan on taking him on, you'd better be real good with that pistol."

"I am," replied Jess. "Is Taggert still in town?"

"Actually, he left about a week ago with another man. He should be back any day now. I didn't like the guy he was riding with though. He seemed like trouble and he weren't exactly a nice fella, if you get my drift. Real young too, like you. As a matter of fact, he kind of looked like you. Always had something smart to say. Quick with a gun though. I heard he taught Taggert a thing or two and from what I hear he's quicker than Taggert, if you can believe that."

"What was his name?" asked Jess.

"Don't know," replied Ted. "He came into town and only stayed one night. Then, he and Taggert took off and Taggert said he would be back in about a week."

"I can wait. Now, how about pointing me in the direction of the sheriff's office and tell me the best place to get a good meal and a room," he asked.

Ted gave him the information he asked for and Jess headed for the hotel first. He figured that since

Taggert wasn't in town right now, he might as well get his room and a meal before paying a visit on the sheriff's office. He got a room at a place called the Boardman Hotel and a meal at Little's Eats, which was a perfect name for the place. It only had four tables, but the food was good, hot, and served quickly. While he was eating, a young boy who looked to be about ten years old ran in and went back to the kitchen area. He could hear the kid talk real quick and the kid ran back out the door without even giving Jess more than a quick glance. He finished his meal and headed for the sheriff's office. The door was open and Jess knocked on the outside wall before entering. He found Sheriff Clancy, a man who looked tired and about in his sixties with more lines in his face than a piece of crumpled paper, sitting behind a rickety old desk. He looked up at Jess but said nothing.

"Afternoon, Sheriff. My name is Jess Williams and I'm looking for a man by the name of Blake Taggert," he said. "I hear he's out of town at the moment, but I hear he'll be back soon. I was wondering if you could tell me anything about him."

"So, you're that young shooter everyone's been talking about," said Sheriff Clancy. "What do you want with Blake Taggert? There isn't any bounty on his head as far as I know and you sure look like a bounty hunter."

"He's got a bounty on his head, but I'm not worried about it, although I'll collect it anyway. I'm just looking to kill him," he said firmly. "He's the last one left of three men who killed my family back in Black Creek, Kansas."

"What happened to the other two?" the sheriff asked, already guessing the answer.

"They died."

"Well, he's not wanted for any crimes here and he has friends here in Red Rock," said the sheriff. "They're not about to just let you shoot him down like some dog."

"Any of his friends who get in my way will go down with him," warned Jess. "That will be their choice, not mine."

"Well good luck, son," he said. "I think you're making a huge mistake, but a man has to make his own decisions. If I were you, I'd make sure you've made your peace with the man upstairs. If Taggert don't kill you, one of the other gunslingers who run through here might, and there sure ain't been any shortage of them lately."

"Sheriff, I'd like to know where you stand in this matter?" he asked. "Are you planning on getting between me and Taggert?"

"Hell no," he said flatly. "You think I got this old by getting in the middle of gunmen hell bent on killing each other? Not me. I just drag out the bodies after it's over. If it isn't a fair fight and someone back-shoots someone, I try to arrest him. I'm not getting shot over wearing this tin star, I can tell you that for sure. If they want better law than that, they can get someone else for the job and I've told the Mayor exactly that more than a dozen times myself."

"I appreciate the honesty, Sheriff."

"Just watch your back here," he warned.

"Don't worry about me, Sheriff. I can take care of myself, and luck doesn't have anything to do with it." Jess turned to walk out and stopped at the door and turned back around to the sheriff.

"Sheriff, the man at the stables said Taggert rode out of town with another man," said Jess. "You know who he is or if you think he'll throw in with Taggert?"

"That sumbitch is one big heap of trouble," replied Sheriff Clancy. "Don't be messing with him if you can avoid it. He was only here one night and killed one of the locals over a card game. I was in the saloon when it happened. It was a fair fight, but almost didn't seem so. That Sloan fella is mighty quick with a pistol, and meaner than a rabid dog." Jess stiffened a little at the name of Sloan.

"Sheriff, did you say his name was Sloan?" he asked probingly. "Is that his last name?"

"I believe so."

"Did he say what his first name was?" asked Jess in a serious tone.

"Jim or Tim, something like that," he replied. "I can't remember for sure. Glad he's gone and I hope he never comes back this way. Don't know what his business with Taggert is."

Jess felt like he had just been hit in the chest with a ten-pound hammer. *Could this be his twin brother he had been told about before he left Black Creek? If it was, is he the kind of man that Jess would hunt? What would he do if that were the case? What was he doing with Taggert,*

*and if it was Jess's brother, did he know that he was riding
with one of the men responsible for murdering their mother?*

Jess calmed himself down. It was too much to
think about right now. He would just have to play
whatever cards were dealt him. If it was his brother,
and he came back to town with Taggert, Jess figured
he would have to face him and get at the truth.
Jess's subconscious was trying to tell him something,
but he wouldn't let it through. It was too awful of
a thought. Jess didn't say another word. He turned
back around and walked out of the sheriff's office.

Jess realized that the sheriff would be of no help,
but at least he wouldn't get in the middle of it. He
didn't want to kill a sheriff, but he might if he were
forced into it. He headed down the street to one of
the saloons. He found a place called Little's Drinks.
He wondered if the same person who owned the
small café where he had eaten earlier owned the
saloon too. Jess pushed through the swinging doors
and looked around. Even though it was early in the
afternoon, the place was quite busy. There were people playing cards, some sitting at tables and drinking, and several men bellied up to the bar.

He picked out the two or three men in the place
that might be trouble. One was playing at one of
the card tables and there were two others at the bar
that he figured for gunmen. One of the two men
standing up at the bar seemed dressed pretty nice
to be a gunman and he seemed to project a friendly
attitude. Jess wasn't sure about him, but his gut
told him to treat the man with caution. There was

a young kid sweeping up the floor and Jess noticed
it was the same kid that ran in and out of the café
earlier. Jess found his usual place at the right end
of the bar occupied by this neatly dressed man. Jess
was forced to take the far left of the bar. He ordered
a beer and took a long pull from it. He noticed that
the barkeep's head wasn't much above the bar,
which made Jess lean over the bar to look. He found
a raised platform behind the bar that was about a
foot high off the floor. The barkeep, whose name
was Paul Little, watched him do this and when Jess
was done looking the barkeep gave Jess a stern look.

"One smart-ass word from you about me being
short and you'll not get another drink from me
and I don't care who the hell you are," warned the
barkeep.

"Sorry. I wasn't planning on making any remarks,
I was just curious," he replied.

"Yeah, well you can be curious about something
else," he said severely.

"Sorry, I meant no offense," he added as he took
another sip of his beer.

Jess glanced down at the nicely dressed man at
the other end of the bar and the man held up his
glass of whiskey as if to salute Jess. The man was tall
and muscular. He was dressed in all black and wearing a very nice black holster tied down low and tight.
Jess noticed the man's hammer strap was removed.
When he had first walked into the bar, it was still
over the hammer. Jess smiled to himself thinking
that's exactly why he always took the right end of

the bar. It could hide such movement from most men, but Jess wasn't like most men. Jess had already removed his hammer strap before he walked into the bar. Jess took another glance around the room and he could tell trouble was about to find him. He could tell from the changed expressions on the faces of the men in the bar. Jess finished his beer and ordered another one.

"Barkeep," the man at the opposite end of the bar said, "put that beer on my bill. I'd be honored to buy Mr. Williams a drink." The barkeep just grunted and got Jess another beer. Jess took a long sip of his beer and then turned to the man.

"Thanks for the beer," he said. "Do I know you?"

"Thought maybe you might," said the man. "They call me Nevada Jackson. I'm a bounty hunter myself. Just finished a job in a small town east of here and stopped off to see if there was some money to be made here in Red Rock."

"Well, it's nice to meet you, but I don't have any bounty on my head," replied Jess. "Well, at least not yet, if that's what's on your mind."

"You sure?" he asked, tipping his head down a little at Jess.

"Pretty sure."

"I'm going to take your word on it," he said. "I always believe a man until he lies to me. I figure that's the right way to go about it. Don't you?"

"I couldn't agree more, Nevada."

"Well, I'd still like to make a little money today and I like a good challenge and haven't had a serious one lately," stated Nevada. "Fact is I'm getting bored. I think I have a way to combine both needs into one." Jess didn't respond. He simply stood there, looking at the man and sipping his beer.

"Don't you want to know what it is I'm talking about, Mr. Williams?" asked Nevada.

"The way I figure it, you're going to tell me all about it sooner or later anyway, and my hunch is whatever I say won't matter much," he replied. Nevada laughed a little and smiled back at him.

"Well, at least you have a sense of humor," he said smiling. "I have to say, I'm quite impressed with you. You're a cool one for being so young and I like that in a man. Now, here's what I propose. Let's each put five hundred dollars down on the bar, and then we face each other and the man standing after the smoke clears, gets to keep all the money. What do you think about that?" Jess thought about it for a moment.

"You know what, Nevada," said Jess, "I've learned that things happen and sometimes you just don't have any real control over them. Things like this: Here you are, and I don't even know you, and yet you're going to force me to kill you in a gunfight that I don't want any part of. One day I hope to understand why; but for now, I'd be satisfied with one simple answer."

"I'd be glad to answer any question you've a mind to ask, Mr. Williams," replied Nevada. Jess took another pull from his beer.

"Have you ever killed someone in cold blood for no good reason?" asked Jess.

"I've killed more than my share of men, but they all deserved dying and they all had a fair chance to defend themselves. Why?"

"Well, if the answer had been different, it would have been a lot easier to kill you. Now, I don't really want to square off with you, but I suppose you're going to push me on the matter anyway."

"Well, I guess so, unless you decide to walk out and refuse to face me," replied Nevada. "I never shoot a man who refuses to draw in a fair fight."

"Of course, you and I both know that I won't do that."

"Of course," he agreed quickly. "I've heard all about you and your fancy pistol you got there. I heard all about you taking down that drifter up in Jonesville who shot that rancher and his boy. As a matter of fact, I was heading up there to collect that bounty when I heard you already took him down. You cost me five hundred dollars on that deal. I guess this would make me whole, so to speak." Nevada pulled a wad of money out of his front pocket, counted out five hundred dollars and placed it on the bar.

"Barkeep," said Nevada, "you hold the money. Mr. Williams, do you have the five hundred?"

I've got three hundred on me, but I can put up my gun and holster for the rest. If you win, I guess I wouldn't need it anymore anyway. Agreed?"

"Agreed on both counts!" exclaimed Nevada quickly. "I'd love to have that pistol of yours. It's worth the five hundred all by itself."

The barkeep took the eight hundred dollars and put a bottle of whiskey on top of the money. Jess took another sip of his beer and turned to face Nevada when everyone in the bar was startled by the words that came from the batwing doors of the saloon.

"Get ready to die, mister!"

CHAPTER TWENTY

The man standing in the doorway to the saloon looked to be about fifty. He had a bushy beard and moustache and looked like he hadn't had a bath or a new set of clothes in several years. Jess didn't recognize him, but he knew for sure the man was talking to him and not Nevada or anyone else in the bar.

"I said get ready to die!" the man repeated, as he walked into the center of the saloon. Jess saw the man had a gun tucked in his belt in the front of his belly. The gun looked as if it was used more for pounding nails than for shooting. Jess glanced at Nevada and then turned to face the old man. Neither Jess nor Nevada saw this man as any threat.

"Mister, I don't know who you are and I have no quarrel with you," said Jess. "What's your beef with me?"

"I ain't got no beef with ya! I just need the money!" hollered the man.

"What money?"

"The three thousand dollars that old man Carter put up for your head, dead or alive," replied the man. "I need it. I ain't had a good meal or a new set of clothes in three years. I've been riding a sorry sack of a mule 'cause I lost my horse and what few nuggets of gold I had left from years of prospecting work to some damn thieves. I figure I ain't got much to live for anyway. I heard about the money Carter had on your head and figured that I might as well go for it. Either way, my suffering will be over with and right about now, I don't much care which way it ends."

"How are you going to collect the money when you don't have a gun?" asked Jess, somewhat sarcastically.

"I got me a gun," the man said defensively.

"Where?"

"Right here," he said pointing the the shabby looking pistol in his front waist. "What the hell you think this here is?"

"That thing?" said Jess, with a look of amusement. "It looks more like a hammer. What are you going to do, throw it at me?"

"Sir," Nevada politely said to the old prospector, "Mr. Williams and I have a business proposition to complete first. You've interrupted us, and I would suggest you wait until we are finished."

The prospector kept his gaze on Jess, but now he recognized Nevada Jackson and he knew of his reputation. He began to have a sinking feeling. He took a few steps back and began to rethink his plan. He knew he was outgunned by either of these two. His senses began to return and he sat down at a table.

When he did, the old pistol slipped out of his belt and fell onto the wooden floor with a thud. When it did, one side of the butt grips fell off the gun. The old prospector just looked up at Jess with a sorrowful look. Nevada turned to the barkeep and told him to get the old man a drink on him. The prospector asked for beer and the barkeep handed it to the kid who worked there and the kid took it over to the man's table. Nevada then turned back to Jess.

"Well, it seems that if I win this thing, I can collect the money on the bar, your fancy pistol and holster *and* three thousand dollars from this Carter fellow," said an enthusiastic Nevada. "It seems to be my lucky day."

"Only if you win," claimed Jess. "And that three thousand dollars is just blood money Carter put up to have me murdered. It's not an official bounty. He's just pissed off because I killed his only son in a fair fight."

"That don't matter," stated Nevada. "If I win, I might as well collect it. If I didn't, it won't make you any less dead."

"Well, I guess talking you out of this is out of the question?" Jess asked him.

"Hell, I was ready to face you for the three hundred dollars and your pistol and holster," said Nevada. "Now with three thousand dollars added to the pot, I mean, who could walk away from that."

"Someone who wants to live."

"You're assuming that you'll beat me."

"I'm not assuming anything."

"So, you're saying I might beat you?"

"Well, I might drop my gun or something like that," replied Jess, smiling.

"A man with a sense of humor," said Nevada with a grin. "I like that in a man."

"Then why push this?" asked Jess.

"Did you forget about the three thousand dollars?"

"I didn't forget."

"Well, neither did I."

"So, you're still going to push this?" Jess asked again.

"I would say that you have a good grasp of the obvious," said Nevada. "Now, since I made the challenge, I think it's only fair that you get the chance to draw first."

"I never draw first," replied Jess. "Besides, this isn't my choice. If you want this fight, you'll have to start it."

What happened next was another lesson that Jess would never forget. Nevada feigned a move so slightly that only Jess saw it. It was so slight that you couldn't really call it a movement. Jess realized in that small fraction of a second that Nevada was attempting to get Jess to draw first. Jess couldn't figure if it was out of some sense of fairness or some way to trick him into stalling his draw so that Nevada had an advantage. When it happened, Jess almost fell for it.

Instead, he turned the tables on Nevada and did the same to him, feigning a draw and when Nevada saw it, he went for his gun. Nevada was fast. He had outdrawn a dozen men and had never taken a bullet yet. And some of the men he had outdrawn were seasoned gunslingers who were fast, which is why Nevada was so shocked at what happened next. After he felt the thud in his chest and looked down at the bloodstain beginning to form on his shirt, he noticed he had his hand on the butt of his pistol, but it had not moved out from the holster. He looked up at Jess with a look of disbelief in his eyes.

"Damn, I didn't even have a chance, did I?" he asked.

"Now it's you who has a good grasp of the obvious," replied Jess. "I guess things just don't always work out the way you plan them."

"I guess not," replied Nevada, a hint of a smile on his lips. He took his right hand off his pistol and went to pick up his whiskey for one last drink. He never tasted that last drop. Nevada slumped to the floor, dead. Paul, the barkeep, who never had much to say and one who was not easily impressed, spoke up.

"I've seen lots of men go at it in here," said the barkeep. "I've seen a few dozen gunfights in my lifetime, but I've never seen anything like that. You ain't normal." The barkeep went back to cleaning glasses. One of the men sitting by the bar was the town's preacher. He looked at Jess with a dreadful look in his eyes.

"I seen it, too, and I don't believe it neither, son," the preacher said, looking right at Jess, "I don't know who you are, but Paul here is right, you ain't normal. Maybe you're a soul incarnate who's been brought back to this world by God Almighty himself or maybe you've been sent here by the devil to do his dirty work. Whichever it is, you're not welcome in my church."

The preacher stood up, picked up his Bible and walked out, not saying another word. Jess said nothing to the preacher. Instead, he turned his attention to the prospector who was still sitting down, holding his glass with both hands so that Jess would see he wasn't even thinking about going for his gun, which was still lying on the floor under the table.

"I hope you're still not going to try to collect that blood money, old man," said Jess.

"No way in hell," replied the prospector. "I saw what I saw, and my mama, whoever she was, didn't bear no fool. I was just desperate and on my last straw when I came in here. I'll be glad to leave here the same way, If'n you'll let me."

"Well, I'll have to think about that for a minute," he said curiously. The prospector moaned a little.

"Damn it," exclaimed the prospector. "I just knew when I opened my eyes this morning that it was going to be a bad day."

"Really, why is that?" asked Jess.

"Because I was able to open my eyes."

"Well, maybe it won't be such a bad day after all," said Jess. The prospector looked somewhat confused. He still wasn't sure what Jess was going to do. Jess picked up the eight hundred dollars from the bar and counted out three hundred dollars. He walked over to the old prospector, who wouldn't move his hands from his glass, and sat down at the table with him.

"What's your name?" he asked the old prospector.

"Name is Dusty Slim," he replied. "I got that name 'cause I don't particularly like baths and I get kinda dusty. I also don't have a chance to eat very often, as I ain't never got any money." He finally took his hands from his glass and patted his chest a little and some dust flew off the old man's clothes.

"Well, Dusty, I want you to take this three hundred dollars and use it to get yourself a new start." Jess threw the money on the table. "And, I want you to promise me you won't try anything that stupid again. Otherwise, I'm making a bad investment in you. "Besides," he said, glancing down at the sorry looking pistol on the floor, "that thing would probably backfire and blow your damn head off even if you did get off a shot. You best let the barkeep sweep it up and get rid of it."

Dusty wasn't quite sure what to say. He had come into the saloon to try to kill Jess for the money and now Jess was giving him money for a new start. This was not a normal day for Dusty Slim. It seemed his never-ending bad luck may have finally changed for the better.

"Mr. Williams, no one's ever done anything like this for me before," he exclaimed. "I don't rightly know how to thank ya. I need the money real bad so I'll take it, but I promise to pay you back every penny and more. I know a secret place that I'm sure still has some gold in it. Not enough to get rich, but enough to pay you back and let me finally quit mining. I'm right sure thankful, Mr. Williams, right sure."

"You're welcome, Dusty. And, you tell the man at the livery down the street that I said to give you Nevada's horse, saddle and his rifle. That is if he had one, and I'm sure he did. Leave the saddlebags or any other belongings though. Tell the stable man I'll be along to claim those later. Anyone gives you a problem; you let me know about it."

"Yes, sir, Mr. Williams, yes, sir," Dusty happily agreed as he headed out the door before Jess could change his mind.

"You're gonna claim Nevada's belongings? You sure that's right?" asked the barkeep. Jess looked at the very dead Nevada and pursed his lips.

"He sure ain't going to need them anymore and besides, that man lying there was going to kill me just as dead as he is right now," explained Jess. "If that had happened, what do you think would've happened to my belongings? You think all my things would just disappear? The way I look at it, his things belong to me now. His money, his horse, his gun and anything else of value he's got. Hell, if right had anything to do with it, I wouldn't be here today; and I wouldn't have had to kill Nevada. I imagine there is some right in this world, but it hasn't been hanging around me for quite some time now."

"Fine by me," replied the barkeep, "but Nevada had a lot of friends and a brother who just might not agree with your way of thinking, if you know what I mean."

"I'll deal with that when it happens."

Jess removed Nevada's gun from his body and found another two hundred dollars in his pockets. He also removed a beautiful gold pocket watch from Nevada's front pocket. Jess didn't have a watch, he never had much use for one, but this one was beautifully engraved on the front. He decided it was time to have one. Sheriff Clancy walked into the saloon and looked at Nevada's dead body.

"Damn," said Clancy. "You took down Nevada Jackson."

"He sure did," interjected the barkeep. "Nevada never even got his gun out." The sheriff got his two deputies to take Nevada's body over to the undertaker. Sheriff Clancy looked at Jess.

"You know he's got a brother," said the sheriff in a cautionary tone.

"So I've heard."

"He's not going to be happy about this," advised Clancy. "And he taught Nevada everything he knew about slinging lead."

"Evidently not enough."

"Well, there's no bounty on him, at least not that I know of," said Clancy.

"Sheriff, I tried to talk him out of this. It was his decision, not mine."

"Hey, I got no problem with it," he said. "As far as I'm concerned, it was a fair fight. I guess it won't be the last one today."

"Why's that, Sheriff."

"Several new toughs came into town a little bit ago," he replied miserably. "Looked like trouble for sure. They went over to Jake's saloon down the street, but they'll end up in here before long, especially once they find out you're here. Sure as shit, at least one of them will be looking to add to their reputation by taking you down. You have time to ride out if you want to."

"You know I can't do that, Sheriff," he replied. "Taggert didn't happen to be one of them did he?"

"Nope, never seen any of these fellows before, but I've sure seen their kind before. I aim to check my wanted posters for their faces. I wouldn't be surprised to see one of them on one."

The sheriff walked out and Jess finished his beer. He thanked the barkeep, gave him a nice tip, slung Nevada's gun and holster over his left shoulder and walked down to the stable. Jess actually felt a little bad about killing Nevada even though Nevada had forced him into the fight. Nevada wasn't a cold blooded killer. He was just another bounty hunter out to make some money and a name for himself.

He walked into the stables and called out Ted's name. There was no answer. Jess was about to turn around when he heard some moaning coming from the back of the stable. He walked over to where the sound was coming from and he saw Ted Watkins laying flat on his back in a pile of hay. He had been severely beaten. Jess grabbed a water pail and took it over to where Ted was. He dipped a rag into the water and placed it on Watkins's forehead. After a minute or so, Ted came around and was startled at seeing someone leaning over him.

"Easy, Ted," said Jess. "Just stay down there for a minute and get your wits about you before you try to stand up." Jess saw several knots on Watkins's forehead and at least a dozen cuts and bruises, along with a real bad gash just below the hairline over the right eye. Someone had really worked him over good.

"Who the hell did this to you?" he asked, after Ted seemed to have shaken some of the fog from his brain.

"That damn bunch that came into town a little bit ago. I told them it was extra for the good grain for their horses and they started to argue with me. They were just looking for a reason and before I knew it, one of them hit me with the grain bucket. I punched the bastard square in the nose and he started bleeding like a stuck pig and that pissed off his friends. They all jumped me and beat the tar out of me. I could've taken the one guy, but I didn't have a chance against all of them," he explained.

"Well, at least you were smart enough not to try using that pistol."

"Hell, I'm not afraid of any fight, but I'm no fool either," he said. "They'd have shot me down like a dog. I've seen their kind before. They make a life out of looking for trouble and a reason to kill someone."

"Well' maybe this will make you feel better," said Jess, as he gave Nevada's pistol and holster to him.

"What's this for?"

"I took this off Nevada Jackson. I figure I don't really need another gun and since you seem to want to wear one, you might as well have a nice one."

"I can't keep this. Nevada will..." Ted's words cut off as his brain began to fire on all cylinders and he remembered the old prospector coming in to claim Nevada's horse and rifle, but not before telling him about the gunfight. Ted stood up and shook the cobwebs out of his head.

"So, you really did outdraw Nevada Jackson?"

"You're holding his pistol and holster," he replied clearly.

"Damn," replied Ted, rubbing his forehead.

"I'm going to head back to the saloon, but I want to ask you for a favor," said Jess.

"Name it. I figure I owe you one," replied Ted.

"Let me know when Blake Taggert comes back to town."

"You got it, Jess. And thanks a lot for the pistol and holster. It's mighty nice," he said examining the pistol and holster.

"You're welcome. I think it's one of the nicest ones I've seen, except for mine that is. And go see someone about that bad cut over your eye."

Ted nodded and walked out right behind Jess, but not before putting on Nevada's gun and holster. Jess walked back into Little's Drinks. As soon as he stepped inside the door, he saw trouble in the form of five men standing at the bar drinking and slamming their glasses down on the bar. All five of them were wearing guns, but only two of the men had them tied down low and tight on their legs. Jess wondered if these were the men who had beaten Ted Watkins earlier.

Jess walked up to the far right end of the bar and ordered a beer. Four of the five men didn't pay Jess any attention at first, but one of the men in the group did. The man had watched Jess walk into the saloon and he was still watching him. Jess didn't return the stare, but was well aware of it and he had already taken his hammer strap off. The man turned back to his other four friends and they suddenly became quiet and then they all seemed to turn so they could see Jess. They drank quietly and spoke amongst themselves for a while, all the time glancing over at Jess. The five men were distracted when Ted Watkins walked into the saloon. The five men smiled at Ted as he walked over to the bar and stood next to Jess.

"Well, looky here," one of them said. "It's the little stable boy. You come to tell us you done raised the boardin' fee on our horses?"

"Naw," said another one of the men, "he just likes the beatin' we gave him and he's come back for another."

Ted ordered a beer and was just about to respond when the one man who had been carefully watching Jess spoke. This man was the leader of the group and his name was Ike.

"Now boys, we done gave the stable boy here enough exercise for the day, don't ya think?" asked

Ike. "I mean, look at that big ole bandage on his forehead. I bet he's got a real nice cut under that bandage." The other four men laughed at that.

"Besides," Ike continued, "I'd like to know more about his friend there at the end of the bar. He's been ignoring us since he came in here and I don't think I like that. Are you shy and hiding behind the stable boy there?"

Ted looked at Jess and Jess gave him a look that Ted understood. Jess motioned his head to tell Ted to move away from the bar, which he did. Ted moved about ten feet away and stood by a table. Jess took another sip of his beer and slowly turned to the men and responded to the question very simply.

"Neither," said Jess. The response from Jess took the man a little by surprise. He wasn't used to getting a simple one-word answer from someone and it riled him a little, although it didn't show on the man's face.

"You ain't one for carrying on much of a conversation, are ya?" asked Ike.

"Nope."

"So is it that you don't like to carry on a conversation, or is it that you just don't want to carry on a conversation with me?"

"Neither," replied Jess. The man laughed for a moment until he finally realized what Jess had answered. That really riled him and this time it showed on his facial expression.

"You smart-ass punk!" hollered Ike. "Don't you know who you're talking to?"

"Nope, and I really don't care either."

"You best care, mister," Ike spat angrily.

"Why?"

"Because I'm Ike Hardy and I was puttin' men in their graves before you were a twinkle in the half-dozen men you call your daddy!" exclaimed Ike. "Besides, you ain't even a man yet, just a young punk who thinks he is."

Ike's face had turned two shades rosier now and the other four men spread out. The one man who had his gun tied down low and tight was looking right at Ted Watkins. Jess knew that he would have to hit that man if he wanted to save Ted. Ike took one step forward.

"Well, smart-ass, why don't we find out how good you are with that fancy shootin' iron you got there?" asked Ike.

"If you want to find out, all you have to do is grab for yours," said Jess. "That should be about the last thing you'll remember."

Ike went for his gun and the first thing he felt was his thumb beginning to put pressure on the hammer of his Colt Peacemaker as he went to jerk the gun from his holster. The second thing he felt was a heavy thump in the middle of his chest from Jess's first shot. Before he fell to the floor of the saloon, he saw three flashes from Jess's gun barrel. It seemed as if it was one continuous blast, but it wasn't. Jess's second shot hit the man who was eyeing Watkins and his third shot hit the man to Ike's left. Ted Watkins had just drawn his gun and had it cocked when the other two men in the group raised their hands high in the air. "We give! Don't shoot! Don't shoot!"

Ted Watkins was standing there in disbelief at what he had just witnessed. He had watched in the blink of an eye as Jess had taken out three men and was ready to shoot a fourth one and not one of the men had cleared leather yet. His mouth was open, but he couldn't speak. He slowly put his gun down at his side, but didn't holster it. Jess continued to keep his gun cocked and ready.

"You men take those gun belts off," demanded Jess.

"Okay. Sure, mister, whatever you say. Just don't shoot," one of the two men said. Both men unbuckled their gun belts and let them drop to the floor. "Okay, now what?"

"Well, I would suggest you men leave town immediately and don't bother taking your friends' horses with you. I'll be taking care of them since they're my horses now." Jess stated plainly.

"You gonna keep their horses?" asked the other man.

"Shut the hell up, you fool," replied the first man. "Let's get our asses out of town while we still have them."

The two men almost ran over to the stables and got on their horses and rode out of town at a dead run. Ted Watkins finally put his gun in the holster and sat down. Jess got two beers from the barkeep and sat down at Ted's table and slid one of the beers across the table toward him. Ted gulped it down and Jess noticed his hand was shaking a little.

"Mr. Williams, I don't know what to say. I'd be dead right now if it weren't for you. Are you for real?" Ted said still somewhat shocked at what he had just witnessed.

"I guess so, at least the last time I checked anyway," he replied. "What the hell did you come in here for? You must've known those men were in here. Are you trying to get yourself killed?" Ted shook his head, still stunned a little by what had happened.

"No, I wasn't even thinking of that," he replied eagerly. "I was just doing what you asked me to do."

"What do you mean?" asked Jess with a confused look on his face.

"Blake Taggert is back in town and he's already heard there was someone in town looking for him," he explained. "He's down at Harry's Place right now and he's got a friend with him. I was just coming to let you know he was back like you asked me to do." Jess's eyes turned darker as he slowly stood up.

"Well, I guess I'll have to go have me a drink over at Harry's. Ted, get these men's guns and take what money they have on them and take it over to your place for me, okay?" Ted nodded.

Jess left Paul a tip and started to walk out. He was at the doorway when Ted stopped him with a question. "Jess, I gotta hunch that Blake Taggert is in a whole heap of trouble, ain't he?"

"You are absolutely right about that," said Jess, as he walked out. Ted turned to the barkeep and asked for another beer. The barkeep poured him another beer and walked it over to his table.

"Well, Paul, I guess you got some cleaning up to do here," implied Ted, looking at the three dead bodies lying on the floor.

"I guess so," he agreed. "I figure Harry's going to be doing some mop work in a few minutes himself."

"Yeah, but I got a real strong hunch that it won't be any of Jess Williams's blood on the floor once it's over."

"If I didn't know any better, I'd think you were one of them mind readers," said the barkeep.

Jess stood there in the street for a moment thinking about everything that had happened so far. He looked up at the sky. It was a beautiful afternoon. The sun was shining and the sky was a deep rich blue with just a hint of clouds here and there. He reloaded his pistol as he began walking down toward Harry's Place. *Yes,* he said to himself, *this is a good day to finish it.* He slowly walked straight down the middle of the street. His thoughts turned to his little sister Samantha and what Blake Taggert had done to her. Blake Taggert's final destiny was finally coming to him and it had a name; Jess Williams.

CHAPTER TWENTY-ONE

As Jess walked down to Harry's Place, he saw a few men running for Little's Drinks. Jess figured they must've heard the gunshots and wanted to see what happened. Jess saw Sheriff Clancy heading toward him from the direction of Harry's.

"Jess, I heard gunshots," said Sheriff Clancy. "I suppose there's some more business for the undertaker back at Little's?" Clancy fell in step with Jess heading back toward Harry's.

"You're an observant man, Sheriff," he replied. "Three men down and for no real reason other than they thought they had to prove something."

"Prove what?"

"That they were tough, but now they're dead," he replied matter-of-factly, as he kept walking and kept his eyes straight down the street, looking directly at Harry's.

"I suppose you're headin' down to Harry's?"

"You're staying right up with my way of thinking, Sheriff."

"Guess you know that Taggert is down there, huh?" the Sheriff asked already knowing the answer.

"I heard."

"I guess there ain't much chance of talking you outta this, is there?"

"Not a chance, Sheriff," he replied, walking slowly and with a meaningful purpose.

"Well, you watch yourself," he warned. "He's got a friend with him and he's a mean one. Don't trust him. He'll draw on you when you ain't lookin'."

Jess stopped suddenly and looked at the sheriff. "Is it the man you said left with Taggert?" asked Jess intensely. "The man you called Sloan?"

"No, I know this man," replied Clancy. "His name is Winn Deets. He's a hired killer and a no good sumbitch."

"Thanks for the warning, Sheriff," he replied. "I assume that you aren't going to involve yourself in this?"

"Now you're staying up with *my* way of thinking," responded Sheriff Clancy. The sheriff let out a little chuckle that he quickly suppressed. "You be careful, Jess." The Sherriff headed back toward Little's Drinks and Jess started back toward Harry's Place.

Jess reached Harry's and stopped outside the saloon and stood in the street looking at the place. He wondered why the place was called Harry's. He understood why Little's Drinks was called Little's because the owner was short and his last name was Little. He thought about calling Blake Taggert out into the street to face him, but decided instead to go ahead and walk right in. He knew they were waiting for him and might be setting him up for an ambush. Jess stepped up onto the boardwalk and before entering the saloon, he pulled the sawed off shotgun from his back sling. He used the barrel of the shotgun to push the batwing doors of the saloon open.

He walked into the saloon and stopped just two feet past the doorway. He noticed there was quite a crowd in the place. There were at least twenty locals sitting around at tables and standing at the bar. The half-dozen or so men at the bar were in two groups. Four of them were standing in the middle of the bar and two men were standing at the far left end of the bar. The two men at the left end of the bar were the men he had to deal with. Those two men slowly turned around to look at who had come into the saloon. Blake Taggert and Jess's eyes locked from the instant they looked at one another. Jess couldn't forget that face even if he had wanted to.

Taggert did not recognize Jess and had no idea who he was or what he wanted with him. All he knew was that someone in town was looking for him and this must be the man. Jess continued to keep an eye on everyone in the room, but his gaze never left Taggert. The place went almost silent with just a whisper here and there. Everyone had noticed the double-barreled shotgun and no one in the place wanted a taste of that. Jess very slowly worked himself around and behind several tables keeping the wall at his backside, making his way to the far right end of the bar. The barkeep walked over to Jess. The barkeep's face was covered with thick hair.

His hair hung down to his shoulders and his beard almost reached down to his waist. The only part of the barkeep's face that showed was two openings for his eyes. Even his eyebrows were unusually bushy. *Another mystery solved,* Jess thought to himself.

"Welcome to Harry's, Mr. Williams," said the barkeep. "I own this place and I'd like to buy you your first drink. What'll you have?" Jess carefully placed the shotgun on the top of the bar, making sure that it was still pointed in the direction of Taggert and the other man with Taggert. Jess asked for a beer, which Harry quickly poured. A few of the other locals who were close to the bar slowly moved away and that left Jess looking straight down the now empty bar at Blake Taggert and Winn Deets.

Jess took a few sips of his beer and stared at Blake Taggert, remembering that day they first met. Jess wondered how any man could be as evil as Taggert. He was certain in his mind that Taggert was the one responsible for the grisly murders recently in Red Rock. Taggert said nothing for several minutes. He wasn't really worried, but he wondered who this kid was who was gunning for him with a shotgun on the bar and a strange looking pistol and holster. Taggert knew he had committed many crimes. Maybe he had done something to this kid, and the only way to find out was to ask.

"I understand you've been waiting for me," said Taggert. "Do I know you?"

Jess didn't respond right away. He wasn't sure if it was because he wanted to savor the moment now that he finally found the last of the three men who killed his family, or if he wanted Taggert to remember who he was. Here he was, his life changed forever in such a dramatic way, and Taggert couldn't even remember him.

"You don't remember me, do you?" asked Jess.

"I can't say I do," replied Taggert. "What's your name?"

"Jess Williams."

Taggert still had a puzzled look on his face. "Sorry, I don't know any Jess Williams."

"Maybe you remember a farm back in Black Creek, Kansas," said Jess. Taggert's body language changed slightly and Jess immediately picked up on it.

"Never been to Black Creek, Kansas," replied Taggert, knowing he wasn't telling the truth.

"Maybe you remember a woman hanging from a doorway, all cut up," he pushed, his voice getting slightly louder.

"I still have no idea about what you're talking about," lied Taggert.

"Remember a man shot several times behind a plow out in a field...do you remember that?" he asked as the anger started to well up inside him. Winn Deets had not said a word up to now, but he was getting aggravated and it showed.

"Hey, kid," snapped Deets. "I don't know who you are and I don't much give a shit. Why don't you just haul your ass out of here while you're still walking upright?"

"Mister, I'm not walking out of here until that man standing next to you is dead and if you want to die with him, that's your decision. I don't much care either way," explained Jess. Jess knew Deets was pissed. He also knew Deets was ready to draw, just as soon as he felt Jess wasn't watching him close enough. Jess turned his attention back to Taggert while keeping a close watch on Deets.

"Maybe you might remember a little seven-year-old girl who you raped and murdered by shooting her in the forehead," Jess pushed further. "Do you remember her? Remember a young boy you met out on the road about an hour before you murdered an entire family? That boy was me and the family you murdered was my family. Surely any man who could commit such brutal acts would remember them. I know that I can still see it in my mind like it was yesterday."

Taggert remembered very well what Jess was talking about. He just wasn't going to admit to any of it. He especially remembered the little girl. He had enjoyed that. "You've got me mixed up with someone else," refuted Taggert.

"You're a damn liar, but I guess that shouldn't surprise me," he countered angrily. "I suppose you ain't going to admit to murdering that family outside of town right here either. That was you, wasn't it?"

"Maybe the man who murdered your family is the same man who murdered that family here in Red Rock," replied Taggert, smiling to himself inside at the thought of the young girl he had so brutally raped and murdered.

"You're finally getting it right," said Jess. "And that same man is you."

"I'm telling you, you've got it all wrong, kid," contested Taggert. "I never murdered anyone, ever, especially in this town." Taggert was getting a little nervous now as some of the men in the saloon started whispering between themselves about the murdered family.

"I've got a message from two friends of yours," said Jess.

"Who might that be?" Taggert asked, quizzically.

"Your two friends Randy Hastings and Hank Beard."

"What was the message?"

"That they'd see you in hell."

"Hell?"

"Yeah, that's where I sent them and that's where you're going next," he replied bluntly.

"And who's going to send me there?" asked Taggert, a contemptuous look washing across his face.

"You're looking at him."

"You?" he asked sarcastically.

"Do I have to repeat myself?"

"And you think you're good enough?"

"You're about to find out."

"Kid, I've been drawing a pistol damn near as long as you've been breathing air," spat Taggert. "What makes you think you can take me?"

"Only one way to find out for sure," he said threateningly. Deets had been listening to all of this and he was getting more and more agitated by the moment. He finally spoke up.

"You might think you can take Taggert, but you can't take the both of us at the same time," claimed Deets boldly. Jess glanced at Deets.

"You throwing in with him?" asked Jess.

"Damn right," he threatened.

"Then you'll die right next to him."

"You gonna use that damn fire breather you got on the bar?" asked Deets, nervously looking at the double barreled shotgun on the bar. Jess smiled.

"Naw, I don't need it," advised Jess, cocking his head a little and grinning a somewhat evil grin.

Jess knew that Deets would draw first. He watched Deets moving his right hand closer to the butt of his pistol. Jess could see a bead of sweat dripping down Deets left temple. Taggert began to move his left hand down to the butt of his pistol and he was watching Deets, trying to time it so they both drew at the same time. As soon as Taggert knew Deets was moving, Taggert's left hand went for his gun. Jess's first shot hit Deets in the stomach. Jess fanned his second shot and hit Taggert in the right shoulder spinning him around a full turn, throwing him down on a table flat on his back, his gun flying across the room. Jess's third shot hit Deets in the chest, punching a hole in his heart and putting him down for good. Jess wanted Deets down and out of the picture so that he could put his full attention toward killing Taggert; slowly. Jess watched the room to make sure no one else was throwing going to be involved. He saw Taggert still lying on the table, but on his side now holding his right shoulder with his left hand. Jess noticed two things simultaneously; a little dust falling from the upstairs railing, and a gunshot going off in the direction of the swinging doors of the saloon. He quickly looked over and saw Ted Watkins and he was holding Nevada Jackson's still smoking pistol in his hand. He heard a thud against the floor upstairs and realized that Taggert had a third man hiding in a room upstairs to ambush Jess. He nodded to Ted.

"Figured I owed you as much," said Ted. "Besides, I had to try it out."

Jess looked at Taggert. He was now standing upright, his buttocks leaning against the edge of the table he had fallen on. He was bleeding, but he wasn't dying, at least not yet. Jess put a slug into Taggert's left kneecap. Taggert fell away from the table, hit the ground and rolled over holding himself up with his left hand and his right knee facing away from Jess.

"Damn it! I ain't got no gun! You can't shoot an unarmed man!" he hollered.

"Is that right? Let's see about that." Jess fired another round, this one ripping into Taggert's right buttock, the force rolling him over onto his back. Taggert pushed and wiggled himself up against the wall.

"You bastard!" Taggert exclaimed. "You can't just kill me in cold blood!"

"You and your dead friend both reached for iron before I did," he barked.

"Yeah, but this ain't right!" hollered Taggert.

"Maybe you should have been thinking that way when you were raping and killing my little sister," refuted Jess. "Besides, who's going to stop me?"

"I know a lot of people in this town," spat Taggert, as he looked at some of the men in the saloon "You can't just let him kill me! Stop him! Go get the sheriff!"

Surprisingly, no one moved. Maybe they were too afraid of Jess or maybe they were beginning to believe Taggert might be guilty of what Jess was accusing him of. Jess had one more round in his pistol. He put that round into Taggert's left elbow tearing it up so bad that his left arm just dangled to the floor. He was bleeding profusely. Jess quickly reloaded his pistol and put it back in its holster. He reached behind and pulled out his knife. He flipped it in the air and grabbed it by the blade and threw it right at Taggert, hitting him in the groin, pinning his gonads to the floor of the saloon. Taggert let out another scream and had an excruciating look of pain contorted up on his face. "You ain't supposed to hit a man in his privates!"

"Now, where have I heard that before?" asked Jess curiously. "Oh, yeah, your friend that helped you murder my family. Now you'll have even more in common to talk about while you're in hell together."

"That one was for my mother," Jess said, coldly. Jess walked over to where Taggert's gun was. He picked it up.

"I figure this is the pistol you used to put a bullet into my little sister's head," Jess said with disgust. "I think it's only fair to finish you off with the same gun, don't you?"

"Just do it, you bastard! I can't take anymore! Finish me!" screamed Taggert writhing in pain.

"Oh, I'll finish you; of that you can be sure," he promised. "But you know all this gun fighting and excitement has made me a little thirsty. I think I need a nice sip of my beer."

"You go to hell, you bastard!" Taggert yelled, as he watched Jess walk back up to the bar where Harry had set down a fresh glass of beer. Jess, keeping his eyes on Taggert, set Taggert's gun on the bar and picked up the glass and took a nice long sip. He wanted Taggert to suffer as much as he could. Taggert tried to remove the knife that had his gonads pinned to the floor, but he was losing what little strength he had from the loss of blood. Jess walked back to Taggert and just looked at him moaning in pain. It would make most men feel a little bad, but Jess felt no pity for Taggert. Not after what he had done to his family.

"You ready to meet your friends, Beard and Hastings?"

"Kiss my ass, you son of a whore!" shrieked Taggert, bloody spittle flying from his lips.

"Just make sure that you give Beard and Hastings my regards," whispered Jess, as he placed the barrel of Taggert's gun about two inches from his forehead, just above the nose.

As Jess pulled the trigger, he closed his eyes and all the events leading up to this point flashed through his brain. When he opened his eyes, Taggert was laying against a fallen chair, his head half blown off. *It's over;* Jess thought to himself, *it's finally over.*

Jess hung his head and closed his eyes for what seemed an eternity, but in reality, it was only about ten seconds. He threw Taggert's gun down on the floor in front of Taggert and retrieved his knife, wiping the blood off on Taggert's pants. Then, he walked back over to the bar and picked up his shotgun and put it back in its sling over his shoulder and downed his beer. Harry refilled it quickly and Jess took a long pull from it. Ted Watkins walked over to him and ordered a beer and took a drink.

"Well, I guess you finished what you came here to do," Ted remarked, looking at the dead body of Blake Taggert.

"I guess so. It seems strange though, as if it's not really finished," said Jess. "What do you think that means, Ted?"

"I don't think you're finished, Mr. Williams," stated Ted.

"What do you mean?"

"There are a lot more Blake Taggerts out there."

"Yeah, and someone has to deal with them," he said realizing his calling. "I suppose it might as well be me."

"I can't think of anyone better suited for the job," said Ted confidently.

Jess finished his beer and thanked Ted for his help. He told Ted to take the guns and holsters back to the stables and Jess checked both men for any money. To his surprise, he found over one thousand dollars between the two. He thought that odd. Most men were lucky to walk around with ten dollars in their pockets. He headed over to the sheriff's office to check on any bounty that might be available on any of the men he had killed today. *Five men,* he thought to himself, *I've killed five men today and it's not even dark out yet.* Sheriff Clancy was sitting outside his office. He had heard the shots and had already heard how Jess had killed Taggert and Deets. Word traveled fast in this town.

"I was hoping to see you again, Jess," the sheriff said standing up.

"You had doubts?"

"No, not really," he replied. "Come on in." Jess followed Clancy into his office and the sheriff picked up a wanted poster he had on his desk.

"Seems like one of those three you killed over at Little's had a bounty of two hundred dollars on his head."

"Well, I'll sure take it, Sheriff," he said. "This bounty hunting business pays pretty well."

"It does for the ones who stay alive, and not too many of them do," cautioned Clancy.

"Sheriff, I found over a thousand dollars on Blake Taggert and that Deets fellow. It's been a highly profitable day, that's for sure."

"A thousand dollars? Really?"

"Well, it was about fifty dollars more than a thousand, why?"

"I just got a wire from a small town about three days ride from here. It seems two brothers who ran a ranch together along with their wives were murdered last week. Both women were raped and killed. Luckily, their two children were staying with relatives and not home when it happened. The brothers kept their earnings at the ranch. One of the brother's uncles says they had almost a thousand dollars saved up to buy some more cattle. I wonder if it was Taggert and Deets who took the money and killed those poor folks," the sheriff stated.

"That would be my guess, Sheriff. I'll make sure the money gets returned to the two children. I'll have Ted Watkins take the money to them personally, along with a message that the men most likely responsible for it are dead," he said pensively.

"That's mighty generous of you, Mr. Williams," said Clancy. "I don't believe I've met a nicer fella who killed five men in one day."

Jess thought about what Sheriff Clancy said. He didn't know what to say in response so he just nodded to the sheriff and walked out. He walked to the livery and told Ted what to do with the thousand dollars. Ted promised to deliver the money right away. He sold the horses to Ted and sold the guns off to a local gunsmith that Ted knew. He shook Ted's hand and said his goodbye. He climbed up in the saddle and nudged his horse into a walk. As he rode out of Red Rock, he thought about the men he had killed and how much money he collected in return. The way he figured it, he was a little over a thousand dollars richer and he had a pretty nice watch to boot. *Not bad,* he thought.

As he turned Gray's head back toward Black Creek, Kansas his thoughts turned to the three men who had murdered his family. August of 1878 was coming to a close and it had been over two years since that horrible day. He could still remember all the details vividly, too vividly. He could also remember killing each one of the three men responsible just as vividly. His thoughts turned to Blake Taggert lying on the floor of Harry's Place in a pool of blood, all shot up with Jess's knife sticking out of his groin. If you looked real close at Jess, you would almost think you could see a slight hint of a smile on his lips.

※ ※

The ride back to Black Creek, Kansas, was a long and somber one. Jess stopped only a few times in small towns to get supplies and his visits were short and for the most part uneventful. He finally arrived back at his family's ranch about an hour before sundown. He sat down by the grave markers under the big oak tree and told his ma, pa, and his sister they could all rest in peace now because the men who had murdered them were all dead. He noticed someone had been putting flowers on the graves. *Probably Sara and*

Jim Smythe, he thought. He would go into town to visit with them tomorrow. It would be nice to see them again. He couldn't bring himself to sleep in the house, although he took a stroll through it. He peeked inside each of the bedrooms and tried to imagine his folks sleeping quietly. He glanced at the floor where his ma was hanging that day and could still see the fading dark spot from all the blood. He cried silently, tears running down his face. It was the first time he had cried since he had left home. He swore it would be his last time.

He bunked down next to the gravesites that night with the big oak tree at his back. There was a slight chill in the night air and he pulled a light blanket over himself. As he lay there, his thoughts turn to his brother, Tim Sloan. He needed to find him and ask him how he knew Blake Taggert. He needed to find out if his brother knew what Taggert had done. If his brother was a killer and a bad man like Taggert, Jess would deal with him in the same way he dealt with other bad men, brother or not. He decided that would be his next mission in life. Find his brother and talk with him. He would start out by talking some more with Sara and Jim. But that was for tomorrow. Tonight, he would again sleep with the family he loved so dearly and wished he could be with once more. He would lie here next to their graves and somehow he hoped that his dreams would take him to them so he could see them and talk to them once more.

As he fell off to sleep he imagined he was a sheriff in a small town and he was facing off with two bad guys and…

That night, Jess had good dreams.

EPILOGUE

It had been four years since Dave Walters's new pistol and holster had mysteriously vanished from his locked gun safe. He had continued to compete in fast draw competition and he was finally in the high twenties, but he still hadn't won the elusive title of fast draw champion. He had continued to use his old pistol and holster, not even thinking about saving up enough money to have Bob Graham build him another one. Truth be known, he was almost afraid to. He sometimes felt that it was some kind of omen having the gun vanish the way it did. It had scared the living hell out of him. The night it vanished he hardly slept. For months afterward, he just kept looking at the gun locker as if some evil spirit would come out of it and take him next. Of course, with the way his wife had been carrying on about how he lost a two thousand dollar gun and holster and she still hadn't gotten any furniture, maybe that wouldn't be such a bad thing.

He didn't really think about it all that much now, only when he had idle time on his hands, like right now. He was traveling with his wife, Jean, heading for Yellowstone National Park. After coming out of Granite Pass, the road to Cody, Wyoming, was a little boring compared to the drive through the pass and that gave him some time to start thinking about that day. He still couldn't figure how it could've happened. After all, he was sitting right in the next room watching television and he could see the gun cabinet through the bedroom door. Sure, he had gotten up a few times to get another beer and to use the bathroom, but those things took all of sixty seconds. Someone would've had to enter the bedroom from the window, break into the gun locker, remove the gun and holster, close the locker and make it out of the bedroom in one minute. Even if you had the combination to the safe it would take at least fifteen seconds just to spin the dial. There had been no marks or any signs of forced entry on the gun locker. No, it had to have just vanished into thin air, taken by some means not known to Dave and he wasn't sure he wanted to know. Although he had always wondered where the gun and holster was, he never reported it to the police. When he told his shooting partner Pat about it, Pat just looked at him like he was crazy.

They pulled up at a local motel in Cody, and checked into a small but clean room. They had planned to go to the Wild Bill Hickok Museum the next day, but in the morning they slept in too late and decided to continue on to Arizona. They headed out on highway 14/16 and when they reached Wapiti, they came to a sign that caught Dave's attention—'Old

Guns of the Old West.' The sign was in the yard of a big white house just off the highway. On the sign it also said—'five bucks.' He decided to stop and check it out. Jean stayed in the car. Dave knocked on the door and a small man who looked to be in his sixties opened the door with a big smile on his face.

"You here to see the gun collection?" asked the man.

"If that's okay," replied Dave. "I always love to see old guns, especially from the Old West."

"Well, come on in. My name is Steve and I have some real neat stuff, but it'll cost you five bucks to see it." Dave paid him five dollars, which the man put in his front pocket.

"I got the stuff in my basement," said Steve. "I collected some of it myself, but a lot of it came from my Uncle Henry who collected guns right up until his last heart attack several years ago."

Dave followed him down to the basement and he was quite impressed. Steve had several tables set up and covered with white cotton material and next to each item was a postcard with a description of the item. There were three saddles sitting on homemade wooden stands and the sign next to one said—"Last Saddle used by Jesse James." Dave wondered about that one. There were several old rifles, a dozen pistols dating back to the eighteen hundreds, and several holsters. Dave took a few pictures. Then, he noticed a stand in one corner of the basement with a fairly long glass case. Steve noticed Dave's eyes focusing on the glass case.

"That's my best piece. Never saw anything like it before. My Uncle Henry said it was given to him by his lifelong friend, Jess Williams, Jr., who passed away several years before Uncle Henry. Dave walked over to the glass case and when he looked down inside the case, he froze as stiff as a tree.

"Oh my God!" Dave exclaimed, his voice trembling.

"I know," said Steve. "It don't look like any pistol from the eighteen hundreds, but my Uncle Henry said he first seen it way back in 1925 when he first met Jess Williams, Jr." There was no response from Dave so Steve walked up next to him and looked at Dave, who was just staring down at the gun and holster. The holster was laid out lengthwise and the pistol was lying flat between the belt of the holster and the strap for the leg. It was the holster that had mysteriously disappeared from his locked gun safe. He was certain of it.

He looked at the pistol very closely, almost placing his face on the glass. He could just make out the stamping on the one side of the gun. RUGER BLACKHAWK .41 MAGNUM. The custom, hand carved stag horn handles were a little beat up, but they were as beautiful as the day he had picked up the gun from Bob Graham four years ago.

There was no logical explanation for what he was looking at, but yet there it was right before his eyes. The gun and holster both showed signs of wear and looked old, but it was the same gun and the same holster. There was no doubt about it in Dave's mind. Dave must have stood there for five minutes thinking about the gun and holster and how it had disappeared that fateful day. He looked up from the case and looked Steve in the eyes. Steve had a worried look about him.

"Are you all right, mister?" he asked.

"I'm not really sure," replied a visibly shaken Dave. "Steve, you're not going to believe this."

"Believe what?"

"This gun and holster that you have in this case is the gun and holster I bought four years ago and it disappeared on the same day I bought it. This is the first time I've seen it since."

"You mean you purchased one just like it?" asked Steve.

"No, Steve. *This* gun, and *this* holster," replied Dave emphatically. "I had this gun built by a custom gun builder by the name of Bob Graham. This holster was made for me by Bob Mernickle, of Mernickle Custom Holsters. I know it sounds crazy, but it's true."

"It can't be," refuted Steve. "I first saw this gun back in 1967 when my Uncle Henry first showed it to me and told me he would give it to me for my collection when he passed on, which was in 1969. I've had the gun ever since, right here in my basement in that glass case."

"You said your Uncle Henry got the gun from a Jess Williams, Jr.?" asked Dave.

"Yeah, he got the gun from him back in 1959 when Jess Williams, Jr. passed away," replied Steve.

"Jess Williams, Jr. was given the gun and holster on the day his father, Jess Williams, passed away back in 1921. That's an interesting story all in itself the way my Uncle Henry told me."

"What was the story your Uncle Henry told you?" asked Dave.

"Well, as the story goes, Jess Williams, Junior's father, found the gun mysteriously hanging up in the barn way back in 1876 when Junior's father was only fourteen. He never figured out how it had gotten there, it just seemed to appear out of nowhere. The strange this is, this happened just after the murders."

"What murders?" asked Dave.

"Back in 1876, Jess Williams's entire family was brutally murdered when he was just a boy. I guess it was quite horrific. They tied his ma up in a doorway and raped her and cut her up so bad you wouldn't believe it. They even gouged one of her eyes out. They shot his pa out in the field. The story is they ambushed him and he never had a chance. The worst part though, is the little girl, Samantha. I guess one of the guys who did the killings took her in the barn and did things to her that you wouldn't think any man would do to a little seven-year-old girl. When he finished with her, he beat her up and shot her in the head.

Well, Jess was crazy with hate and revenge for the men who killed his family and he went hunting for the men. Jess had gotten pretty good with his pa's gun; but when he used this gun and holster he found in the barn, he found it gave him an advantage that no other man had. He had a gun and holster that seemed to be designed for a quick draw. That, combined with plenty of practice and a burning desire to hunt the men down, made Jess Williams truly the fastest man on the draw in the Old West, although the history books don't even mention him. As a matter of fact, Jess Williams turned to bounty hunting and was never beaten on the draw, ever. He finally settled down in 1899 and Jess Williams, Jr. was born in 1902. Jess Williams, Jr. and my Uncle Henry became friend's early on in life and that's how Uncle Henry came by the gun and holster. So you see, this can't be the gun and holster you had four years ago. This gun has been in my family for over forty years and I've had it here in the display case since 1969."

Dave had listened to this whole story and somehow, in a strange sort of way, it made some sense to him. This Jess Williams had somehow found his gun back in 1876 in the same mysterious fashion that the gun and holster disappeared in 2002. And Jess Williams had a burning need for the gun, more than Dave Walters needed it, and they both needed it for the same reason, to be the fastest man at drawing and shooting a pistol. It was almost as if, in some unexplainable and unimaginable way, Dave had done something to help Jess Williams find justice in a land and a time that didn't see much of either. Yes, in a strange surreal sort of way, it made sense to Dave. He had lost an expensive gun and holster, but something good had come of it. He wished he could have met Jess Williams.

"Steve, I'll bet you five bucks that I know the serial number stamped on the other side of the gun, as well as the serial number on the back side of holster," Dave challenged.

"How could you possibly know that?" asked Steve. "I've never met you before and you've never been in this basement before."

"What if I told you that the serial number on the gun is 40—01079?" asked Dave. Steve had a strange look on his face. He reached inside his front pocket and got a set of keys. He unlocked the case and picked up the gun and turned it over. He read the numbers off, not believing what he was seeing. 40-01079.

"I don't understand," exclaimed Steve. "How can this be? How could you possibly know that? This gun has been locked in this case since I put it in there in 1969."

"Now, turn over the holster and you'll find the serial number stamped in the leather. It will be SN020679 and it will also have the name BOB MERNICKLE CUSTOM HOLSTERS and MADE IN CANADA stamped on it," Dave challenged.

Steve turned over the holster and it was exactly as Dave said it was. The serial number was exact. Steve was absolutely and totally dumfounded.

"I just don't understand," muttered Steve. "How could you possibly have known that? I've never met you before and I'm sure you've never seen this pistol and holster before. My Uncle Henry never displayed it or showed it to anyone except family as far as I know."

"Steve," Dave asked, "Do you believe in destiny and fate and all that?"

"I sure do, always have."

"So do I." replied Dave.

"Well, what do we do now?" asked Steve, a little worried. Dave simply put his hand out.

"I guess you owe me five bucks," replied Dave. Steve took the same five-dollar bill that Dave had paid him and Dave put it in his front pocket.

"Are you going to make a claim for the gun?" asked Steve, a worried look forming on his face. Dave didn't have to even think about it for even one second.

"No. I believe things happen for a reason," he said bluntly. "I think Jess Williams was destined to have this gun and I simply played a small part in his destiny. Some things that happen in our lives, no matter how unexplainable, are best left unchanged, don't you think?"

"Yes, I believe that's true," replied Steve, with a look of relief.

Dave thanked Steve again and headed up the stairs. As he walked down the driveway to the car he thought about how destiny had intertwined the fate of both his life and Jess Williams's life together in such a strange way. He got in the car and closed the door. His wife Jean looked up at him.

"Dave, are you okay?" asked his wife, a worried look on her face. "You look like you've seen a ghost or something."

Dave let out a sigh. He decided right there he wouldn't tell his wife what he had just seen. She probably wouldn't believe him anyway. She still often wondered about his sanity after his claim that the gun simply vanished into thin air.

"I'm fine," replied Dave. "Maybe it's the altitude. I'll be fine."

"Well, was it worth the five bucks?"

"Oh, yes. I would have paid five hundred bucks to see what I just saw." Jean looked at him, puzzled. He offered no explanation. He knew better than to try.

Dave started the car and drove down the driveway and back onto highway 14/16. As he drove, his thoughts turned to Jess Williams, the bounty hunter and fastest draw in the west. He could picture him wearing his gun and holster and beating the bad guys to the draw. Then he pictured himself there in Jess Williams's place, back in the old days, shooting it out with the best and always the man standing in the end. As Dave hit the first hill going into Yellowstone Park, his wife looked over at him and noticed he had a strange smile on his lips.

Dave was imagining he was facing down some bad guys in the Old West, and he had Jess Williams's gun and holster and…

READ ALL THE BOOKS IN THE JESS WILLIAMS WESTERN SERIES

Made in the USA
Lexington, KY
07 September 2018